THE TRIAL LAWYER

JOHN ELLSWORTH

SUBJUDICA HOUSE PRESS

DEDICATION

For Chase and Skittles

1

Killen Erwin wanted Mary Roberta to come home to him and the kids. He wanted her to stop drinking and dancing with other men as she did several nights a week. Most of all, he wanted her to stop picking them up and bedding them. He begged, he bribed; he appealed to the mother in her: "Celena and Parkus miss their mom. They cry themselves to sleep!"

But nothing worked.

So he followed her to the Copperhead Tavern and got himself good and drunk while he watched her dancing and rubbing up against Dave Daniels. A slow song played. Killen tried to cut in. Dave laughed at him, and Mary Roberta turned her face away, burying her beauty in the man's shoulder. She refused to look at her husband, refused to acknowledge him and wouldn't give him even one dance.

Killen poured down the booze. There was a fire down below, and it refused to die.

As he watched his wife dance a slow dance, he saw the man

take a step to the side and the woman step into his groin with her own. It was intentional, and it was sexual and they hung there together, joined through their clothing, missing a full step of the dance. Killen broke a Cutty Sark bottle on the bar and threatened the old-timers who were perched along the bar like magpies on a wire. They scattered and broke for the door.

Then he screamed, the sound of a cougar with its foot in a trap, "Mary Roberta! I'm coming for you, baby!" And he began making his way across the floor. He held the broken bottle out in front of him like a lance, away from his body, slashing at the air, scattering the dance crowd left and right.

Mitt Henry, the massive bartender, pulled his baseball bat from behind the bar. It was a thirty-two inch Louisville Slugger spotted with blood.

It was Killen's luck that he had an ally in the crowd of drinkers that night, a young, quiet man named Johnny Albertson. Johnny liked Killen and knew what he was going through. Johnny ran to him and slapped away the bottle. The green glass hit the cement dance floor and shattered, shards spinning out and out. Johnny shook his head at Mitt, who was stalking Killen with his baseball bat like a pinch-hitter intent on ending a tie game. "He's knee-walking," Johnny said and positioned himself between Killen and Mitt. Mitt pounded the sweet spot of the bat into the palm of his hand.

"You've got ten seconds," Mitt told Johnny.

Johnny bear-hugged Killen and began pulling him away.

"Johnny?" Killen said. "You saved her!"

Johnny dragged Killen outside. In the parking lot, he demanded the keys to Killen's pickup. Killen refused.

So Johnny climbed in the passenger seat, resolute, arms crossed on his chest. "Then I'm coming too," he said. He would make sure Killen got home safely.

Then the driver's side door opened and, as Killen was climbing in, Johnny heard a woman's voice tell Killen, to "Move your ass over, sit down and don't throw up."

"Mary Roberta?" said Johnny. "What are you doing?"

"If dumbass kills himself I lose my best babysitter!" She spat. "I'm taking him home. Then I'm coming back."

Five minutes of bouncing along and Killen was passed out, chin to chest, bobbing and swaying with the road.

"You think that string of slobber makes you irresistible," Mary Roberta said to her comatose husband. "But I'm onto your tricks," she laughed. She rapped Killen's head with her knuckles. He didn't move except to swing and sway with the road.

Five minutes later they were coursing through the pitch black Illinois countryside, images of tall corn swaying in the soft summer breeze, dry leaves clashing together above a screaming chorus of riverine bugs and night fliers so in love and lust they soundtracked the landscape. Mary Roberta, chain-smoking, intent on the road, but every so often turning her head to answer or query Johnny on some fine point of furniture refinishing, his day job at his mother's antique shop.

The pickup's headlights swept a quarter mile ahead and illuminated the Algonquin Levee Bridge. Mary Roberta's eyes were turned to Johnny and then swept to the front as Johnny's mouth fell open, and he soundlessly pointed at the road ahead and she turned to see what he had seen. Johnny heard the driver curse. "Son of a—" she cried as their lane ended.

Upon impact, the bridge girder sheared away the truck's right side and Johnny went airborne in the night sky over the edge of the bridge. The spinning crew cab door tattooed him. He plunged to the sandy river bed where once there had flowed water but now there were dredge marks from the scoop line that had reclaimed that good earth. Shoes were found twenty yards beyond; one contained a foot. The catastrophic crash caused a farmer two miles north to sit up in bed.

Killen survived. His Ford truck spun 360's along the asphalt, blocking all lanes where it came to rest. Traffic snarled and backed up. Someone dialed 911.

A state trooper named Bill Janes, who lived on a farm less than two miles back the way the Ford had traveled, took the call. He dressed and fired up his squad and ran Code 3 out to the scene. The driver was ID'd as Killen Erwin. Sergeant Janes observed Erwin, smelled his breath, and spoke briefly. He needed no first aid. Erwin found himself handcuffed in the rear of the squad.

(*The driver was sitting in the center of his Ford's front seat, now sitting on the asphalt, cursing because the truck wouldn't go. He still possessed the steering wheel* said the police report.)

The trooper placed flares and reflectors. Traffic was stopped in both directions. Now he could look the scene over while help came on.

Sergeant Janes pulled out his Canon and began snapping. He gave particular attention to the northwest lane, which was under repair. The vehicle had shredded the blinking sawhorses and sent the orange cones flying. The paint markings on the roadway remained as at the time of the accident.

Erwin cursed from the back seat. He vomited down his Rolling Stones T-shirt.

(*Words were slurred and the eyes bloodshot and there was a strong odor of alcoholic beverage* said the police report.)

The officer backed up fifty yards, lights flashing. He snapped the approach to the bridge. He pulled forward. He snapped the roadway paint indicating a lane drop. The paint job puzzled the veteran highway cop. He made a note to check the traffic engineering rules adopted by Illinois.

EMTs came and scattered into the dry river bed, looking for the shorn half of the Ford. Among the debris, they found Johnny. Stethoscopes returned only silence. A stretcher was packed in and the body loaded.

The Ford was removed. Wreckers tugged and hoisted as the frame, the engine, glass and debris were winched and swept away. Then an EMT dually removed the body from the scene and headed to the morgue.

After the Ford had been taken away, Sergeant Janes spoke to the two vehicles waiting to cross from the south. These would be the vehicles that were following Killen's truck when it struck the bridge. In the first car, a yellow Mitsubishi, sat a seventy-year-old woman named Anita Brushkart. She told Janes that she had witnessed a figure fleeing the scene of the accident. Was it a man or a woman?

She said she could only guess because the figure was wearing blue jeans and a shapeless top, but she would have to suppose that was a woman.

"Where did the fleeing woman go?" asked the officer.

"Why, she run off the bridge and jumped in a pickup that stopped ahead of the one that crashed. It was already across. It was red and had lights on the roof that was pointed back at us. Blinded us but I could clearly see the gal run up to the truck and then she was gone. Ain't nothin more to add."

Anita Brushkart lived in Summer Hill, and she had been going to the hospital in Orbit because she was dizzy, and her chest felt tight. Later that morning, Sergeant Janes filled out some of his police report. But he left out the part about the fleeing woman. The witness was sick and probably hallucinating, so he purposely omitted her comment. She had agreed to ride into Orbit with Sergeant Janes as he was going to the hospital anyway. Nothing further had been said about the phantom woman driver.

Sergeant Janes rushed Erwin and Brushkart into Orbit. She was admitted to the hospital for tests. Erwin refused to submit to a blood draw, so Sergeant Janes read the mandatory consent form and Erwin fell to his side on the examining table, asleep.

(*Subject passed out and physician revived with smelling salts and requested consent for blood draw. Consent to blood draw was refused* said the police report.)

So Sergeant Janes ordered the blood be drawn: the sergeant's legal right and obligation.

The needle bit into the vein. Erwin struggled awake. His free arm beat the air. "I want to see my lawyer."

"Mr. Erwin, it's Sergeant Bill Janes. You *are* a lawyer."

"I'm a lawyer? Well."

"You are the District Attorney. We have cases together."

The ER physician capped a purple tube of blood. "He is? How's that gonna work?"

"It will be politics as usual," said the sergeant.

Sergeant Janes drove the District Attorney back to the Orbit Jail. He was single-celled because the District Attorney couldn't be commingled with the general jail population—consisting of two drunks and a domestic violence enthusiast.

By noon the next day the DA was regaining sobriety. He demanded to make his phone call.

"Hello, Thaddeus?" he said into the pay phone in the jail hallway. "It's Killen Erwin. I've been arrested."

2

He turned off the ignition switch.

Here he was back in Orbit, south of Chicago on a slant to the Mississippi River. The stately Hickam County Courthouse filled his windshield like a wedding cake.

A woman walking by on the courthouse sidewalk recognized him through the windshield. She was well-fed and round and looked to Thaddeus like a woman who served pork chops every week. She waved and smiled. He waved back and smiled at her. He was a clear-eyed, hard-driving attorney with almost eight years of experience in the trial game and he felt every minute of it deep in his bones where he carried the pain of the people he represented. Their agony always became his own; he was just that kind of lawyer. Thaddeus was tall—he had played college basketball—and wore his brown hair down to his collar in back and short on the sides. Sunglasses were Oakley amber with interchangeable lenses for mountain biking and skiing. A day's growth—maybe two—wasn't unusual. But wife Katy hated it and made him shave before entertaining his advances.

The clerk had faxed him the police report. Thaddeus read it while he listened to Pearl Jam and kept time with his fingers drumming against the leather seat.

He drew a deep breath and looked up again.

A silver dome capped the courthouse. Each ninety on the compass offered stairs and double doors. An acre of green August grass, sprinklers tossing long combs of water, enough dandelions to rank second on the agenda of the County Board, and very busy mom-and-pops all around the square—a postcard of a town. On the north side was a state bank; on the south a federal bank. According to their digital signs, both were paying less than two percent on savings. They also blinked out hog prices, time and temperature and a welcome back to the seniors of 2015-16.

At least fifty pickups sat nosed-in all around while their owners did their weekly shopping, for it was late Friday afternoon, and everything would be open until nine.

At the moment he shut off his engine, both the federal and state bank had it at 4:10 p.m. Just enough time to accompany his best friend to court.

Killen Erwin had called when Thaddeus was chewing his first bite of lunch pita stuffed with hummus and walnuts—wife Katy's idea—no mayo. Nine hundred feet above Chicago in his office at Federal Tower, Thaddeus accepted the collect call.

"I'm in jail, man. I need you."

"Slow down, Kill. Have you been charged with a crime?"

"Last night, man, I was driving—"

"Don't say it on the phone."

"I've already said too damn much."

"Just stop there. You've been charged with a crime?"

"Yes. I go to court today. Four forty-five.'

"What crime?"

"Negligent homicide."

"Okay. Don't speak about the facts. Is it in Hickam County?"

"Yes."

"That's where you're going to court?"

"Yes."

It just so happened it was Thaddeus' birthday. He would miss the surprise birthday party. But he had no choice. His wife was his best friend in the world. But Killen was his second best. He had referred Thaddeus' first hundred clients to him; Thaddeus felt he owed him his law practice.

"Who's the judge?"

"Richard Mason Wren."

"Bird Nest? What's he doing in Hickam County? Judge Veinne recused herself?"

"Sure she recused herself. We're bridge buddies."

"Okay, sit tight, I'm on my way."

"Sitting tight is easy. No bail. Johnny Albertson was in my truck. I didn't know it. He died."

"I say this to everyone, Kill. I'll say it to you: Don't talk to anyone about the case. Got me?"

"Hell, I already have. I've talked to everyone."

"Why?"

"Waggle tongue. It comes in a Stoli vodka bottle."

"Okay, that's enough."

Drinking and driving. Hard cases to beat under the best of circumstances. But a dead body in the aftermath? Damn near impossible. Thaddeus had tried hundreds of fender-benders, rear-enders, and DWIs—he was an expert on vehicle cases—and none was so hard to beat as a drunk-driving case. Why? Because the cops loved those cases. The evidence was chemistry and physics—easy to prove in court using the right experts, plus the state provided the experts free to the prosecution. The HGN test, the heel-to-toe test, touch your nose test, alphabet test—hard to pass even stone cold sober; impossible if you were knee-walking drunk.

So that's what it sounded like. Drunk-driving and a negligent homicide. Thaddeus wouldn't have wished that on his worst enemy.

Much less his best friend.

"Cancel me out," he told Janet on the intercom. "I'm going to Orbit. Call Katy, tell her I'm sorry about the surprise party but it's about Killen and I had no choice. JT will pick her up from the shelter."

Three bottles of Aquafina went with him when he pulled out. Two hours south of Chicago, a mad dash inside a rest area. Another two hours and he was on the Orbit town square recovering from road hypnosis.

An internal debate was underway as his eyes roamed over the wedding cake courthouse. Did he go inside and defend the guy or did he just throw up his hands and leave? The case was crap to begin with, and any trial lawyer would tell you that crap cases don't get better with time. But he was Thaddeus' best friend, and he had killed a guy. Which didn't reduce him in the young lawyer's sight because he'd seen all the sins. None of them offended him, and he forgave them all because he wasn't put there to judge. He was put there to defend.

It was the only way he ever found it possible to do such dirty work.

~

The Mustang's A/C popped as it cooled.

He looked both ways across the square.

Now both banks agreed it was 4:20 p.m. In a fit of what could only be price-fixing, they both blinked they would pay 1.04% on savings.

He resisted going inside. He would give it another ten.

His mental image of Killen was of a professional District Attorney, a guy maybe mid-thirties, five-six, weighing in at 125, dressed resplendently in expensive suits with pocket squares, tie tacks, and a heavy gold Rolex on his wrist, something with serious diamonds. He was effusive when he talked, explosive almost. High, high energy level, forever challenging everyone about the facts of any case in court when he was prosecuting. He thought himself always right. He protected his cops and to hell with those who did evil. He made sure he returned evil tenfold with long jury trials and refusals to plea bargain, preferring prison terms to probation.

Now there he was in jail, with it all falling down around him.

Thaddeus considered what he would tell the judge about Killen when he made an argument for bail. He knew Killen was an ex-jock. When he was sixteen, he started racing thoroughbreds at county fairs. Wearing silks sewn for men, he swam in the garments and people often laughed.

But he loved racing. He loved being a jockey.

The horses got bigger and faster. Some of them got clumsier.

He told the story of the conclusion of turf and thoroughbreds.

Churchill Downs. Betty's Erotic Handicap hauling ass with Killen up top charging the final turn when she stepped in a gopher hole. Of course there was no gopher, and there was no hole. Betty just made that up. So she had an excuse for going down like she'd been head shot. The Daily Racing Form said Killen was a human comet, head-over-heels into the turf. Betty the horse? Twice a mother since her retirement to Tennessee.

When he hit the dirt, the hoof of the lead horse caught his eye and pitted his eyeball from its socket, leaving him without a left eye. Worse, he heard the bones in his neck pop as he skidded on his chin.

After he broke his neck, he never swung a leg over another

nag. And that was lucky because *Betty's Erotic Handicap* cratered the next Sunday and popped the jock's head like an egg. It was a jockey tradition, roses for the funeral, so Killen wired one dozen. Jocks attending their dead colleague's funeral said he had finally made the winners' circle.

When news of the dead jock first reached him, Killen grimaced from his hospital bed. He questioned whether he had in fact been all that lucky. Spinal fusion—enough pins, wires, and metal to supply an Erector Set. Followed by three months facedown. The guys in the white coats said the next stop was diapers if he torqued his neck just once more.

How to pass three months facedown? Killen read everything the nurses brought him. One, working on her master's degree, forgot it was her day to bring books and so she left behind her college catalog. Curious, Killen cracked it and tried on a hundred possible careers, archeology to zoology. Two weeks later he found himself enrolled in law school. A titanium rod in his C-Spine corrected his posture like a West Point plebe.

He graduated law school and purchased *Money's* "100 Best Places to Live." Into a bowl twelve of the hundred best places were dumped. Shutting his eyes and plunging his hand into the choices, he surfaced clutching Orbit, Illinois.

Thaddeus was waiting in his Mustang for 4:30, watching Mr. Hatch drag the sprinkler around. What a great job, he was thinking. Mowing, watering, painting, snow plowing, changing neons. No clients, no stinking jails, no bad cops, no temperamental judges and other mental losers in black robes. He had almost forgotten it was his thirtieth birthday. Then his watch beeped, and it was time to go inside.

Goodbye Mr. Hatch, goodbye grass rainbow.

Up the stairs he trotted, each step seeming higher than the last. A few heads turned in the Circuit Clerk's office as he passed. A few smiles of recognition, then he was entering the second-floor courtroom.

It was packed; the arrest of the District Attorney on murder charges was a guaranteed draw.

The Hickam County Democrat was represented by no less than the publisher along with the local reporter. The police reporter from the *Quincy Herald-Whig* was in the crowd, and an anxious team of TV journalists were poised as they waited for the judge to rule on their motion to allow TV cameras inside.

Killen Erwin was already at counsel table.

From the back, as Thaddeus came up the aisle, the jock looked like a large boy. His shoulders were hunched, and Thaddeus knew that was because he was handcuffed.

Just behind him sat Mitt Gaffney, the rotund deputy who had walked Killen over from the jail. He wasn't smiling like his usual jocular, double-dipping self. He was all frowns.

They'd all been there a thousand times, but this time was different. Thaddeus realized it was the light that was different: in every surface, every wood and linoleum and wall he could see stark reality. Something had gone bad in Orbit. Really bad.

Killen turned when he heard Thaddeus step through the gate.

"Thaddeus. Thank God.

"Hey, Kill. How's tricks?"

"I was afraid you wouldn't come."

The young lawyer laid his hand on the DA's shoulder. "That, little brother, would never happen. You need me; I'm here."

"How can I ever pay you back, man?"

"Give me a surprise birthday party."

"What?"

"Nothing. So where's Bird Nest?"

"Judge Wren? He's back in chambers conferring with the special prosecutor the Twelfth sent down."

The Twelfth Judicial Circuit had rallied from the shock of Killen's arrest enough to locate an experienced prosecutor and send her to court that afternoon.

"Sounds like a blow job to me."

"You never know," Killen said at Thaddeus' weak attempt at humor.

They were alone at the table, so Thaddeus went for some particulars.

"You told me Johnny Albertson died last night?"

"Johnny Albertson."

"He was a passenger?"

"Yeah. We hadn't been drinking together. He saw me leaving and asked for a ride."

"And you said what?"

"I told him no. I said it wasn't smart, that I'd had too much to drink."

"So how was he in your truck?"

"The truth is, I don't even remember pulling away. I was in a blackout."

"Down at the Copperhead?"

"Yep. Three day weekend to kick off Pork Week."

Hickam County proudly touted itself as "Pork Capital of the World," a dubious honor in most circles, but one to which its citizens clung like fat on lean. There was the annual *Miss Pork County* contest and a thousand dollar gift certificate from the Orbit Chamber of Commerce.

"How'd it happen?

"Hit a bridge."

"Where?"

"Algonquin Levee Bridge. Smacked it head-on. Shit, did I just say that? Oh my God!"

"This was last night?"

"It was. I'm still drunk. Head's on fire, seeing spots."

"Okay, take a deep breath and count to ten."

At that moment, the courtroom's double doors flew open.

"Oh shit," muttered Killen.

"Who?"

"Johnny's brothers, Markey, and Mikey. They're here to hang me."

Thaddeus shot a look back over his shoulder. They were identical, the two young men. Sandy hair, unkempt and silvering as their natural blonde gave it up for the nagging gray of middle age; eyes rheumy and lackluster; arms and shoulders powerful enough to wrestle tag team—they were just the sort of survivors it would take all the guile and cunning Killen could muster if he were to avoid them and stay alive.

The twins took over the front row and turned on the harangue. Thaddeus knew they were the type who would watch their sons play football and curse the coach anytime the boys fell short. Fair-minded they were not.

"Who's the loser with the killer?" Asked one twin in his loud, sideline voice.

"Thaddeus Murfee. He used to live here. I remember his picture from the paper. He sued the state and made off with a hundred million of taxpayers' money. Total asshole." It was the almost-identical voice of the identical twin.

"Hey, Murfee," the first twin said. "What are you driving? We wanna be sure we don't run you off the road after court."

Thaddeus shook his head, trying hard not to provoke them.

Just then the Honorable Richard Mason Wren of the Twelfth Circuit entered the courtroom from offstage left. He looked very elegant in his black robe. Silver hair combed back on the sides and top and clipped to perfection around his ears, he looked like a soap opera businessman, the guy who owned the company. He happened to be the Chief Judge of the Twelfth, and he was a no-nonsense jurist who'd never been overturned on appeal. A phenomenal record, to say the least. Steely eyes with the ability to pierce a defendant—or hapless defense attorney—like a bug under the pin. The local bar called him Bird Nest in their futile effort to downsize a man larger-than-life.

"All right," said Bird Nest, "we're back on the record."

"I don't hear no record!" said one of the twins in a rancorous drawl. While Hickam County was all-Yankee, it was far enough south in the state that many citizens spoke in a southern patois. It was strange to hear "Y'all" in the north, but it happened.

Bird Nest ignored the remark and the few sniggers it elicited from the crowd.

"Counsel, identify yourselves for the record, please."

The special prosecutor went first. "Eleanor Rammelskamp," said the stout middle-aged woman with thick neck and eyeglasses hung from a gold chain. She reminded Thaddeus more of a member of the local garden club than the seasoned prosecutor he knew she was. She was nobody's fool, and she would be throwing the proverbial book at Killen Erwin, for he had let down the elite: the prosecutors. "I represent the people of the State of Illinois."

Now Thaddeus stood. "Thaddeus Murfee for the defendant Killen Erwin. We are prepared to enter our plea of not guilty, Your Honor."

Before His Honor could respond one of the twins erupted with, "Not guilty my ass! Killed my brother, the son of a bitch did!"

Whereupon Judge Wren's eyes narrowed, and he moved his gaze to the twins.

"Gentlemen—yes, you two, no need to look around. That will be quite enough with the outbursts in my courtroom. If I need to hear from you, I will tell you. Otherwise please shut the hell up!"

His words settled the courtroom. The participants knew his reign was a *fait accompli,* and he wasn't going to allow anything to detract from his station. Much less a set of hillbillies from a lesser county than his own.

"Sorry, Judge," said the verbal twin. "We thought this was like wrestling."

"Well, it's not. So silence, please, gentlemen."

"You got it judge," said the same idiot voice, and Thaddeus turned just in time to see him make the zipper motion across his mouth, turn the key and toss it. Judge Wren nodded and got back to his script.

"Counsel, has your client received a copy of the charging document?"

"He has, Your Honor. He showed me a copy of the information he'd been given as soon as I walked in."

"And he's aware of the charges against him?"

"He is, Your Honor."

"Mr. Erwin, please step to the podium with your attorney."

They stepped to the podium. Killen stood on Thaddeus' right, and the young lawyer would have sworn he saw him wobble.

The judge saw it too.

"Are you all right, Mr. Erwin?"

"Yessir. Just upset."

"Damn well oughta be," drawled verbal. "Killed my baby brother!"

Judge Wren snapped his gavel hard against its base plate. "Enough! Sir, one more outburst and you will be held in contempt and removed from my courtroom. No more!"

That time there was no reply. The judge and defense counsel then went through the standard question-and-answer dialogue interspersed with the occasional standard response of the defendant himself. It was rote for all of them.

"Now, the question of conditions of release. Madam District Attorney, you may be heard first."

Ms. Rammelskamp was quick to her feet.

"The defendant is a resident of the county, owns property here, and has well-known contacts with the area. All of that is true, and defense counsel will hammer on these facts. But the truth remains, Judge, this is a murder case. The court must set bail enough to guarantee the defendant's return to court. We're asking bail of one million and his passport."

"Counsel?" said the judge to Thaddeus.

"Your Honor, it's true there are a great many connections

between Mr. Erwin and this county. He owns real estate here, owns livestock here, has a wife and two children here, and even holds elected office here. More important, perhaps, is the fact he has no prior convictions—much less indictments—for anything. He's an example of decency and good citizenship to all of us. I say this keeping in mind he hasn't been convicted of anything. The information the state has filed against him is allegations only. There's no proof of any wrongdoing, not yet at least. So the court is asked to release him OR—on his own recognizance. No bail bond necessary, Your Honor. Thank you."

"What the fuck!" cried a twin in his twangy drawl. "Fuck that no wrongdoing kind of bullshit talk. He killed our fucking brother!"

Without a word Judge Wren nodded at big old Gaffney, the luckless deputy who was the sole law enforcement officer in attendance. Gaffney pushed up to his feet from the bailiff's chair and made a beeline for the twins. Thaddeus turned to watch the fracas.

Gaffney grabbed the closer one by the arm and the twin immediately twisted free of his grasp. "Back off, fat boy," said the twin. "I'm gonna have to hurt you, son." The twin danced away and taunted the deputy now with some distance between them.

Gaffney then reached for the arm of the second twin—now the closer one—only to have his hammy fist pounded away by the much faster fist of twin two. A startled look passed over Gaffney's face. He'd never been physically over-whelmed in the courtroom. Not in twenty years. He reflex-ively felt for his firearm, but all guns were checked downstairs in the clerk's office before law enforcement was allowed upstairs in the courtroom. Gaffney was outnumbered, and the force he faced was overwhelming. He turned and looked at the judge.

Judge Wren was momentarily dumbstruck. In Quincy, where he regularly held court, he would be joined in the courtroom by a dozen or more police officers, deputy sheriffs, and state police on any given day. But now he found himself in this backwater without recourse to force. What to do?

Which was when Thaddeus climbed to his feet.

"Your Honor," he said, "can I be of any help? As an officer of the court, I too want to see justice done here in an orderly manner. These outbursts are contemptuous, and I would join Deputy Gaffney in his effort to remove the offenders." Thaddeus was way outside his weight class. It was all an act.

Judge Wren's expression changed to relief.

"Thank you, counsel," said the jurist. "I think Mr. Gaffney can show them the door, and I think they'll leave now without any further outbursts. Gentlemen? Am I right?"

The twin with the fast fist waved off the judge.

"We're just leaving," he declared.

The two left the courtroom, sputtering and cursing as they departed.

So Thaddeus sat back down, but he knew he had made his spurs with the judge. It was the exact moment to renew the defendant's motion for release OR. This meant Killen might leave the courtroom without posting a dollar.

"Again, Judge, we ask OR release," Thaddeus said.

"That is certainly appropriate, given the circumstances of the case," said the judge. "It is so ordered. Preliminary hearing on Monday at ten a.m. Anything further?"

They shook their heads. They had nothing further.

Court fell into recess, and Killen and Thaddeus stood up. Handshakes and thanks followed.

"Thanks, Thad," Killen whispered. "Now what?"

"Now I start interviewing witnesses. My weekend is spoken for."

"Too bad. I could use your help shoveling shit."

"I could do that for an hour."

"Well, come by the barn in the morning."

"I'll be there. Put the pot on."

"Done."

"And say hello to Mary Roberta. Tell her I'm on it."

"She doesn't give a damn. I go to jail, and everything falls into place for her."

"Sure. I've heard." Mary Roberta's lifestyle was common knowledge and even though Thaddeus had been away he'd heard things through the grapevine.

"How can I thank you enough?"

"Don't worry about it. Just keep inviting me out to shovel shit and we're good."

He left the courtroom after the judge had, to everyone's surprise, granted bail. He escaped out the back, down the judge's private entrance, avoiding the milling press. It was a violent death, and it had attracted a loud, insistent crowd of journalists bent on a sound byte.

As he drove off to the motel, he looked around the square. Same buildings—though some with different names above the stores. But everything pretty much just like he had left it five years ago.

It was good to be home.

Two miles west of town, Thaddeus parked and checked into the motel Killen owned. He carried his laptop, briefcase, and suitcase inside. He made the two cups of coffee in the mini-pot. In the bathroom, he ran water and lifted it to his face. Then he called Katy.

The disappointment was evident in her voice when she heard he wasn't coming home yet. He would miss the birthday celebration they both knew she had planned in secret. She sounded resigned.

Another client had stepped to the head of the line.

3

That same Friday night, Katy Murfee called the wife of the District Attorney. Mary Roberta Erwin was ten years younger than Killen Erwin but didn't look it. Alcohol, cigarettes, and late nights had prematurely etched her face, a condition she fought with foundation and Botox. She was twenty-six years old and had once been a beautiful woman whose inability to find level ground on which to make a stand had left her forever troubled—and in trouble—both with those she was forsworn to love—husband and kids— and those she picked off in the dance halls and taverns. She was always the life of any party until the third round was bought and served. But then the alcohol took over and put her imagination in charge of her life where once her common sense had tried to prevail but had failed. At those times, anything could happen and often did. Killen was left behind with no peace, suffering children, and loneliness so profound and unremitting that it only happens in marriages of this type.

Katy had never lived in Orbit, so the two women didn't

know each other, but Katy wanted to reach out anyway. So she placed her call at eight.

"Mary Roberta, this is Katy Murfee. I'm Thad's wife."

"Oh, hi! I know all about you, Katy. Killen's told me how you and Thad met after he left town."

"Well, the reason I'm calling is—there're two reasons. The first is, you're probably scared to death about your husband. I know I would be. So I just wanted to say that I'm here for you. If you need anything or need anyone to talk to, I'm just a phone call away. Plus I only live four hours away by car, so I can get down to you in a blink if you need help with the kids or anything while court's going on or about jail—"

"That's very sweet of you, Katy, but my mom's helping me and we've got it under control."

"How do you feel about everything?"

"I could kill him! Did Thaddeus tell you everything that was going on last night?"

"I haven't talked to Thad but just a minute. He said he had to stay over until Monday."

"Killen was furious because I was dancing with someone else. I had no idea he was in the bar. I'm getting all this second-hand from Johnny Albertson's mother. She runs an antique shop and has spoken to lots of people who were at the Copperhead Tavern last night. They're all saying the same thing; that Killen proceeded to get knee-walking drunk when I wouldn't let him cut in."

"How could you do that?"

She ignored Katy's question.

"I threw his ass out a long time ago. He's got a room at our motel. He's over there."

"Would you like to talk about what's really been going on?"

Again, Mary Roberta ignored the question.

"Serves him right, he wants to follow me around on my night out. I don't wanna hear about it. Ten good years I've given him and two beautiful kids. None of us deserves this."

"It seems like maybe you're both—"

"I'm seeing Elizabeth Melendez on Monday about getting a divorce. I'm so fucking mad at Killen I want half of everything and want him gone!"

"Well, maybe we could talk about that first. Maybe you'll feel—"

"I don't need to talk about it first. I need to take action. You don't know what Killen's really like."

"I do know what it's like to live with a drinker. We went through some of that."

"Well, it's divorce city for me. I've got my kids to think of."

"Can't you maybe give it a week first? See how you feel then?"

"No way. I want out yesterday!"

"Listen, how about if you came up to Chicago and stayed with me for a week? I think you need someone to talk to, someone who isn't all wrapped up in your life. I'm a good listener, and I would love to have you. Especially with Thaddeus down there doing the court stuff. It would be good for you to come here."

"Can't. Kids in school. Plus I run the motel."

"Maybe your mom would stay with them while just you came up?"

"Mom's a scatter-brain. I wouldn't leave the fucking dog with her."

"Oh. Well, what if I came down there, and we spent an afternoon or two together? We could talk, get lunch, try to get through the next few days together."

"Now that would work. I could put you up in our motel suite with Thaddeus. It's three rooms and a living area. Includes kitchenette and cable TV."

"Sounds perfect. Tell you what, I'm on my way. I won't tell Thaddeus, I'll just bring my youngest and zip right down."

"How many you have, Katy?"

"Turquoise is eighteen and Sarai is my baby. Turq will be fine alone, of course."

"Well, let me know when you pull into town. I'll come by and say hello."

"Now that sounds great. It'll probably be tomorrow."

"Check-ins anytime after noon. So feel free."

"Thanks, Mary Roberta."

"See you then. But here's the deal. You don't try to talk me out of a divorce. My mind's already made up."

"No, I won't try to talk you out. I just want to be there for you."

"That'll work then. Maybe we'll find a good place to eat anyway. Somewhere out of Hickam County."

"I'm sure we will."

"But first thing Monday, I'm filing for divorce."

"I understand. So I'll see you tomorrow."

"Yep."

4

Katy drove in on Saturday, and Mary Roberta moved the Murfees into the motel's large suite. While six-year-old Sarai went up the hill to play with Mary Roberta's girl, Celena, the wives went to coffee. Mary Roberta's nanny was watching the kids.

So Thaddeus walked up to the barn where he knew he'd find Killen. Ostensibly he was going there to help the DA with his chores. In reality, though, Thaddeus was going there to have a man-to-man. They both knew that, but neither wanted to say it. There were things between them that needed to be said and the Saturday morning choring was the opportunity for that.

Two tons of horse manure. That's how much Killen and Thaddeus often scooped out of the Hackney stalls on a Saturday morning. Killen had built a new barn since Thaddeus was last there. The new one was twice as long and wide as its predecessor. As Thaddeus approached it from the motel, he judged it was maybe a hundred and fifty feet long by maybe half of that wide. It was red, barn red, of course.

The parking area in front was concrete, and there were designated parking spaces. One was taken up by Killen's sedan. There was a small office up front and a tack room. Thaddeus went right on through.

"Hello, Killen!" He called out.

No answer. So he started walking back between the stalls. Horses could be seen in every stall. It looked like they had just been fed. He called out again.

"Down here, Thad!" Killen called back and waved an arm through a stall door.

The far end of the barn was open. Backed half inside was the old blue Ford tractor with a manure spreader attached. Killen was busily shoveling manure out of the stall. Thaddeus' job would be to move it from there onto the manure spreader. Not exactly the kind of work you might expect to find the young lawyer at on a Saturday morning, but he liked the manual labor. It always got him in touch with a side of himself that he sometimes missed:the young, hapless Thaddeus Murfee who had come to the barn seven years ago on Saturday mornings because, truth be told, he had nowhere else to go. Killen had befriended him then, given him something to do that made him feel good about himself and, most of all, that brought them together so the old pro could further enlighten Thaddeus about the practice of law. They would talk about Thaddeus' cases back then, and Killen would give his two cents worth as far as strategy. It was a priceless education, and Thaddeus knew he owed a lot of his early success to that graduate school Killen invited him to long ago.

He looked inside the stall where Killen was shoveling.

"Hey," he said over his shoulder, never breaking stride, as it were. "You're up early for a city boy."

"It's already seven," Thaddeus said. "That's actually late for me."

"Well, grab a shovel. Or a pitchfork. Whichever flavor you prefer."

"I'm a shovel guy," Thaddeus said and removed his blue work shirt. He had arrived wearing roper boots, jeans, a white T-shirt and an open, untucked blue work shirt.

Then came the shovel.

"Need gloves? There's some on that bench across there."

Definitely needed the gloves. He retrieved them and momentarily felt like OJ as the gloves were a size small, but he worked them on anyway. They were leather and would loosen up with sweat. Then Thaddeus grabbed the shovel and began moving horse manure in a mindless, repetitive effort at staying up with how fast Killen was digging the stuff out of the stall. But there was no way. Killen moved to the next stall while Thaddeus was still on the first one. It was always that way. Killen was in better shape and worked like a machine. Always had.

Thirty minutes later they took a break.

"Coffee up front in the office. Follow me."

Killen took the desk chair, and the young lawyer took an old, comfortable but well-worn easy chair. Thaddeus sank in it to his hips and found himself sitting with his knees higher than his hips. And that's when it happened: in the blink of an eye his lower back suddenly spasmed. A look of pure shock and pain came over his face, and Killen saw it.

"Hey, Thad. What's hurting?"

"My back. It just seized up."

"Need some aspirin?"

"Yes."

"Hold on."

Killen rummaged through his desk and finally surfaced with Tylenol.

"Take three of these. Five-hundred each."

"Good."

Killen held up the plastic bottle and shook it. The pills were tightly packed inside.

"If you're ever looking for these, I keep them right in here," Killen said and replaced the bottle in the top right-hand drawer. "Just help yourself."

Thaddeus did as directed and fought to pull himself up out of the chair. As he did, the spasm increased in intensity until he was standing on both legs with his upper body bent nearly horizontal.

"Try the desk chair," Killen said and came around the desk.

Thaddeus took Killen's seat and immediately felt some relief. "Better. A little anyway. So let's talk. What the hell, Killen?"

Killen shook his head. "I know. I know. Please don't beat me up over it. I've been doing that myself for two days."

"You deserve it. What a rookie mistake!"

"I know, I know. Still can't believe it."

"What, were you just mad at the world? What happened?"

Killen's face tightened. His lips pursed as they did when he was suddenly angry.

"There was a man involved with Mary Roberta."

"How did I not know that?"

"I'm in love with that woman, Thaddeus."

"So she's still sniffing around the bars looking for a stiff dick?"

"She is."

"Okay. So you're still in love."

"Last week one night, I'm out at Lemony Crickets having dinner after work when she walks in with that mother of hers."

"That would be the infamous, the tawdry, Mary Aseline Kittenforge of Kittenforge Orchard, Dooley, Illinois. Road dog number two."

"Exactly. They walk in, and Mary Roberta sees me. I might be her husband, but there is zero sign of recognition. She and mom walk through the restaurant and disappear into the bar. I'm stunned she didn't even so much as nod at me. Or smile. Or come over and—"

"Screw you on the spot."

"It was one of those moments when lightning strikes. I got it:

she was done with me. I came unglued. Suddenly I just had to talk to her."

"So you followed her into the bar."

"By the time I paid for my meal and got back to the bar, she was rubbing up against Dave Daniels."

"Dave the pipeline welder and all-around pussy hound?"

"The same. They're both leaned up against the bar. She's got her arm around his back, and he's nuzzling her ear. Then they see me come in; she whispers something to him, they both look over and smile. Then they laugh. An inside joke and it's about me. So I took a seat underneath the picture of Secretariat and ordered two vodka martinis. Bam! The first one slides down like water. Then I'm into my second when the thought arrives inside my thick skull that she either hasn't recognized me—impossible—or that she is actually going to make her way over to me—possible but not likely, the way she's rubbing up against Dave, the welder. So I sit and stew."

"This was what night?"

"This would have been Wednesday night."

"The night before your accident."

"Exactly."

"Okay. So what happened next?"

"I got drunk, and the cops took me home. Fast forward to Thursday night."

"Down at the Copperhead Tavern."

"Yes. I followed her there, doing my own detective work.

She walked in and found Dave and latched on. Dave loaded the jukebox. An old song by Jim Croce played, 'Time in a Bottle.' They started to slow dance together, and his hands were all over her ass. I was nuts. So I decided to cut in."

"You didn't."

"Yeah, I did. I was a little wobbly on my feet, working on number three, and I touched Dave on the shoulder and told him I was cutting in. But he ignored me. Then he said, 'Scat, Erwin.' That's it, just 'scat,' like I was a barnyard cat."

"What did Mary Roberta do?"

"She laughed and turned her head away from me. Wouldn't even look at me."

"So what did you do?"

"I turned and looked around. Everyone in the place was watching me and pointing and smiling. Some were laughing."

"So you got embarrassed. Were you angry yet?"

"Just at that exact moment the anger train pulled into the station, and I climbed onboard. So I touched Dave on the shoulder again."

"Now Dave's built like one of Mike Ditka's linebackers. Not smart, pushing at him."

"Right. This time he batted my arm away. So I touched his shoulder again and told him I was cutting in, what doesn't he understand about that?"

"And he knocked your dumb ass on the floor. Am I right?"

"Not yet. No. But he told me to sit down and leave them alone."

"What did he say, exactly."

"'Tonight's my night in the saddle. You already had yours, Erwin!'"

"His night in the saddle! What's the girl do?"

"Turned and laughed at me. Said, 'Bug off, Kill-joy. Can't you see we're busy here?' So I broke a bottle. I was going after Dave Daniels. At that point, Johnny Albertson appeared out of nowhere. He came up and took me by the arm and steered me outside. I was feeling like shit. I threw up. My steak dinner and three martinis. What happened inside that bar made me sick."

"What did Johnny do?"

"He walked me around and told me to give him my keys. Then I went into a blackout. Next thing I know, I'm sitting on the bridge all fucked up. Bill Janes arrested me and well, here I am."

"So that's the story."

"Yes. How's the back?"

Thaddeus shuffled in the chair and winced. The pain was still there; maybe even worse.

"Not so hot. I think I need to see Mike Cheever."

"He'll be working the ER this weekend. They lost their weekend ER doc, and Mike's been filling in. The city is trying to lure another doctor to Orbit. The big deal in the newspaper the past month."

"So I'm thinking I show up at the ER and get some muscle relaxants or something. I can't be folded over like this when we have your hearing on Monday."

"Hopefully not. Hopefully, you'll be walking more like a man and less like a knuckle-dragging ape."

Thaddeus smiled. "You driving?"

"Sure. On my temporary license."

"That'll do."

They continued their discussion on the way into town. They passed by the Case tractor dealer, passed by the new cut-rate pharmacy in the strip mall with the Safeway grocery store, passed by the cemetery on the left, passed by the Red Bird Inn, and then passed the other motel in town, Killen's competitor. The next block on their left was taken up by the Hickam County Hospital. Killen pulled around back.

"Wait," Thaddeus said before they climbed out. "Got a question."

Killen withdrew the key from the ignition and began spinning the keychain in his hand. "I'm listening."

"Do you really love this girl?"

"You know what? I really do."

"Why? Where's your pride, Kill?"

"All I can tell you is, whenever I see her, my heart flips over in my chest."

"What do you like about her?"

"Well, I love the page boy haircut. And I love the black hair."

"Wait, that's the beauty queen stuff. You don't love someone for physical features only. Think about my question. What is it about her that you love? We're talking character traits, personality features, Killen."

"She's fun to be with. Lots of laughs."

"Okay, you laugh a lot with her. What else?"

"She's a great joker."

"Okay, lots of laughs. We've already got that. That's item number one in 'likes' column. What's item number two?"

"I don't know. Something about how free-spirited she is. She's not all hung up on social dogma. She's free, man."

"Meaning she spreads her legs on command."

"Come on, Thaddeus, don't make her sound like a hooker."

"Okay. Item number two is free-spirited, parenthesis, spreads her legs on command, parenthesis."

"She's intelligent, smart."

"Name some of the things you two have discussed. The intellectual stuff."

"Well, she knows a lot of the history of the Beatles."

"Are you kidding me? That's the depth of her intellect you want to lay on me? Sorry, pal, but I'm not buying Beatlemania as evidence of someone's depth. Try again. For example, is she a nihilist? A Buddhist? An existentialist? Has she read the Russian novelists? Does she discuss Renoir's underpainting? What is it exactly that equals intellectual accomplishment?"

"Don't make her sound stupid, man."

"I'm not. I'm asking you to make her sound smart. Intellectual, like you said."

"I can't think of specifics."

"That's the same as saying it doesn't exist, dumbass."

"Okay, so she's no—not—"

"The Mary Roberta I've noticed around town is good looking, large-breasted just like you lust after, and a party girl without limits. You tell me what I'm missing."

"You know what? The hell with you, Thad."

"Yeah. That's what I thought. Come on, my back's killing me."

"Good. I'm glad."

"I don't know if it's the horses' horseshit that did me or *your* horseshit."

"Come on, city boy."

"Coming."

5

Mike Cheever was Thaddeus' doc when Thaddeus lived in Orbit. Dr. Cheever was a general practitioner who was unafraid to tackle any area of medicine. But he also knew his limits and would refer a patient out whenever indicated.

Thaddeus limped inside the ER and showed the admitting clerk his insurance card and ID, and then waited in a stiff plastic chair for a good thirty minutes. In the meantime, Killen left to find coffee. He finally gave up after turning down the hospital's machine coffee and left to find the good stuff. He would bring it back, he said as he passed back through the waiting area.

Thaddeus read an old *Field and Stream* article that featured the 2014 line of Orvis rods and reels and gear. It was interesting and made him miss the trout stream out on Katy's reservation. He decided it was time to visit Henry Landers—Katy's grandfather—and catch some native rainbows. They would be hitting the August fly hatch hard.

At long last a tech came and told him the doctor had ordered X-rays when he was told of Thaddeus' complaints. Mike Cheever and Thaddeus went way back, so the young lawyer wasn't surprised there would be films even before the examination. There had been back spasms before, since being shot in Orbit, and there had been X-rays before.

After the radiologist, Thaddeus was shown to a curtained-off exam area. Mike came briskly striding in and shook his hand and asked about things. They caught up. He then asked about Thaddeus' back and what he thought had caused the muscle spasms. Thaddeus explained about the manure work and Dr. Cheever laughed. "Typical thing, weekend wannabe farmers. Hurt yourself 'cause you're out of shape. When we get in our thirties, Thad, it's a whole new ballgame. We're not as resilient and hard-wired as we once were. Stuff starts to deteriorate, although you're still quite young."

He then examined Thaddeus' leg reflexes, made him walk on his heels, made him lie on his stomach while he palpated his spine and remarked that he could feel the spasm. "Probably at L5-S1," he said. "Which is very typical for the work you were doing."

"So what's my prognosis," Thaddeus asked.

"Well, you're going to be taking some Skelaxin tablets and Tylenol for about a week. That should help with the symptoms. In the meantime, I don't want you lifting anything over twenty pounds. And when you do lift, lift with your legs. Here, let me show you." He then demonstrated proper lifting fundamentals and made sure Thaddeus could see how he wanted things done.

"What about sex?" Thaddeus asked.

"Have all the sex you can stand," he said, "but make sure it's your wife."

"Ha-ha, Mike. Katy says it's time we have another baby. So we've been trying."

"That's funny. She didn't mention that."

"What?"

"She was here earlier. Maybe an hour ago."

"What? The ER? Was someone hurt?"

He shook his head. "There's patient confidentiality I can't violate."

"Mike, come on. Katy and I have seen you together lots of times."

The doctor nodded slowly, deciding. Then he relented.

"No, she came in because she felt a lump. In her armpit. She was at coffee and scratched and happened to feel it. It alarmed her. I checked her over and told her it was probably an ingrown hair, but I couldn't be sure."

"She's a doctor, she would probably know the difference."

"I know she's a doctor. I tried to hire her to work our weekend ER rotation while you're down here on Killen's case."

Thaddeus smiled. "I'm sure that went over big. She's been working in her homeless shelter for quite some time now. I don't know if medicine fits her any more."

"She said she wouldn't be down from Chicago that long."

"So what about the lump thing? Did you do anything? Do a biopsy?"

"No. She'll follow up when she gets back home. A specialist can decide what to do."

"That worries me, Mike. Should I be worried?"

"Well, if it's an inflamed lymph node, maybe yes, maybe no. I couldn't feel any other swellings, but you never know. It might be early in whatever is going on. Or like I said, it could also be an ingrown hair. Though that's doubtful, to tell the truth. It's something to follow up."

"Now I'm worried. I'm going back to the motel and have a talk. We can't afford to wait on something like that."

"Don't hit the panic button, Thaddeus. But next week some-time wouldn't be too soon to see someone."

"Okay. Now. Where do I get these prescriptions filled?"

"Well, you drove right by the new discount pharmacy when you came from Killen's barn. Best prices in town."

"You own a piece of it, don't you?"

Mike smiled.

"Who said anything about a mere piece?"

"Thought so. Good work, Mike."

"Take your medicine, don't lift, and I'm sending a set of back exercises we give all our back people. Do them twice a day. By the way, the X-Rays show minimal osteoarthritis, no disk narrowing, nothing that indicates any bony process involved in your complaints. So that's all good."

"Roger that."

Thaddeus left in a hurry, found Killen returning with two coffees, and asked the DA to drop him by the motel.

There was something Katy hadn't called him about, and he wanted to know why.

6

Back at the motel Thaddeus met Katy at the door. She was just returning from checking in on Sarai. Sarai begged to stay up the hill at Mary Roberta's. Sarai was first grade, and Celena was second grade. But Sarai was large for her age, so it was a good fit, Katy explained. Without a word, Thaddeus took his wife in his arms and drew her close to him. He inhaled the smell of her hair and felt her firm body press against him.

Katy was above-average height, lithe, and wore her black hair shoulder length, parted down the middle. Her dark eyes absorbed the world around her—especially her husband and children—and responded with a lifelong drive to do good, to give back, to make the world better than how she had found it. These were the same traits that had taken her to medical school and every day confirmed that she was correct in her choice of a helping profession. She laughed easily and listened to those around her with the natural concentration of the physician she was, a graduate of Stanford Medical School and a Board-Certified Internal Medicine doctor.

She moved against Thaddeus and drew his face to her and kissed him hard on the mouth. "I missed you," she said, referring to his being away from her in Orbit.

"I'm glad you're here," he said and kissed her back. "Really glad."

Thaddeus and Katy went inside the room, and she was humming while she put more of their clothes into the dresser drawers and the small closet. For the life of him he couldn't make out the tune she was humming, and then it came to him: "You Must Have Been a Beautiful Baby." One of those ancient songs that maybe his grandparents sang. He asked her where she'd heard it, and she thought maybe the radio. Or a TV quiz show. But it was about babies and that wasn't lost on him. Katy wanted another, and he was hesitating. They already had Sarai and Turquoise and his law practice was putting a horrendous dent into his schedule. He didn't wish to deprive a baby out of time with its father, so he was slow on the uptake. At least that's what Katy said. "You can't plan for kids like that. You just have them and then do what's indicated. That's how you parent."

But he still felt the world closing in on him from all sides. He had his practice in Chicago, and he still maintained a presence in Flagstaff and now, to top it all off, here he was back in Orbit taking on what would have to be a tremendously time-consuming case. They had airplanes—they had two now, a Gulfstream, plus a Lear for shorter hops—and they had leased cars at all the airports, but Albert and Thaddeus were still running thin. It occurred to him several times a day that they needed another attorney or five in the practice, but Albert always balked. Albert liked the big bucks, and once they started hiring more attorneys the pie would be smaller—or so he thought. Thaddeus thought just the opposite: that with more bodies they could take on more cases and do less of it themselves. Albert would prepare the cases, and Thaddeus would take them to trial. Or Albert plus two or three more attorneys would prepare the cases and Thaddeus would take them to trial plus he would locate and groom a second trial attorney. His thoughts turned to Christine Susmann. Christine was Thaddeus' long-time paralegal and best friend. She had gone from legal support to the practice of law herself, and now ran her own criminal and personal injury practice out of Chicago. Why she had never practiced law with Thaddeus was a subject about which neither had much clarity. At any rate, she was hugely successful in her own right and they were still fast friends, jumping in to help when the other asked. Still, it would be a dream if she would come in with him, but that was never going to happen. She'd gotten too successful too fast and throwing in with him would be a step backward for her. She was launched. He was the launching pad, but the rocket was in outer space.

So, back to his point: he wasn't convinced another baby was a good thing while Katy wanted to give birth yesterday. They were at a stalemate, and they discussed the issue endlessly. So much so, it seemed like that's all they had to talk about anymore.

But that day, with Sarai away at play, he wanted to spend some time with Katy. Get away from the motel, away from the phones, away from the Killens and the Alberts of the world. Just the two of them.

"Hey," he said on the second time through *Beautiful Baby*, "what do you say we take a drive?"

"Cool. Where to?"

"Summer Hill. I want to see where Killen had his wreck."

"Oh. I thought you had something romantic in mind for the day after your birthday."

"I do have something romantic in mind. Later."

"Sure, I'll go. Let me hit the john and I'll be right out. Start the car."

"Okay," he said. But he didn't leave the room. He had a hunch. And when he had a hunch he followed it.

He stepped backward into the bedroom and opened and closed the outside door. Then he crept back to where he could see inside the bathroom. Spying on his wife? Sort of. He watched her while she stood before the mirror and slipped her Stanford T-shirt up around her neck. Then he watched while her physician's fingers probed under her arm. Bingo. He knew she'd be doing that. How did he know? Because she was his wife and he loved her. That's just how it was when you loved someone. You *knew* them.

Then he jumped back and opened and closed the door again. Sound effects.

"You ready in there?" He called.

"I'm peeing. One second, Hurry-Up."

"No hurry. Just cooling my jets."

"Okay. Just about done. Let me wash."

He heard the sink run and then the light being flicked off.

She came out air drying her hands and retrieving her sunglasses from the top of the TV. She pushed them up on top of her head, tucked in her Stanford Cardinal T-shirt, and gave the room a quick once-over. Then she announced she was ready.

They pulled out of the motel and headed west. A mile west of town, two federal highways join in a Y coming east and split into a Y going west. They took the southern leg of the Y, going southwest.

They followed the Mississippi River down through bottom-land—the richest farming land in North America. Basically if you spit a watermelon seed on that soil, an entire fruit orchard would spring up. Or record-yield soybeans and corn. The fields were German-neat, and the forests ran up to the west roadside from the river. Very manicured. Top Husbandry.

Then they entered into the drainage district known as the Algonquin Island Levee Drainage District. This was where millions of dollars received from bond issues had been spent reclaiming priceless bottom land from the river. What had once been useless swampland was dredged and leveed, and farm land with ten feet of topsoil was left when all the water was gone. Incredibly productive and valuable, the land returned five thousand dollars for every dollar spent. An amazing district and they were driving down the center of it, north to south, where it followed the Mississippi.

It was August, and the sun was at two o'clock, the cumulus clouds were building in the west, and the airliners were laying down lazy contrails forty thousand feet overhead.

Summer in the Midwest meant green everywhere you looked, and that day was no different. Summer also meant cornstalks reaching above your head and soybean bushes higher than your waist. A bread basket to the world, the American Midwest. He knew there were lots of jokes about "Flyover country," and the like, but the Midwest, while it was conservative, was also rich, clean, pretty, and a damn fine place to raise a family. Plus, there were very few droughts and other natural calamities. The occasional tornado would break loose and run the table now and then, but nothing like the plains of Oklahoma and southern Missouri, and Kansas. Truth be told, Thaddeus was glad to be back in the Midwest. He could afford to live anyplace in the world, literally, and he was happy right where he was.

With the exception that their room was too small.

"Hey," he said after they'd driven maybe twenty minutes in one of those comfortable silences you can have with your best friend, "I'm thinking we should find a living arrangement a little more permanent now that I've got Killen's case going on here."

"What are you talking about?" She had lowered her sunglasses over her eyes and her tone, while not irritated, was clearly about avoiding one of his schemes.

"I'm thinking maybe we should buy a house here."

"Here? In this farmland?"

"In Orbit. Find a big old barn of a place and fix it up."

"Why in God's name would we do that? We live in Chicago. And Arizona. We don't live in Orbit."

"I'm not saying we'd live here full-time. Just some of the

time. I mean, if you really want another kid, I can't think of a better place to raise him. Or Sarai, for that matter."

"Him? Are we having a son? Are you sure about that?"

He looked across at her. "If we're lucky, we're having a him."

"You've changed your mind?"

"I'm thinking seriously about it. We're not getting any younger. Why, you're not backing out on me, are you?"

"No—just surprised, that's all."

"Well there's nothing holding you back, is there?"

A look came over Katy's face. She was nobody's fool.

"When you went to see Mike Cheever. He told you I dropped in, didn't he?"

Thaddeus nodded. "Yes."

"Fool. That violates the doctor-patient confidentiality rule."

"Hey, he knows we're joined at the hip. When he treats you, he's treating me. When he treats me, he's treating you. I see his approach as holistic."

"Nice try. I'm going to kick his ass. He's got one Indian maid plain old pissed at him."

"So...were you going to fill me in?"

"What?"

"Tell me why you went to see Mike?"

"It's nothing. I just felt something under my arm, and I panicked. I'm like the first year med school student who catches every disease she reads about in her textbooks. That's what it was like this morning. Nothing going on after all."

"We're sure about that?"

"Sure as sure can be."

He drummed his fingers on the steering wheel. He adjusted the outside mirror on his side.

"So, does this mean you're not going to follow up on it, or you are?"

"The little bump? Working diagnosis is an ingrown hair."

"Whose diagnosis?"

"Mine. Me, myself, and I."

"Uh-uh. You can do better than that. I want a second opinion. Monday, when you get home to Chicago."

"I'm going home to Chicago?"

"Yes, tomorrow. I want you in a physician's office by Monday noon. And I want a biopsy done or whatever she thinks. No ifs ands or buts."

"But—"

"Silence, woman, Baal has spoken."

"Well, Baal, please tell me how I'm supposed to—"

"Call in a favor. Some doctor in Chicago owes you a favor. And he or she is an expert in what you need. Don't argue with me, just do it."

"Okay." She turned her head away and looked obliquely out

her window. The tips of her hair across her forehead were catching patches of light as they passed through the trees. Her beauty was fantastic to see, and he was suddenly struck with how much he loved her and how much he wanted her to be okay. Then he chided himself for jumping into a huge plate of worry. It was more than he could think about. He fished his sunglasses out and plopped them over his eyes. Now the tears could trickle out, and she'd never know.

"You're getting all weepy on me," she said gently. "Don't do that, Thad. I'm okay."

"Promise?"

She touched the back of his neck. "Promise."

"And you'll see someone Monday?"

"Promise."

"And you'll come back to me Monday afternoon and let me get you pregnant once we've got the all-clear?"

She sat upright. "Well, if there's a biopsy it won't be back Monday. More like Wednesday or Thursday. We shouldn't try until then."

"So, that means you *are* worried there might be something to this lump. Or else you'd jump right into making a baby with me on Monday."

"Shit, I hate being married to a lawyer."

"Come on, admit it. You're holding back now."

She looked at him full-on, leaning forward in her seat and looking at his face, removing his sunglasses. "Earth to Thaddeus. I think we should get a definitive answer about mom's armpit before we get pregnant. That is all. Over and out."

"Okay. Next time just come clean."

"Yeah. You do that too."

Which opened an avenue for another argument, but neither was in the mood, so she snuggled as close to him as possible from inside a shoulder harness and on they drove in silence.

7

One of the first things Thaddeus had learned as a new lawyer was to see for himself. He had learned to go to the scene of whatever a case was about and look it over for himself. The difference between how the client described it to him and how it really looked was most often jolting. But there was a problem. When he woke up Sunday morning, his lower back was still in spasm; he medicated with a Skelaxin and decided to push ahead.

Katy had left early with Sarai for Chicago. She would see the doctor on Monday.

Thaddeus couldn't be with her because Killen's preliminary hearing was Monday. So Thaddeus was stuck in Orbit. He decided to go with Killen to the scene of the accident, his thought being that maybe Killen would see something that would trigger a helpful memory.

From his motel room, he climbed upstairs. Killen was lodged on the second floor, directly above his suite. When he opened the door, the inside air came swelling out in a cloud of stale alcohol and cigarettes.

"Hey," he said. His eyes were bloodshot and his voice husky. Thaddeus' friend was not doing well at all. He stepped inside.

"Hey," Thaddeus said. "It stinks in here."

"I know. Please don't get started or you'll sound like Mary Roberta."

"Maybe Mary Roberta's on to something, Kill."

"So what's up? It's not even nine o'clock."

"I'm going down to the Algonquin Bridge. I need you to come with."

"I can do that. Can I grab a shower first?"

"Definitely."

"Will you sit down and wait?"

"Sure," Thaddeus sat in the desk chair.

He looked around and tried not to judge. Which was difficult. Because clothes were strewn about, the chest of drawers was serving as a makeshift dry bar populated with whiskey bottles, two ice buckets, four drinking glasses and an ashtray overflowing with butts. The air was rotten.

The closet door was open; Thaddeus could see two suits still in dry cleaners' bags and three pairs of shoes neatly arranged at attention. A grocery bag sitting on the floor was overflowing with what looked to be dirty clothes.

Unmade bed, cigarettes on the bedside table, half a six pack of warm Coors—everything about it said that here was a man who was not doing well. And how could Thaddeus blame him? He had just killed a man while driving drunk and he was estranged from his wife and kids. No one survived that mental hell. It was ugly.

Killen was going downhill fast, and Thaddeus wanted only to help. Deep down, the lawyer in Thaddeus wasn't willing to accept that Killen had all but murdered an innocent man and now had to pay the price for such terrible conduct. There had to be something he could do to help though for the life of him he had no clue what that might be.

He yelled into Killen, "Daylight's burning! Let's go!"

"Coming!"

Killen emerged from the bathroom wearing Jockey's and aftershave. Thaddeus was grateful for the one and over-whelmed by the other, as the Old Spice was thick enough to limit visibility.

"I know you're feeling like dog shit," Thaddeus said, "but you need to get ahold of yourself. You're living on a mental skid row, Kill."

Erwin began picking up discarded T-shirts and smelling them. Then he chose one that extolled the advantages of King Corn Seed on the chest.

"I know I am," he said. "I'm turning over a new leaf today."

"Have you thought about taking in an A.A. meeting?"

"Not really. What do you program people say, you hit your bottom? I'm still dangling several inches above mine. My feet haven't touched down yet."

"Hey, if killing Johnny Albertson Thursday night didn't make you hit bottom, then I don't know what it will take."

Erwin shook his head as he pulled on a pair of clean blue jeans. They had been tucked away in a dresser drawer as if he was saving them for a special occasion. Maybe that time had arrived: the first sober look at the tornado damage in his room.

"So we're going to the Algonquin Bridge?" he asked.

"We are. That's the best place to start."

"The scene of the crime."

"The scene of the crime."

Fifteen minutes later they were in Thaddeus' Mustang and headed south on Illinois 54. They had stopped at the Red Bird and picked up two tall coffees to go and were doing their best to handle the steaming brew.

"So, tell me what you remember about the crash."

He looked out the window. He looked back and blew across the surface of his coffee.

"I don't remember. I guess I was in a blackout."

"You don't remember driving?"

"I don't know, Thad. The truth is, I was in a blackout and can't help much."

"So you don't remember driving to the bridge?"

"No, I don't remember driving to the bridge. Does that make me a bad guy?"

"You don't sound remorseful. A judge would put you away with that attitude."

"I guess there's remorse. I don't know; things are pretty mixed up inside my head."

"We'll let's think about that. If we have to work out a plea we're going to need remorse for the judge to buy-in."

"All right. Let me work on it."

"Agreed."

They turned east on a county road back toward Summer Hill. The Algonquin Bridge was two miles down the road. They crossed the bridge and parked along the right-hand shoulder. Then they ran across the road and had a look.

There was still construction. It was Sunday, so there was no one around, but there were plenty of construction signs and temporary lane markings on the concrete bridge and the approach.

While standing there, Thaddeus pulled out his phone and began snapping pictures. Which was all right, but the pictures he was taking didn't necessarily reflect the state of the bridge and the construction zone when Killen had crashed into the bridge in the right-hand lane. Things had been moved around since that night if for no other reason than that the road crew had had to do cleanup.

"Do you remember what the road looked like just before the wreck?"

He shook his head. "Sorry, Thad, but I don't. Looking back, it's like I'm looking at it underwater like it's all swirling around me in a dream. I don't have an accurate video playback in my head that's going to be useful. Not at all. Damn, man, I'm sorry."

"And Bill Janes arrested you, right?"

"He did. Arrested me and took me to the hospital for a blood draw."

"Have you talked to him since?"

"No."

"Did he get pictures?"

"Probably, I don't know. I passed out in his back seat. Threw up and passed out. He was really pissed Friday when he stopped by the jail."

"No doubt."

They were standing about thirty yards east of the bridge. Thaddeus was eyeballing it, trying to get a feel for what might have happened. It came to him that he needed whatever pictures Bill Earl might have taken if he was going to begin even to understand what happened. What happened beyond the garden variety drunk-driving crash and death. It was a hunch, but Thaddeus felt there was more than met the eye. So he needed the pictures.

"Let's hit the Copperhead," he said. "Let's see what we can find out there."

"I don't think so," Killen said. "I'm embarrassed to go there with you. Besides, they eighty-sixed me."

Stony silence. Then, "What about Mary Roberta herself? I made a total ass of myself with her," Killen said

"I expect you did. But what's done is done. This is no longer a backstreet romance we're tap-dancing around. This is a main street homicide investigation and if feelings get hurt tough shit. That includes your feelings, Killen. So get in the car with me and hold on, because we're going to jump right into the heart of that night."

They jogged back across the road, climbed into the Mustang, and set out for a visit to the Copperhead Tavern.

"I've been thrown out and banned," Killen complained.

"You can wait in the car. I haven't been banned."

8

T haddeus had been to the Copperhead twice before: one time to interview the bookkeeper, whose boss was charged with embezzlement of Illinois State tax funds, and one time to buy a sandwich and a beer at lunch when he was trying a drug case in the south county. It was a desolate, lonely looking place from the road. It had once been a farmhouse. Out front, a wide porch rambled beneath a cross-gabled roof covered with green shingles. Wrapping the sad package was a frame exterior badly in need of paint. A simple black-lettered sign said above the door COPPER-HEAD TAVERN.

"Wait here," Thaddeus said to Killen.

"Believe me, I'm not about to set foot in there," Killen said. "I know my limits."

"*Now* you do. A day late and a dollar short."

Thaddeus threw it in park and climbed out. His cowboy boots crunched in the parking lot gravel as he made his way to the entrance. He touched the pocket of his sports coat. He had his cell phone for the snaps.

Removing his sunglasses, he stepped inside. Three old farmers turned on their barstools to look him over. This was a country tavern on a secondary road; everyone expected to know everyone who came inside. The apparition of Thaddeus in the doorway was disconcerting to the tavern's habitués; here was a man no one knew.

Thaddeus sauntered to the bar and had a seat. He pulled a twenty dollar bill off his money clip and pressed it against the shiny wood. A willowy bartender in her early fifties moved his way. She had blowzy, fly-away hair, a pair of orange reading glasses around her neck on a coral chain, and gray-rimmed, puffy eyes. Thaddeus smiled at her and she stone-faced him.

"Diet Coke," he said. "And give these guys whatever they're drinking, on me." He indicated the three ancient farmers perched at the bar, who, when the purchase of the round was announced, returned to their conversation. The guy had bought them a drink; that meant he passed all necessary good-citizen tests.

The barmaid slid the brimming Coke glass down the bar. She nodded at him.

"So what's your name?" he asked.

She returned the question with a blank look. "Margaret. Call me Margie if you need another."

She turned her back to Thaddeus and began mopping imaginary spillage from the far end of the burnished oak bar.

Thaddeus tapped a quarter against the countertop. "Margie, I have to ask you something."

Margie turned around. Thaddeus flashed his badge. Margie approached him.

"Liquor Control?"

"No, not Liquor Control. Lawyer."

"Forget about it."

"Were you here two nights ago?"

"I forget."

"Did you serve District Attorney Killen Erwin? Please help me."

She held out her hand. He peeled off a hundred and laid it in her hand. "Well?" he said.

"I served him, and Mitt Henry served him. Mitt owns the place. Thursday night the place was jumping, so we were both on."

"Why was the place jumping Thursday night?"

"Start of Apple Festival down in Ford County. People were stopping here headed south to the party."

"Was there a band?"

"In here? Never. Fairly decent sound system. I installed it."

"Good for you. Did you happen to see Mr. Erwin when he left here that night?"

"Did I know he killed someone five miles down the road?

Yeah, I knew that. Everybody in the county knows about it, I guess."

"Answer my question, please. Did you see him when he left here?"

"Not particularly. You know how it is. They come and go, and you don't pay no attention. Just an endless river of faces. Some pretty some ugly, most drunk or on their way there."

"Sure. Do you know whether Mitt saw Mr. Erwin when he left that night?"

"Couldn't say. We never discussed it."

"Did you ever form any opinions that night as to whether Mr. Erwin was intoxicated?"

"I'm not supposed to discuss that. Mitt says the dead man's widow will probably sue us for dram shop."

"There is no widow. Only a mother."

"Well, then, she'll probably sue us for getting the DA drunk and letting him drive."

"Who told you not to discuss it?"

"Mitt's lawyer."

"Who would that be?"

"Louis M. Crankles."

"Did he come all the way out here from Orbit to talk with you?"

"He did. This morning bright and early. I was still out back in my trailer. Mitt knocked and got everyone rounded up."

"So you've been told not to discuss Mr. Erwin's demeanor."

"I've been told not to tell anyone he was drunk."

"Was he drunk?"

"You betcha. He came behind the bar, grabbed a Cutty bottle, broke the neck on the counter and chased a bunch of old coots out. They was raisin' their hands tryin' to surrender to Erwin. It was hilarious, but naturally we don't cotton to that down here."

"So what happened next?"

"Mitt stepped up. He threw him out."

"Why did Johnny Albertson leave with him?"

"Dunno. Wanted to hitch a ride back to Orbit, I expect. Never asked."

"Were any women involved that night? Any I might need to talk to?"

"Just that whore Mary Roberta Erwin. She had Killen tied up in knots."

"Tied in knots? How's that?"

"She was sitting at table nine with her mom and some others. The mom is from Ford County and thinks her shit don't stink. That's because she owns lots of apple trees, and she's a millionaire. Some shit like that. So the daughter is with the mother and they're dancing with this and that guy. The thing is, I notice Killen keeps asking this Mary Roberta to dance and she keeps shaking her head No. But he don't give up. He keeps goin back every song."

"How old is this Mary Roberta?"

"Probably thirty-two, three."

"You called her a whore. Why's that?"

"When she comes south to see her mom she screws every Tom, Dick, and Harry. We've had to ask her to leave our parking lot before; there was a line of guys waiting to get in her car and a fight broke out. Another time she was on her knees in the men's room, back stall, and some guy was laughing his head off over it. You could hear him clear out here, louder than the sound system. 'Faster!' he was yelling at her. 'Faster!'"

"So why was she so tough on Killen?"

"Mitt tells me Killen is still in love with Mary Roberta, never mind her ways. He's head-over-heels. But that's just hearsay."

"How does Mitt know this?"

"Mary Roberta's mom, the apple queen, tells Mitt about it after Killen chased those guys with a broken bottle."

"Why did she tell Mitt?"

"Cause Mitt walked up to their table and asked what the hell they did to Killen to make him act so crazy. Killen's been here lots. Always a perfect gentleman. Something sure'n hell set him off that night, though. Whooee!"

"What did they tell Mitt?"

"She didn't wanna dance with him no matter what. She told him she fucked for fun, not for serious. Something like that. I forget the exact words she told him."

"All right. I think I want to talk to Mary Roberta's mother. How do I get hold of her?"

"Her mother's that bitch Mary Aseline Kittenforge of Kittenforge Orchard in Dooley."

"Never heard of her. But Dooley, you say?"

"Yep. Dooley. She's a whore herself and can drink any two men under the table. I know, I seen her do it."

"Okay, Margie. I think that about answers all my questions. Anything else you think I should know that I haven't asked?"

"Just talk to the mom. Bitch."

Just as he was leaving, a second cocktail waitress came on duty. She was medium height, a peasant blouse with pleasant curves rising from the scooped neckline. Her face was freckled across the bridge of her nose, and her hair was coarsely braided in short, stiff-looking braids with red elastic on the ends. She'd been in the sun that day, and it looked good on her; he figured she was more than likely skiing on the river before she came on. The name tag said it all: FANCY PANTS.

"Can I get a word with you?" he said when she started up behind the bar.

"You a cop?"

"I'm a lawyer. And I have a question for you."

"All questions, one hundred dollars, no exceptions. It's about that Killen Erwin thing, ain't it?"

"It is."

Thaddeus peeled a hundred dollar bill off his walking-around roll and passed it to Fancy Pants.

"Shoot. What's your question?"

"Did you see Killen leave here that night with Johnny Albertson?"

"No. But I did see him leave here with his wife, Mary Roberta."

Thaddeus felt the hair stand up on the back of his neck.

"Mary Roberta left with him?"

"Uh-huh."

"Did you see who was driving?"

"Uh-huh. That's another hundred."

Thaddeus quickly paid off. "Who?"

"She was. Mary Roberta was driving when they left."

"Where was Killen?"

"Passed out with his face pressed against the passenger window. Drooling, feeling no pain."

"Was Johnny with them?"

"If he was, I didn't ever see him."

"Have you told anyone else this?"

She shook her head and crossed her arms over her chest.

"Nope because no one's asked me."

"No cops have asked you?"

"Nope, you're the first."

"Look. Would you put your digits in my cell phone?"

"No."

"Why not?"

"That costs extra."

He sighed. "How much?"

"Name and number is two hundred."

He peeled off another two bills.

With his smartphone held close to her waist, she entered her name and phone number.

"Carla Knight, that's me."

"Carla Knight. Fancy Pants."

"One and the same."

"Will you testify to what you saw?"

"You payin'?"

"Of course."

"Sure, then. I'll tell what I saw."

"I'll be in touch. Fancy Pants."

"It's like a stage name."

"I know. Thanks again."

9

Thaddeus returned to his motel room. Killen went upstairs to take a nap. Thaddeus was certain Killen was also going to have a drink or maybe several.

So he decided to keep moving the ball down the field by himself. Thaddeus called the State Police Sub-Station on the west end of Orbit. He made arrangements to meet with Sergeant Bill Janes later that afternoon when Janes came on.

He made coffee and worked on his laptop for ninety minutes. Then he went to meet the investigating officer.

Thaddeus pulled into the sub-station on the west end of Orbit, out beyond the city cemetery. The Ford's engine popped and sizzled as it dripped air conditioning condensation onto the asphalt parking area.

He pulled open the front door and approached the counter. An officer wearing sergeant's stripes was standing behind a trooper who was peering at a computer screen while the sergeant bent behind him to follow his explanation.

"Help you?" said the trooper without looking up.

"You can," said Thaddeus. "I have an appointment with Sergeant Janes."

"You that lawyer representing Killen Erwin?"

"I am. I'm Thaddeus Murfee." The young lawyer extended his hand, but no one shook it.

"Sergeant Janes just called in. He's running five minutes behind. Why don't you have a seat over there?"

"Roger that."

"Listen to that, Sarge. The lawyer knows radio talk."

The sergeant shook his head. "Forgive him, Thaddeus, I'm just happy Killen has you to stand up for him."

Thaddeus began flipping through last week's edition of the local rag. He found himself engrossed in *Who's Doing What* when the sergeant spoke up.

The sergeant nodded at the front window of the sub-station. "Your man just pulled in."

"Sergeant Janes?"

"Yep. Why don't you take the conference room off to your right. It's private in there."

Thaddeus stood and followed the sergeant's suggestion. He opened the door to the room and went inside. Against the far wall was a six by six cork board on which were pinned the police shoulder patches of every sheriff's department in Illinois. It was an impressive display and Thaddeus nodded. "Sweet," he muttered.

He took a seat at the far end of the small conference table and laid his pad before him. He withdrew a ballpoint and made a note about the date, time, and location. Then he heard Sergeant Janes enter the outer office, and he heard the trooper telling him Thaddeus had arrived and was waiting.

Sergeant Janes stuck his head in the door. "Wait one, Thad. Gotta pee."

"Go for it," said Thaddeus with a smile. "I'm not going anywhere."

Thaddeus began counting the shoulder patches. At sixty-seven, he was joined by Sergeant Janes, who came into the room and shook his hand. The sergeant's hand was cool and damp.

"All right, Mr. Murfee," said Bill Janes, "how can I help you?"

"As you know from my call, Sergeant, I am representing Killen Erwin."

"Understand. So...ask away."

"I've viewed the road and bridge. It's my impression that the roadway was improperly signed, striped and marked for the lane drop."

"Are you asking me about it?"

"Did you form an opinion about that?"

"I'm not an expert on traffic engineering, Mr. Murfee."

"I appreciate that. But as a law enforcement officer, how did the road appear to you?"

"I thought the lane drop looked sudden. Not enough

advance warning. I can see how someone would miss it and hit the bridge like Killen did."

"Anything else?"

"Not really. It was dark, and I remember some ground fog. Hard to see that night, which made the lane drop that much more hazardous."

"By the way, did you speak to anyone at the scene other than Killen?"

"Mrs. Brushkart. She was having a heart attack, and I took her to the hospital when I ran Killen in."

"Did Mrs. Brushkart tell you anything she'd seen?"

"She said she saw a woman flee from the accident scene. She thought maybe a woman was driving Killen's truck."

Thaddeus' head jerked up. "She what?"

Sergeant Janes shrugged. "I know. She said she thought a woman was driving."

"What happened to the woman?"

"She was seen by Mrs. Brushkart to run north off the bridge and climb into a red pickup waiting there."

"Did you tell this to the Special Prosecutor?"

"Nope."

"Seriously? Why not?"

"She never asked."

Thaddeus got the impression the sergeant and the special prosecutor weren't fans of each other.

"How can I contact Mrs. Brushkart?"

"Well, you can try a seance."

"What does that mean?"

"It means she's dead. She never left the hospital alive."

"Why isn't her comment included in the accident report? It doesn't say anything about a woman driving Killen's truck."

"Honestly? I thought she was hallucinating. I mean she was having a heart attack, Thaddeus."

"It should have been in your report."

Sergeant Janes leaned back in his chair. "Maybe so. It's been bothering me."

"How about if I asked you to amend your report to include her statement?"

Sergeant Janes thought about that. Finally, he said, "I'd have to talk to my lieutenant."

"Is he here?"

"In his office."

"Well, there's no time like the present. Please."

Sergeant Janes stood and left the room.

Thaddeus clasped his hands behind his head and stretched. He again studied the shoulder patches on the wall.

Sergeant Janes returned. He looked grim, and he appeared hurried, brushing by Thaddeus and bumping the back of his chair.

"Well?"

"It's done. I went online."

"What did you add?"

"An addendum of my original traffic accident report. It says, 'Officer Janes was also told at the scene by Mrs. Anita Brushkart that a woman was driving the truck when it hit the bridge. She further said that woman fled the scene in a red pickup truck with bright rear lights on the cab. The officer was unable to find any other witness to corroborate this statement.'"

"Good enough. Thank you, Sergeant."

"We done here?"

"We're done."

"So what now, counselor?"

"Now I'm going to talk to Killen's wife."

"Well, keep your dick in your pants."

"Not to worry."

"She's pretty slick."

"So's my wife. Nothing gets past her."

Thaddeus accompanied Katy when it was time to pick up Sarai from Mary Roberta's house. Thaddeus took the opportunity to ask Mary Roberta if he could stay behind and talk about last Thursday night. Mary Roberta laughed and said she didn't want to talk about Killen's accident or the stuff leading up to it. She had spoken with a lawyer, she said and had been advised to make no statements.

Thaddeus thanked her, and he and Katy held Sarai's hand on each side and swung her between them as they walked back down to the motel.

~

By Sunday evening, Thaddeus was tired. He realized he had pushed his investigation about as far as it was going to go.

But he was satisfied in part because he had done what lawyers are supposed to do: he had gone to look. While he did, he had found a cocktail waitress and a state police officer who indicated—in very different ways, as one was an eyewitness, and one was relying on hearsay—there was a woman driving Killen's truck when it wrecked.

All in all a very productive weekend.

Except that, the phantom driver had refused to talk to him. He worked on a subpoena he would serve on her that would require her to appear at the preliminary hearing and give testimony.

He had only just begun.

10

P reliminary   Hearings   were   his   favorite   court
appearances for two reasons.

First, the defense was supposed to lose. Defendants were
always bound over for trial at preliminary hearings. Except
occasionally the state's case was so bad the judge had to
dismiss it. It happened, but it was very rare.

The second reason he liked preliminary hearings was
because they were all about shooting from the hip. For
example, hearsay was admissible. This meant the investigating officer could take the witness stand and recite what
everyone connected to the case had told him and even
though it was hearsay it was still admissible. Why was that?
Because the standard for binding someone over for trial was
much lower than the standard for finding guilt. With the
latter, there was no hearsay and proof must always (almost)
pass certain rigid tests before it was admissible. Conversely,
preliminary hearings were made up of "He said, she said,
they said" testimony. The witness could also testify to *written*
hearsay: reports from police officers, doctor's reports, expert

witness reports—all of it came in which meant none of it was subject to the test of cross-examination. Because Thaddeus couldn't cross-exam what Joe Blow told Officer X when Joe Blow wasn't in court, and his comments were being provided by Officer X as hearsay. The whole damn thing was a joke, and everyone knew it. Which made it a sport of sorts.

Monday's preliminary hearing was on the calendar for nine a.m.

Thaddeus met Killen at the Silver Dome Inn at eight, and they began going over what to expect. They knew Sergeant Bill Janes would be a key witness because he made the arrest. But there was also the chance that his testimony would be provided—as hearsay—by Illinois Bureau of Investigation Special Agent Wells Waters, who did the actual witness interviews. Either guy was unimpeachable; either guy had been around the block ten thousand times when it came to preliminary hearings, and they knew how to act.

But there was also the new matter of the amended accident report. It added Mrs. Brushkart as an eyewitness who had seen someone else driving. It could prove to be fertile soil to examine the police officer as to who else was asked about a fleeing female because, most likely, the inquiry had stopped with Mrs. Brushkart, leaving the full investigation undone. At times, even these minor matters could result in a defendant walking free after a preliminary. So Thaddeus had his hopes.

But there was one witness no one was expecting. His name was Al Hodges, and he was a traffic engineer who had done thirty years of professional work with the City of Los Angeles Department of Transportation or LADOT. LADOT

was the world's largest employer of traffic engineers, and Al
Hodges had been one of them his entire career until his
retirement in 2010 when he began his private consulting
practice. Since 2010 Thaddeus had used him a number of
times in catastrophic injury cases involving an aspect of
traffic engineering beyond the basic questions like "Was the
light red?" or "Was there a stop sign?"

The key mover and shaker for traffic engineers in any city,
county, or state or private practice anyplace in America was
the manual titled the *Manual on Uniform Traffic Control
Devices*, or MUTCD. It was the traffic engineering bible.
Luckily the book was available to Thaddeus online and last
night he had done a cursory survey of its standards for
highway construction zones.

Al would be in town in time for the preliminary hearing. He
was flying into Chicago and taking the firm's Learjet from
Chicago to Orbit. He would sit in on the preliminary
hearing testimony and, if Thaddeus saw the need, his testimony would be introduced. Would Thaddeus need his testimony? Would he actually call Al to the stand? He had no
idea. He was clueless. But he wanted him there to back him
up. There was one aspect of the case that Thaddeus had a
hunch about, and Sergeant Bill Earl's photographs of the
scene the night of the accident might be priceless to the
defense.

When they walked across Washington Street from the Silver
Dome Inn, they found the courthouse square was mobbed.
News of the extraordinary prosecution of a sitting District
Attorney had spread far and wide; the press was there in full
force. Three TV trucks with satellite dishes held up traffic
along Madison Street. A team of TV reporters was eagerly

waiting like hounds after the rabbit. Thaddeus felt Killen linger a step or two behind, and it became apparent: he would be running interference for the DA.

"Thaddeus," said the young blonde anchor from NBC Five out of Quincy, "have you come up with any rabbits to pull out of the hat? Anything you can share with us."

Thaddeus paused and gave her his best smile. "Let's just let the testimony speak for our side. They expect to win this thing, so let's hear what they have."

"Sure, Murfee," called one of the idiot twins from the top step. "You dumb shit you wouldn't know the truth if it bit you in the ass!"

Thaddeus could only smile. The thought occurred that he might be weak when it came to knowing *all* the law, but it was a mistake to call him a dumb shit. He was anything but dumb.

"Hey Killen," said the other twin, "are you getting any sleep? Or is Johnny's ghost haunting you?"

Killen kept his eyes downcast as they ascended the courthouse stairs. Just like Thaddeus had told him to do.

Having run the exterior gauntlet, they made their way inside, only to discover more press and more gawkers. Many merchants from around the square were there as well. But this time there was also a significant police presence. City cops, State Police, Sheriff's deputies were everywhere. Thaddeus felt good about the cops. And he felt a hell of a lot safer than he had on Friday when he'd almost had to join Gaffney in ejecting the brothers from the courtroom. Thank God that had passed without Thaddeus getting beat to hell,

because he was anything but a street brawler and wanted no
part of it. He'd do his fighting inside the courtroom. That
was his room to rumble.

They made their way through courthouse security and took
off their belts and shoes as they passed through the check-
point. It appeared that neither Killen nor Thaddeus was
armed or carrying a bomb, so they were allowed to replace
their belts and shoes and proceed upstairs to the courtroom.
It was eight forty-five a.m.

Court was called to order by Judge Wren at precisely
nine a.m.

Seated at the prosecution table was the special prosecutor
Eleanor Rammelskamp who, Thaddeus had learned,
belonged to no garden clubs and was extremely competent;
and at her side was Sergeant Bill Janes, clean-shaven,
proudly showing off the starched short-sleeve summer
uniform of the Illinois State Police with the trademark gold-
and-black shoulder patches. Thaddeus sat at the other table
with Killen. He was wearing his navy off-the-rack gabardine,
and Thaddeus was wearing his Monday morning Zegna
with a light pink shirt, red tie, and his hair perfectly in place.
The two lawyers, Thaddeus and Killen, wanted to look innocent and prepared, although, as Thaddeus sat there, he
believed "prepared" was the only look they were pulling off.

Directly behind Thaddeus, in the first row of public seating,
was Al Hodges, the expert with the briefcase full of books
and studies. Al was wearing SoCal cool: loafers, Lauren
slacks, Polo shirt and no necktie. He was a fit sixty-year-old
engineer with a quick smile and the ability to give the oppo-
nent a point for a serve well-played while at the same time
not giving up the match. He never lost control. Never mind

how relentless and pounding the cross-examination delivered, Al would keep his cool and continue with his soft smile and bottomless fount of traffic engineering expertise. That was why Thaddeus had wired him fifteen thousand dollars to be earned at one thousand per hour and had personally guaranteed more to come should the case persist beyond the preliminary hearing stage. Which they guessed it would.

Sergeant Janes took the stand first.

The Special Prosecutor began asking questions.

He recounted taking the 911 call from the ISP dispatcher at 9:35 Thursday night. He was already asleep as his wife was expecting, and he knew they could be headed for the hospital at any moment, so he slept whenever he wasn't pounding the highway in his squad car.

"What did you do after receiving the call, if anything?"

"Jumped into my uniform and drove to the scene."

"What did you first see?"

"Lights stopped on both sides of the bridge and a long black gap between them. That was the bridge."

"What did you do?"

"Activated my emergency lights and drove around the stopped traffic. I parked in the oncoming lane and got out. I left my emergency lights flashing, and my vehicle turned off. SOP. I then ran to what was left of the car to check for survivors."

"Take us through what you found there."

"I came up to the left side of the vehicle. The right side was missing. It wasn't even on the bridge. Not that I could see with my flashlight. Of course I didn't know at that moment that the right side of the car had plunged off the bridge and taken Johnny Albertson with it."

"What happened next?"

"I located the defendant, Killen Erwin. He was sitting on the bench seat, on the roadway, trying to start what was left of the truck."

"Describe him, please."

"He was angry. He was disoriented. I asked him if he was okay."

"What, if anything, did he say?"

"He was angry. He told me to go screw myself. Words to that effect."

"Exact words?"

"Go fuck yourself, Sarge."

"What did you do?"

"I asked him again. 'Are you okay?'"

"Any different response this time?"

"He stretched out his arms and smiled. 'Nothing hurts, so I guess I'm okay. Help me get this thing started, Sarge.'"

"He said Sarge, so he knew you?"

"Evidently so. We've been acquainted for ten years or more."

"He recognized you."

"Yes."

"Describe his manner of speaking."

"Slurring his words."

"And you said he was disoriented?"

"Well, trying to start a non-existent truck is pretty disoriented to me."

"All right. Did you get close enough to smell his breath?"

"I did. I leaned down and unfastened his seat belt. I helped him climb to his feet. I smelled his breath. A very strong odor of alcoholic beverage."

"What about standing up? Was he able to?"

"He swayed and at one point lunged. I thought he was going down, and I put out my hands to steady him."

"Then what happened?"

"I asked him whether anyone else was in the truck."

"What did he say?"

"He didn't say anything—not at first. At first he looked around the bridge and took in what you could see in the dark. Then he said, 'I don't see anyone else.' Something like that."

"So he couldn't seem to recall whether he had a passenger and instead looked around to see if there was anyone?"

"Yes."

"What happened next?"

"I took him to my patrol car and put him in the back seat."

"He was under arrest?"

"Yes, and for his own safety. He was intoxicated enough to fall off the bridge into the river bed."

"What happened next?"

"I had already called for backup, ambulance, and tow trucks. I could hear sirens off in the distance. So I backed up my squad car and tried to shine my headlights from the side of the bridge. I was looking for the rest of the truck. Couldn't see anything. Tried my flashlight. Still couldn't see the rest of it. So I straightened my squad car out and took pictures of the bridge. Then I drove forward and took more pictures."

"Did you give me those pictures?"

"Yes."

"Your Honor, I have had the clerk mark the pictures as State's Exhibits fourteen through forty-four. May I pass them to the witness?"

"Yes."

"Sergeant Janes, please review the exhibits."

He shuffled the pictures and quickly checked them over.

"All right. These are the pictures I took."

"Any others taken?"

"No."

"Do these pictures accurately and truly depict what you viewed of the accident scene as of last Thursday night?"

"They do."

The pictures were moved into evidence without objection by Thaddeus. He wanted them in, after checking them out before agreeing to their admission. Definitely he wanted them in evidence. But he was also angry that the special prosecutor hadn't made them available before the hearing. That would have been a common professional courtesy. Evidently she didn't feel that applied to her.

More questions followed about the scene, weather, lighting conditions, traffic conditions, roadway conditions, signs, road stripes, and road markings, and the like. He then testified about the EMTs locating the body of Johnny Albertson and more wreckage from the truck and how Johnny was removed and the debris gathered. Then he testified about the blood testing at the hospital and the blood test results.

"What was his blood alcohol level?"

"Point two-one."

"Almost three times the legal level of blood alcohol?"

"That's right."

"Thank you, that is all I have."

Then it was Thaddeus' turn to cross-examine. He didn't have all that much but did want to clarify a few items.

"Mr. Janes," he began, "is it possible my client was in shock at the scene when you saw him?"

"Definitely."

"It wouldn't be unusual for an accident victim to be in shock?"

"Not at all. It would be expected, I'd say."

One thing about Bill Janes in Thaddeus' questioning of him over the years he'd practiced in Orbit: he was fair. And truthful and didn't try to embellish.

"So when you saw him trying to start his truck, that could have been the result of shock?"

"I suppose so. I'm no doctor, though."

"I appreciate that. So you weren't telling the court that his trying to start the truck was definitely because of his intoxication? It could just as well been from shock?"

"I suppose so. Again, I'm not a doc—"

"I appreciate that. But I just wanted to be clear that you weren't saying all of what you observed him do at the scene was alcohol related. It could just as easily have been the actions and demeanor of someone suffering from shock after a horrendous motor vehicle accident?"

"Except for his breath. He reeked of alcohol. That wasn't from shock."

Even honest cops will stick the knife in if you give them the chance. Unfortunately, Thaddeus had done that, and now he paid for it. So he did the next best thing: he ignored his comment.

"Was Johnny Albertson alive when you arrived on the scene?"

"Unknown."

"He could have been alive?"

"I didn't see him. I would have no way of knowing."

"Mr. Janes, do you know CPR?"

"Sure."

"Basic first aid?"

"We get that at the Academy."

"Did you try to administer CPR or first aid to Mr. Albertson that night?"

"Like I said, I never saw him that night."

"So he might have been alive when you arrived, and he might even have been saved if you had located him, but you don't know?"

"From what I've been told, he was dead before he hit the ground."

"Who told you that?"

"I don't know. Several people, I think."

"But you have no first-hand knowledge of that? So you're reciting hearsay?"

"Yes and yes."

"Now, one last question. When you backed up your squad car and viewed the roadway along which Killen Erwin's car traveled that night. Did anything stand out in your mind?"

"Like what?"

"Like how it was signed, striped and marked?"

"Yes."

"Please tell us about that?"

"The lane drop wasn't marked right. At least not to me."

"Might that have caused the accident?"

"Objection! Foundation! Calls for an opinion outside of this witness's area of expertise."

"Sustained," said the judge. "Move along."

"Thank you, Sergeant, that is all."

"State rests," said the Special Prosecutor.

The judge looked at Thaddeus and nodded. It was his turn to present witnesses.

Thaddeus had decided to call Al Hodges as Killen's only witness.

"Defense calls Al Hodges."

Hodges came through the gate, a nice smile for everyone, and stepped up onto the witness platform, where he remained standing, his right hand raised. The clerk administered the oath, and Hodges took his seat.

"State your name."

"Albert J. Hodges."

"Mr. Hodges, what is your business, occupation, or profession?"

"I'm retired. Five years now."

"Prior to retiring?"

"Traffic engineer at LADOT."

"That would be the Los Angeles Department of Transportation?"

"Yes."

"Now, tell us about your educational background."

He recited his years at UCLA and USC and his master's degree in traffic engineering, his time at Northwestern, and the rest of it.

"You worked thirty years at LADOT?"

"I did."

"Tell us about your career trajectory."

"I started as a Traffic Engineer I. Graduated to a II after eighteen months. Then a TE III. Then I was given my own group to chair. This was three years into my career. After that, it was some management but mostly I was an in-the-field traffic engineer with responsibilities running from maintenance and rehab to new construction."

"During your time on the job, did you become experienced with the *Manual on Uniform Traffic Control Devices*?"

"I did."

"And has LADOT adopted the *MUTCD* as its standard for traffic engineering in the City of Los Angeles?"

"It did. Shortly after the *Manual* was first published."

"I'm going to pass you the State's exhibits fourteen through forty-four and would ask you to review them."

"All right."

"Your Honor, while Mr. Hodges makes his review, I would ask that we take the morning recess."

The judge nodded. "We're in recess for twenty minutes."

He stood up and floated out of the courtroom into chambers.

Thaddeus nodded at Al. "Please continue your review, Al."

He nodded back, already engrossed in the pictures.

Twenty minutes later, after restroom stops and quick gulps of coffee supplied by Deputy Gaffney, they took up again.

"Mr. Hodges," Thaddeus began slowly, "have you now reviewed Mr. Janes' photographs taken the night of the crash?"

"I have."

"Are you able to offer any opinions as a result of that review?"

"I am."

"What is that opinion?"

"Objection, foundation."

To the lay onlooker, this objection seemed innocent enough. But to the attorneys it was the most critical moment in the hearing. The judge's ruling on the objection would basically decide whether Al would be allowed to give an expert opinion or not—because the foundation had not been made and wouldn't be made on any other facts except that he had looked at photographs and made a hurried visit to the scene just after he landed. In short, the foundation was lightweight, and the judge might have stopped the defense right there.

But he didn't.

"Overruled. Rules 702 and 703 allow expert opinion testimony with follow-up foundation. Rule 703 provides that the facts or data in a particular case upon which an expert bases an opinion may be those made known to the expert at the hearing. If of a type reasonably relied upon by experts in the particular field in forming opinions or inferences upon the subject, the facts or data need not be admissible in evidence. Please continue, Mr. Hodges."

"What is that opinion?" Thaddeus asked again.

"One major opinion, three lesser ones."

"Yes?"

"The roadway was improperly marked the night of the accident. In fact, the marking that was there fell so far below the traffic engineering standard of care that in my opinion the roadway approach itself is what caused the accident."

Thaddeus was all but dumbstruck. Without the photographs before the hearing he hadn't been able to hear Al's opinions, of course. But now there he was, testifying without rebuttal expert testimony from the Special Prosecutor, that the roadway markings caused the accident.

"Are you saying," Thaddeus continued slowly, "that the defendant's ingestion of alcoholic beverage that night was not a cause of the accident?"

"I am. Drunk or sober, the way the workers had left the roadway after they finished working that day—anyone could easily have been misled and had an accident. With or without alcohol."

"But would alcohol make it more likely?"

Al gave one of his soft smiles. "Honestly? I'm not an accident reconstructionist in that sense and am unable to testify about alcohol consumption and degrees of impairment. But I can say that that roadway was a killer. It's no wonder someone hit that bridge."

"Why is it no wonder?"

"Well, look at Exhibit thirty. See this lane leading up to the bridge? This lane suddenly ends without warning. That's known in my profession as a lane drop. A lane drop is a situation you have where a lane of travel comes to an end. If lane drops are properly signed, striped, and marked, they're acceptable. But where, like here, they're inappropriately signed and marked, they're deadly. It is my opinion that the roadway caused the death of Mr. Albertson—"

"Objection! Foundation."

"You're probably right, but there's no jury here. I want to hear what he has to say so I'll let it in. Please continue, sir."

Hodges nodded. "Well, just that there was no fault on the part of the defendant. This is based on what I've seen and heard."

Thaddeus decided to back off a bit. It was true that Hodges probably wasn't qualified to give that particular opinion, but it was also true the judge was probably going to ignore it. So he moved away from the fault portion of Hodges' answer.

"What else can you tell us about the roadway?"

"Besides this unfortunate death trap of a lane drop? My other opinions don't have that much to do with my opinion that it was the highway that caused the decedent's death that night and not the driving by the defendant."

They then covered a small number of fine points that really would have no bearing on the case, but that were required to connect the dots. Then the young lawyer quit.

"Very well. I believe that's all I have for now."

The Special Prosecutor rattled her papers and opened her mouth to begin her cross-examination.

But the judge cut her off. He spoke directly to Sergeant Janes, seated beside the Special Prosecutor.

"Sergeant Janes, how long have you had the pictures in your possession?"

"Since Thursday night."

"Were the pictures turned over to the Special Prosecutor last Friday?"

"Yes."

"What time were they turned over?"

"Friday morning. As soon as Ms. Rammelskamp arrived in the DA's office."

"Do you know whether she turned them over to the defense?"

"I don't know."

"Tell me about the pictures. What do they depict?"

"They depict the roadway at the crash scene."

"Shortly after the crash?"

"Within the hour."

"Were you able to tell, had anyone changed around the debris you found or the construction zone signs?"

The judge was repeating some of what Thaddeus had covered in his cross-examination of Sergeant Janes. Slightly different questions, same answers.

"They had not. Everyone there had remained in their car except for one off-duty male nurse. He was checking over the defendant when I arrived."

"How many cars were in the immediate area when you arrived?"

"Maybe four, two on either side of the bridge."

"And the occupants of those vehicles had remained with their cars or trucks?"

"Correct."

The judge then focused on Eleanor Rammelskamp.

"Ms. Special Prosecutor. Were the photographs ever turned over to the defense?"

"No."

The judge's face clouded over. His lips pursed and turned purple with anger.

"Any particular reason you haven't turned the pictures over?"

"The rules don't require me to until formal discovery."

Now his cheeks were purple as well.

"What about justice? Don't you think justice would be served by you giving the defense the photographs prior to today's hearing so they could better prepare?"

"I don't know."

"Well, wouldn't it be fairer?"

"I don't know."

"You don't know, why?"

"Because I don't know what difference the pictures would or wouldn't make."

"So that's your rationale for your failure to turn over the pictures? The fact that you don't know whether it would have made any difference?"

Thaddeus couldn't help but smile, but only for a second that no one saw. When judges begin talking "your failure", they are about to lower the boom. Look out, Ms. Garden Club, Thaddeus thought.

"I don't know what I was thinking. Or even if it crossed my mind."

"Did you hear Al Hodges testify about the importance of the photographs and what they tell him?"

"I did."

"Knowing that, wouldn't you concede that your failure to turn over the photographs might have compromised the defendant's ability to defend himself against your charges?"

"I concede."

"What remedy should I consider, counsel, given that the Special Prosecutor failed to prosecute her case in good faith?"

Thaddeus realized he was speaking directly to him. His head jerked up.

"Well, the defense requests that the case be dismissed for prosecutorial misconduct."

There, he had it. The exact remedy he guessed the judge might have in mind.

"It is so ordered," said Judge Wren. "The court finds the Special Prosecutor guilty of prosecutorial misconduct resulting in the defendant's inability to properly prepare his defense. Accordingly, the charges herein are dismissed. Without prejudice, of course. Counsel, we are done here, and the court stands in recess."

With a flurry of swirling black robe, the judge came down off his perch and left the courtroom.

Thaddeus immediately turned to the Special Prosecutor. "I assume you're going to re-file the case?"

She shrugged. "I'm going to take it before the grand jury. I'm sure they'll indict him."

"I'm sure they will too. I'm sure we're not finished here," Thaddeus said so Killen could hear.

"I know that," Killen said with a small smile. "But just for today it feels good not to have it hanging over my head like the sword of Damocles."

"I'm sure."

"In fact, I owe you big time, Thad."

Killen was hugging Thaddeus when Markey and Mikey burst through the swinging gate.

"You're dead!" they cried at Killen. "Dead, dead, dead!"

Several deputies restrained them and steered them out of the courtroom.

"You need to get yourself some protection, Kill," Thaddeus told him.

"I can go back to my office now that the charges are dismissed?"

"Yes."

"Walk me over to my office?" A direct reference to the lurking twins and Killen not wishing to be confronted while alone.

"Sure I will. You're still the District Attorney of Hickam County."

"Good. Let's go put someone in jail."

"Are you thinking death threats from the idiot twins?"

"Maybe. You heard it. You can be my witness."

"Uh-uh. I'm headed back to Chicago in one hour."

"Don't blame you for that. But first I need to write you a check for your help."

"No need. You owe me nothing, Killen."

"Please, Thad. How much?"

"Zero. You helped me way back when. I owed you."

He shook his head. "Then I'll mail a check to your office. Fair's fair."

"Mail away. It won't be cashed, so save the paper."

"We'll see."

By now they had cleared the courthouse, and the two friends were walking north across the square, headed for Killen's office.

From their truck, the twins witnessed the procession.

They began talking revenge. If the court wouldn't do its job, they would.

11

By Monday afternoon, there was new activity on the Killen Erwin/Mary Roberta Erwin front. A new lawsuit was filed that got everyone in town talking. How much more interesting could the day get? The gossips wondered. First, the case against the District Attorney had been dismissed just that morning by the judge; now Mary Roberta had exploded a bombshell of her own.

Mary Roberta insisted on accompanying her lawyer to the clerk's office for filing.

The divorce papers were spell-checked, signed, attached to a summons, and ready for the clerk's stamp.

Heads turned in the Circuit Clerk's office when lawyer and client approached the counter.

"This is a new divorce case," Elizabeth Melendez told the assistant clerk. "Please file and issue the summons for service."

"Will do," said the clerk, a female in her early thirties. She slammed the clerk's seal and date stamp on the original and stamped the summons for service. She passed that back to the attorney.

"And here's my check for the filing fee," the lawyer pointed out.

"So noted," said the clerk.

The lawyer turned to her client.

"So there you have it, Mary Roberta. Your divorce is now officially filed."

Mary Roberta pushed a short lock of hair off her forehead.

"And it's about time. Now maybe the kids and I can settle down like normal people."

An assistant clerk in the back of the office raised an eyebrow. "Normal?" she mouthed to the next clerk with the facing desk. "Normal? Seriously?"

"Well, I hope it works for you," said the assisting clerk. "And good luck."

The attorney and her client, heads high, departed the clerk's office.

Killen Erwin was officially named as the respondent in his own divorce case.

The town criers couldn't have been happier. The Erwin's soap opera was in full swing and who knew what might happen next?

12

In early September, the fight broke out over Killen's glass eye.

Killen had walked up the hill from his room at the motel. It was Saturday night, his turn to watch a movie with the kids. They had one all picked out, and Killen was happy he was going to get some quality time with his offspring. He loved those little guys more than he loved life itself and would have done anything for them. Celena was eight—second grade, and Parkus was five, pre-school. They weren't quite old enough to accept that Daddy wasn't living with them in the same house anymore, but Daddy tried to assuage their hurt by inviting himself into his own home as often as Mary Roberta would allow and spending an evening with them. That happened more frequently, as she was now down to calling him on her "nights out," and getting him to babysit while she ran the table at some honky-tonk, often not getting home until three or four in the morning or maybe not even at all.

Saturday night—rather, Sunday morning, early—Mary Roberta came dragging in just after three a.m.

"You look rode hard and put away wet," said Killen, coming awake in his recliner in the family room. He had been interrupted out of a deep sleep that had set in around midnight and had him making a closing argument to a jury in his dream. His glass eye was beside him on the end table beside his chair, as he always removed it for sleep.

She had giggled. "I am wet," she said beneath her breath.

"Whoa," he said. "Say that again?"

"You know what I'm up to, husband of mine."

"Meaning?"

"Meaning our divorce is about final."

"Have you thought about the Church at all?" He asked. He realized he was grasping at straws, but nothing else had worked.

She giggled. "If the Church won't let me take communion anymore, or whatever it does, I'll just have to live with that. It's better than the alternative."

"The alternative being what?"

"Living with you, stupid."

She was intoxicated, and it came out "Shhtupid."

Which only angered him even more than the original, "I am wet," comment.

He slammed his hand on the end table, and his glass eye jumped up and rolled across the floor like a marble. Mary

Roberta, lucky as much as accurate, managed to trap the rolling object beneath her cowboy boot and stop its wander.

"How's the view from down there?" She said to the prosthesis. "Underfoot, as always."

"Damn you, Mary!" Killen cried. "Get your damn foot off my eye!"

Whereupon Mary reached down, grabbed the object out from under her boot, and retreated to the kitchen, taunting Killen as he came after her. "Come and get it, Big Boy," she said in a catty taunt. The kind of taunt that fourth graders do to each other on the playground. Whatever; it worked. He became infuriated and lunged for his eye. Mary Roberta stepped aside and dropped the eye into the right-hand side of the stainless steel sink, where it plunged down through the opening, into the garbage disposal underneath. In a continuing motion, she flipped the switch on the unit and the garbage disposal could be heard grinding the optical illusion into fine bits.

"My frigging eye!"

"Hush. Your insurance will buy you another."

"You ruined my eye!"

He lunged at Mary Roberta and connected against her, shoulder into waist. She was thrown backward and hit the floor with a thud, her skull making the sound of a dense melon falling to concrete.

"Mary?" Said Killen. "Are you all right?"

She didn't move.

Again, louder, urgent: "Mary? Talk to me!"

He moved on his knees up to her head and cradled her upper torso in his arms. He felt a smattering of blood and hair on the back of her head. Within minutes, his shirt and bluejeans were covered in her blood, and more was coming. He stood to find something with which to wrap her head and slipped and fell across her, as blood was making the floor slippery. He tried again, careful this time to step beyond the red flower.

As with any head wound, the blood was all but impossible to staunch. He tried paper towels and dish cloths but still it came.

Finally, he panicked and dialed 911.

Within minutes, the EMTs were churning into the kitchen and removing Mary Roberta on a backboard and hurrying her out to their truck.

Killen couldn't follow. The children were fast asleep upstairs.

Thank God.

But Michael Dunleavy, Patrolman First Class with the Orbit PD, showed up. He was alone, and his face was white as he came inside the house while the paramedics were leaving.

"Mr. Erwin," he said. "What happened?"

Without a thought, Killen admitted there had been a fight and that Mary Roberta had been tackled and thrown to the floor.

"Isn't that some crime?" Officer Dunleavy asked. "I mean, you're the DA and all, but still—"

"No, no, I'm at fault," Killen said. "I was wrong as rain."

"I'll have to take you in and book you, Sir."

"Yes. You should."

"Let me call Thaddeus and Katy. They're down at the motel. I'll get Katy to watch the kids."

"Sure."

Ten minutes later, Katy and Thaddeus arrived. By now, Officer Dunleavy had placed Killen in the backseat of his patrol vehicle. He was still wearing the bloody pants and shirt, which were only just now beginning to dry and stiffen.

The first thing Thaddeus said was, "Has he made a statement, Officer?"

To which Dunleavy replied, "No, no statement.

"Did he tell you what happened?"

"He said he tackled Mary Roberta."

"Okay, here's what's going to happen. You're going to take Mr. Erwin down to the jail and book him. You are not to try to discuss this incident with him. Not you or any other peace officer. Are we clear?"

"Yes, sir."

"Good."

"So I hold him in jail?"

"I think you have to," Killen said.

Thaddeus raised up his hand. "And you," he said to Killen through the back door of the squad car, "Have said all you're going to get to say tonight. No more talking, okay?"

"Fine."

"Now I'm going to the hospital and find out what I can," said Thaddeus. "After that I'll come up to the jail, we'll contact Judge Veinne, and we'll get bail set. I can help make the bail."

"I can make my own bail," the DA said.

Thaddeus gave him a dour look. "We'll make the bail out of your money. I'm just going to facilitate that. Now, what did I just say about talking?"

"Not to."

"So don't. Please don't."

"Fine."

~

Officer Dunleavy maneuvered Killen through mugshots and booking. He decided against the blaze orange jumpsuit change because he knew Killen would be bailed out in the morning. He then told Killen good night and went back about his duties.

Killen was shown to an empty cell by the jail staff and given a blanket. He stretched out on the cement slab, pulled the blanket up to his chin, and fought the chill of the air conditioning, which smelled of sweat and violent men. His shirt and pants still clung to him, damp with his wife's blood.

He shuddered to think what her reaction would be; he wouldn't be surprised if she came after him or sent one of her boyfriends. He had no doubt she loathed him enough to see him dead.

Then he closed his eyes and, for the first time in twenty years, said a prayer. He prayed for Mary Roberta's full healing and prayed for the healing of their marriage and prayed for the willpower to stop drinking.

Then he fell asleep.

~

M ike Cheever was still on duty at the ER. It had been almost a day since Thaddeus had been in to see him about the pulled muscles in his back. The ER doc looked faded and exhausted. But he met Thaddeus back at the coffee machine, as Thaddeus had asked, out of sight and earshot of the front reception area.

"How is she?" Thaddeus asked.

"I can't say. Confidentiality."

"She's going to make it?"

"Yes."

"Long term injury?"

"Too early to say. CT scan is clear."

"Which must be a good sign."

"She's conscious. But I didn't tell you that, Thaddeus."

"No, it's off the record. But I needed to hear that. Killen needs to hear it, too. He's horrified he's permanently injured her."

"Concussion and blunt force trauma resulting in laceration.

Something like we get in here at least once every Saturday night."

"Got you. Okay, then."

Dr. Cheever laid a hand on Thaddeus' shoulder.

"Who's got the kids?"

"Katy and Sarai came up to Killen's. It's all under control."

"Good, I was going to say Alice could help too."

"No need. I'll have him out of jail by nine or ten in the morning. We're good, Mike."

"Well, if we can help. But remember, off the record with the Mary stuff."

"My lips are sealed."

"Good. Hey, admit or deny for me, okay?"

"Sure."

"She mumbled something about Killen's glass eye in the garbage disposal."

"Admit."

"OMG. Now that just made my whole night."

"Admit. Mine too."

13

It was ten o'clock Sunday morning. For the second time that week, Thaddeus found himself getting Killen out of jail. Again Judge Veinne recused herself and again Judge Wren from Quincy was called in. He assigned the case to himself, as an initial appearance deadline was looming. The judge entered his order setting bail on Sunday morning, and Thaddeus had the full amount posted for his friend. But having earlier learned his lesson in Flagstaff, this time the source of the bail money was Killen himself, not Thaddeus.

"Your record this week is a dismal oh-and-two," Thaddeus said as they waited at the front of the jail for the bail receipt."I think you've done all the damage your rep can stand around here."

"You're coming through loud and clear."

"But have you noticed that your troubles are always preceded by your being in the company of Mary Roberta?"

"Now that's instructive."

"So what's your takeaway?"

"Stay the hell away from my wife."

"That's a good start, Killen."

"Yes."

T haddeus had already heard from County Supervisor Flanagan T. Stoops. Supervisor Stoops was asking for Killen's immediate resignation. "This has gone on way too far, for the chief law enforcement officer of this county," said the Supervisor. "I want his resignation on my desk by nine o'clock Monday morning, or I'm filing for a recall election and I'm going to embarrass the living hell out of your client."

"Understood," Thaddeus told him. He was trying to manage the Supervisor's tone and position but was having little luck at either. The man was rancorous, wronged, and had a son who had just passed the July bar exam in Illinois. Iggie Stoops, Esq. was being curried to step right into the shoes of the outgoing DA—at least in his father's mind. They had talked at length about it, father and son, and they thought it totally made sense. There was no other local attorney without a caseload who could step into Killen's shoes and take right up where he would leave off. Iggie was the clear choice. Then, in the general elections in twenty months, he could officially toss his hat in the ring and try to hang onto the plum job. His father's name was gold, and the son would probably ride his coattails right into the elected office. Thaddeus knew all this, of course, and had no problem with it. Killen Erwin had overstayed the party and had no other choice but to resign. All credibility was lost among the law enforcement community and the community as a whole with this latest domestic abuse/felony battery charge. It was the second felony Killen had been accused of that week, and it was time for him to step quietly down.

Which he did.

Supervisor Stoops had the signed letter of resignation from Killen Erwin on his desk at exactly nine o'clock Monday morning, delivered there by Thaddeus. Now life could go on, and Thaddeus could begin the difficult task of defending his friend on yet another charge, this one every bit as serious as the negligent homicide stemming from Johnny's death.

Killen stayed home that day. He visited his horses in the barn and talked to them. He visited his kids up at the house, but that was short-lived as Mary Roberta's mother had arrived, and Killen was no longer welcome. The fact was, he was ejected, and as he was turning to go, the mother produced a court order of restraint. Killen was ordered to remain at least five-hundred-feet away from Mary Roberta and his children until further order of the court. He would comply with the court's order, and left without complaint.

Mary Roberta was released from the hospital Tuesday morning and went straight home to her mother and her kids. David Daniels' pickup was seen in her driveway that night, which Killen noticed from his motel room, but he drew away from the curtains and retreated to his bed, where tears came, and he finally lapsed into the emotional outpouring he'd felt coming for a long time.

Thaddeus came by to see him at eight o'clock.

Red-eyed and pale, Killen opened the door to his friend.

"Getting to you, huh?" said Thaddeus as he stepped inside Killen's room. "Not surprised."

"She's killing me."

"Sure she is. That's an evil woman. Course you giving her a concussion doesn't help your upcoming custody battle over the children."

"I've been thinking about that. I'm not going to fight for the kids."

"Yes, you are. Those little guys need you. We are fighting all the way for reasonable visitation and vacation time."

"We are?"

"You've got the guilties right now, Kills. Let me guide you through this. It won't be pretty, but you're not giving up the kids. Later you'll thank me for it."

"I will?"

"Guaranteed. Now, what say we go over to the Red Bird for coffee? Katy's gone back to Chicago, and I'm all alone too. We might as well lean on each other, little brother."

"Sure."

14

"Do you want sole custody or not?" Mary Asline Kittenforge asked Mary Roberta, her daughter.

"Of course I want sole custody. Killen's a drunk."

"He is a drunk. But the kids love him. What if the judge asks the kids?"

Mary Roberta shook her head. "I don't think he can. They're too young for their opinion."

Mary Asline sniffed. "Here's hoping. Be just like some judge to give them to Killen, for all your running around. No, you'd best do what you can to make sure."

"How am I supposed to do that?"

"I don't know. Have him thrown in the river, I guess."

Mary Roberta at times didn't know whether she should take her mother literally. This was one of those times.

"Really? Have someone get rid of Killen?"

"Why not? He's worthless to you now. And if he contests the divorce you run the risk of him getting custody. Even visitation is too much. Plus, think of this, Miss Puddin'head. If he's alive, he gets one-half of all the assets. That means he can sell your house and take half. Sell your motel and take half."

"But he paid for everything. I've never worked."

"That's not how it goes, stupid. You get one-half just for putting up with him for all these years. That and the fact you've got the kids to raise. He got you pregnant; he's gotta pay."

"So what should I do?"

Mary Aseline's gray eyes filled with a new gleam. "If it were me, I'd talk to Johnny's twin brothers."

"And say what?"

"Tell them how to snatch Killen out of the motel room where he's staying. Offer to open his door in the middle of the night. Hell, girl, *I* don't know. Make it up but do it fast, before he gets to talk to a judge."

"Okay, okay. I'm talking to them."

"And here's something else, Mary Roberta. You keep up stealing ladies' husbands, one of them's gonna do you in. I kid you not. What's wrong with the single men?"

"Not as much fun. I like taking them away."

"Not smart, girl. Some wife's gonna shoot you."

"They're all so afraid of doing anything. They're all embarrassed to have the world know they couldn't keep their husbands."

~

She dropped in at the Copperhead Tavern where Markey said the twins would meet her. Her head was still throbbing from the concussion, and the stitches were dry and pulling at the scalp and back of her head. She gingerly touched the bandage and grimaced. It hurt like hell and right then she could have killed Killen. He had done it to her, and payback was required.

Her eyes adjusted to the dim light and she spotted the twins at the back wall.

In a dark corner, they had their talk after two pitchers had been downed.

"Markey says you had something to tell to us about Killen," Mikey said, to get the ball rolling. "You want we should leave him alone?"

Mary crossed her eyes. "Not hardly! I'm here to ask you to rough him up. Beat him silly. I know where he's staying. It's my motel. And I've got a passkey to his room."

Markey squinted at the wife. "Beat him silly? What the hell does that mean, woman?"

"Well, it means what it means. I just don't want any more trouble outta him."

"So do we—" Markey leaned on the table to whisper, "do we cut him?"

"Maybe yes, maybe no," said Mary Roberta. "I'm not a guy. I don't know what it takes."

Markey nudged Mikey. "Look at who's not a guy, brother!"

"How about proving that, Mary Roberta? We've got the Dodge outside."

"You're serious, aren't you? Well, I don't see why not. Both of you or just one?"

"Both," said Markey. "Then we make sure he never bothers you again."

"I guess so," said the wife. "Yes, all right. Let's go."

"We're leaving now. You come out in ten minutes."

"You worried Mitt's gonna be watching?"

"Just don't want no witnesses, lady. You're asking for some serious help here."

"All right. I'll wait ten then I'm coming to your Dodge."

"See you there."

The twins left the bar.

Mary Roberta ordered a grilled cheese with pickle and slowly ate it, chasing the cheese with a bottle of Lowenbrau. Then she belched and patted her belly.

"Let's get you outside, sister. Two on, two off, one gone. It's a fair trade."

15

Two-forty a.m and Killen Erwin was dreaming of green pastures and horses dancing in the bright sunlight, rearing up and pawing the warm summer air. He was there as well, sitting on his tractor, watching them across the thick grass as they cavorted and expressed the joy he felt in being alive. In his dream, he knew that Mary Roberta and the kids were just over the hill in the yellow brick house he'd built for them, doing Saturday morning cartoons and making breakfast. Soon he would hear the clang of the triangle and break away from his heaven long enough to eat with his loved ones. He was glad he was alive, in his dream, and very grateful for his blessings.

"Click!" The motel door swung inward.

Stepping inside came Markey and Mikey, shotguns raised, their faces white disks in the dark, air conditioned room. Adjoining rooms wouldn't have heard the sound as their air conditioners were roaring as well, removing humid summer air from the guest rooms.

"What?" Killen exclaimed as the leering brothers replaced the dreams. Outside the window, fleetingly, he thought he saw Mary Roberta dart past. Or was he dreaming?

"Got you," hissed Markey, "you son of a bitch!"

"Get your ass outta bed," commanded Mikey. He shoved the muzzle of his shotgun against Killen's face and pushed him back. "Now!"

"Can I put on my pants?"

"You don't need no frigging pants where you're going, dumb ass. Up, now!"

Killen jumped to his feet. He was wearing white boxers and a frown. A good foot shorter than his unwelcome visitors and totally without any defense, it was clear he would do as they said.

"What happens next?" he asked, trying to remain calm and keep his voice level.

"You walk out that door and come with us. That's what happens next, stupid."

"Now!" shouted Mikey. He placed the muzzle of his gun against Killen's bare chest and pushed him backward. Killen stumbled and found himself sitting on his bed again.

"Up now and walk out that door!"

Killen obeyed. He said a prayer that they would leave Mary Roberta and the kids alone, that their revenge would involve only him.

Quietly he stepped down the exterior stairs, down to the

landing, turned, and down the stairs again. He stopped at the bottom step and waited for the intruders.

"See that Ram? That's us. Climb in the passenger's seat. You're riding shotgun!"

The brothers couldn't help but laugh at the shotgun joke. Killen went around the front of the truck to the passenger's side and climbed in. Mikey climbed into the crew cab behind him and laid the barrel of his shotgun on top of Killen's left shoulder. Markey climbed onto the driver's seat and turned the key. The truck started right up. The diesel engine thumped in the early morning air.

They backed away, and Killen felt his breath snap in his throat. He was caught, trapped, the raccoon with his paw held by steel jaws over which he had no control.

He was their toy.

They could do with him as they pleased.

He had no doubt he wouldn't return to this place alive. He would never see Mary Roberta and the kids again, would never witness his horses knee-deep in summer pasture, would never know the freedom of an early Saturday morning where the full, beautiful day stretched before him.

The muzzle pounded against his ear.

"I'm gonna count to ten, and then I'm gonna blow your head off, Mr. Erwin," said Mikey.

"All right," said Killen. He had no other response.

"One-two-three—"

"Mikey, you shoot this piece of shit in my truck, and I gonna bash your head!"

"Four-five-six-seven—"

Suddenly Markey twisted the wheel and ran the truck off onto the shoulder. He turned from the driver's seat and seized the barrel of Mikey's gun. He shoved the muzzle away from Killen's head.

"I told you, boy, you ain't shootin' shit in my truck. Now get your shit together, boy!"

"I wasn't gonna—"

"Yes, you was. You're stupid enough to do it. Now I've got a plan for this piece of shit and it ain't shootin' him in my truck!"

"All right."

Markey turned back around and eyed his brother in the rearview.

"We good, boy?"

"We good."

"All right."

The truck leaped from the shoulder back onto the asphalt and continued moving southwest. The speed increased.

Killen watched the late summer corn rows flash past his window. Hickam County corn was taller than most men that time of year. He wished he had the courage to open the door and flee into a field. But the impact would kill him. Jumping was not the answer.

"You know, Mr. Erwin," said Markey, "I had a dream about you. I had a dream about you all tied up and me pouring gasoline on your head. You was screaming and begging and crying like some pig with its throat cut and bleeding out. Then I lit my cigarette and dusted ashes on your head. You was praying there was no spark. And you know the best part of my dream? Johnny was there with us. Johnny was there, dressed all up in a white suit of clothes and sitting on a throne. He was holding out his arm, and I was waiting on a thumbs-up or thumbs-down. Just like the gladiators. Should you live or should you die? And you know what Johnny did?"

"No, I don't know. It was your dream."

"That's right. It was my dream. What happened was, Johnny gave off this very sad look and tears started rollin down his face. He was crying and the floor around his feet was getting wet from his tears. It was a terrible thing to witness, Mr. Erwin, because those tears just wasn't gonna stop."

"So which was it, Markey?" said Mikey from the back seat.

"Tears. A pool of tears."

"I mean was it thumbs up or thumbs down?"

"Neither one. Johnny stood up from his throne and held out his hand to me."

"What for?"

"He wanted my cigarette lighter."

"Oh, boy!"

"Then he walked up to the asshole and clicked the lighter and the flame shot out."

"And he dropped it on the asshole?"

"He clicked it off. Then he dropped the lighter and walked out the door. The lighter didn't have no flame. No spark. So he just left me there with the asshole."

"What did you do?"

"Nothin'."

"You mean nobody burnt this bastard?"

"I told you; it was a dream."

"But we're gonna burn him, right Markey?"

Markey turned in his seat and cuffed Killen on the side of his face.

"Yep. We're gonna torch his dumb ass."

Killen had no idea the twins had a cabin on the Mississippi. They pulled up a dirt road off the gravel lane and there it was.

It was a wood frame structure with what looked to Killen like a tarpaper roof. But it was dark, and he couldn't be sure about that or if it was corrugated tin like the neighboring cabins. Neither did it matter: the thing looked like a tinderbox just waiting for a match.

"We just using it," Markey told him as if reading his thoughts. "It ain't ours or nothing. We just borrowed it."

"It's not your cabin?"

"'Smatter, boy? You got shit in them drunkard's ears? Not

guilty, my ass. That judge sure fucked up."

"It's not over. I'm going to be indicted then I'm probably going to prison."

"Sure you are."

"I mean you don't have to do this. The system's going to take care of me."

"You mean let you go like that idiot judge did."

"I was surprised he let me go," Killen said, lapsing into the bad feelings about himself that had become his new norm. "I wouldn't have let me go."

"Then we agree on something," said Markey. "'Cause you ain't leaving here alive, boy."

"I figured as much."

"You figured right."

"How's about shooting me right here and getting it over with? You can throw me in the river, and I won't be any more trouble. I've certainly got it coming."

"You think we're looking to ease up on you, boy? You trying to cheat us out of our fun with you? Think again. We gonna filet you, Mr. Erwin. Just like a big old fish. We goan slice away a chunk of you at a time."

"Then what? Throw me in the river?"

"Only when you bleed out. Then we gonna torch your ass right before you dead."

"Okay. Have at it."

Killen felt all hope sliding away as if it was a boat pushing away from shore into an undeniable current. Nothing could save him here. No one knew where he was. Worst of all, he didn't deserve saving. He wasn't kidding himself about that. He had to admit he had it coming, whatever the idiot twins did to him. He was guilty, and he had been set free. That had been wrong, and now it was time to pay up. The twins were right. He should be filleted and burned. He blinked hard against the night and followed them up the steps into the cabin.

A kerosene lantern was lit. Its yellow light spilled across the floor of the cabin. Faces glowed as Killen watched the brothers make their preparations. He recognized the Rapala filet knives they settled on after a lengthy discussion about the merits of the various knives available in the cabin. The long, curved blades caught in the wooden handles would do the job perfectly, Markey said. Mikey's eyes gleamed. Clearly he was ready to pare away the hurt and anger he had for Killen. As for Killen, he was totally resigned. Whatever would come, would come.

He made no resistance as they stuffed his mouth with a ragged T-shirt that tasted of engine oil. He imagined the shirt had been worn on some fishing expedition or other and that the brother who wore it had operated the Evinrude motor. He closed his eyes and sucked hard, drawing life-giving air up into his lungs through the cotton cloth. Which became all but impossible when they then ripped duct tape into long strips and wrapped it around his mouth and jaw and head. Two strips were used, and then he could access air only through his nose.

Then they cut his boxer shorts away. Now he was bare.

Markey whetted his blade on a gray stone. The stone was

next passed to Mikey. He drew his blade repetitively up and down like his twin had done.

The nude Killen was placed on a wooden ice cream chair, and duct tape was wrapped around at navel level, at neck level, and at ankle level. His hands were pulled behind the wood frame, and his wrists taped together.

Markey stood before his prey and studied him. He held one hand to his chin and thought long and hard. Then, with a flick of his wrist, he leaned and carved away a one-inch strip of Killen's right pectoralis major muscle—a bacon-sized strip out of his chest. Killen shrieked, but the T-shirt muffled the sound. The duct tape around his mouth sucked in and out as he struggled to breathe through the excruciating pain.

His mind raced. He watched as a stream of blood sprung into view where his chest muscle had been. It was as if a surgeon had decided to deftly relieve him of muscle mass. The blood wouldn't coagulate as wide as the cut was and as deep as it was; it continued slipping down his chest and across his pubis and right thigh. He closed his eyes and thought of his children, Celena and Parkus. They would be looking out the window in just a few hours, hoping their dad would come up the hill for breakfast with them. But Killen doubted he would ever have the privilege of dining with his children again.

He became regretful. He thought about the cheating his wife had done and the damage it had caused their marriage. Why had she done that? And why hadn't he handled it differently?

Eyes closed, he was reliving his time with Mary Roberta and

hating every minute of it when suddenly and without warning it happened again. Pain! Another strip of flesh gone, this time from his left chest. Another length of bacon dropping to the floor beside him as his eyes flew open, and he watched in agonizing silence. Were they going to filet him, his mind asked. Yes, it answered its own question. Yes, they were going to filet him.

They pulled out the gag.

"Tell us what you're thinking *now*, brother!"

Although he was Catholic, he hadn't attended confession for twenty years. Since the age when he rode his first thoroughbred for pay and a piece of the purse. That was the beginning of his downfall, the lust for profit and worldly things, which began to come clear to him—sublimely and painfully clear as he awaited the next flick of the silver knife blade.

"Forgive me, Father," he muttered, "for I have sinned."

"What the fuck?" said Markey.

"I have sinned!"

"You damn right you sinned," cried Mikey. "You killed Johnny!"

"I killed your brother, and I am sorry. I ask your forgiveness."

"Too late for that, Mr. Erwin," said Markey. "We ain't forgiving nothing."

"You in the wrong church, son," said Mikey. "You took a wrong turn somewhere along."

"You a drunkard, boy. Wait 'til we get to your tongue. You won't be swallowing shit after that."

"Gonna de-tongue you, Mr. Erwin. That's my job, for sure."

"I ask your forgiveness by all that's holy."

"I ain't your priest, boy. I don't gotta forgive shit."

"Forgive them, Lord."

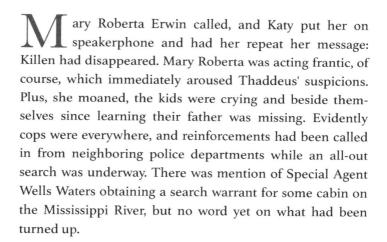

Mary Roberta Erwin called, and Katy put her on speakerphone and had her repeat her message: Killen had disappeared. Mary Roberta was acting frantic, of course, which immediately aroused Thaddeus' suspicions. Plus, she moaned, the kids were crying and beside themselves since learning their father was missing. Evidently cops were everywhere, and reinforcements had been called in from neighboring police departments while an all-out search was underway. There was mention of Special Agent Wells Waters obtaining a search warrant for some cabin on the Mississippi River, but no word yet on what had been turned up.

16

Katy beat Thaddeus to Chicago. Along the way, she had made four cell phone calls. Ultimately she scored a two p.m. appointment with her doctor.

"Is it an emergency?" asked the doctor's receptionist.

"No. It's a swelling under my arm. I'm guessing ingrown hair."

"And you said you're a doctor?"

"I am," said Katy. "Internist."

"Then you should be able to diagnose your underarm swelling, wouldn't you?"

"We don't self-diagnose. We have our own doctors for that."

"Of course. Is two p.m. good?"

"Perfect."

"Because he might want a biopsy, and he's got a thirty-minute cancellation at two."

"Put me down."

"Done."

Arriving home, she left Sarai with her nanny and turned back south to her physician's office. By 1:55 she was waiting in the exam room after having vitals taken. Blood pressure and heart rate were within normal limits; complaints were underarm swelling and—she hadn't told Thaddeus about this part—a lump in her breast.

Dr. Maria Coates was a small woman with a bright smile and cheerful attitude. Her specialty was internal medicine, which was specifically the background Katy had chosen for her primary care physician. "Internists know medicine," she told Thaddeus. "Strongly suggest you use the same type of doc."

Dr. Coates came into the exam room and folded her arms across her chest. The two women then spoke for five minutes, doctor-to-patient and doctor-to-doctor. Katy was then asked to remove her blouse and bra. Next she reclined on the examining table while Dr. Coates felt the lump Katy had discovered by self-exam. She stared at the ceiling as she felt around, lips pursed, nodding.

"All right. Let's do a fine needle aspiration on this and see what's what."

"How long before we know anything after that?"

"I'm going to have someone walk it down the hall. We can have a report back before three."

"Oh, that will help," said Katy. "I'm very anxious about it."

"You should be. It's probably just a swollen gland, but it

could be something worse. Well, we'll know within the hour."

"Excellent."

Dr. Coates explained to Katy that different techniques could be used to perform biopsy but that she was going to opt for the least invasive procedure possible. Katy said she knew that, that she had performed hundreds of breast biopsies herself. Dr. Coates caught herself. "Forgive me. Old habit."

Her choice was a Fine Needle Aspiration biopsy. She proceeded by first injecting local anesthesia to numb the breast. Katy was lying down when this was done. Five minutes later, Dr. Coates inserted a thin needle into the breast, locating the lump with her fingers and penetrating it with the needle. A sample of cells was then returned into the syringe.

"Now, Katy, I'm going to treat you like my other patients and tell you some things that you probably already know. Bear with me, I must have it in your record that I told you these things, or my malpractice carrier goes nuts."

"I know, so please proceed."

"The samples I have taken will go down the hall to our pathology lab. Our pathologist will examine them under a microscope. A detailed report will be provided in writing, but today I'll also have a phone conference with her too. She will talk about the type of cells seen, including any suggestion that the cells might be cancer."

"Understand. Is that your speech?"

"There's more. Aspirate samples can be benign, meaning no cancerous cells present. They may also be atypical, indeterminate, or suspicious of malignancy. This would mean the results are unclear, and further study is necessary. A surgical biopsy would be indicated in that case. Or she might tell us flat out that the cells are malignant, meaning they're cancerous, uncontrolled, and have the potential to spread to other areas of the body. Given this possibility, I'm going to take a sample from the lymph gland in your armpit. The swelling and tenderness there. Fair enough?"

"Fair enough. I understand and appreciate your thoroughness."

"You would offer your own patients no less."

"True."

Again the injection of anesthesia, this time into the armpit, followed by the same process of needle, withdrawal of aspirant, and labeling for the pathologist.

Then Katy was returned to the waiting room where she would spend the longest forty-five minutes of her life as she waited to hear from the pathologist who even at that moment might be fixing her tissue on a slide and beginning the study.

Her eyes misted over and despite her determination not to, she felt sorry for herself. She missed Thaddeus and the girls and swore that she would become a better wife and mother if only she could survive the lump and whatever it meant.

She even closed her eyes and prayed to Grandfather.

∼

By three forty-five she was driving home without the radio playing, which was unusual for her. Her mouth was twisted in a grimace, and her eyes were teary and swollen. The anesthesia had worn off, and her breast and underarm were burning and far more swollen than when she had gone to Dr. Coates.

Against anything else she might have imagined, she finally had to admit: she was sick. She was a doctor but now she was a patient. The cancer cells were present, and they had spread to at least one lymph node. The diagnosis made her a breast cancer IIA, which meant her tumor was under two centimeters, and a lymph node was involved.

Beyond that, nothing else was known.

Treatment would begin the next day.

17

The twins cut away the tape holding Killen to the chair. "We want to watch you dance, boy!" cried Mikey. Killen looked around just in time to see Markey unscrew the fill cap from the kerosene lantern and slosh its contents at him. He stood dripping from chin to waist. Then Mikey ignited a highway flare and swept it down Killen from his chin to his waist. The kerosene flared up and burned the lawyer in one long flash. The twins ran for the door, down the stairs, and headed for their Dodge Ram.

Killen recalled the army blanket on the single bed and immediately pulled it over his upper body. The flames were smothered, and he fell to the floor of the cabin. Several hours later he awoke in such pain that he began crying. He made his way out into the night and ran to two cabins where no one answered his pounding and pleas, before finding an old fisherman in the third he tried. An ambulance was called. Killen was rushed to the hospital.

On the way, he managed to tell the deputy taking his statement in the ambulance who had kidnaped him. The deputy went to his shoulder mike and broadcast the identity of the perps to Dispatch. Dispatch contacted the duty sergeant, and an APB was put out for the twins.

Wells Waters organized a shoreline watch for boats on the river. Sheriff's deputies made dozens of interceptions and numerous boardings as river runners were interrupted due to the search for the twins.

The State Police were on high alert. The Dodge Ram was located on the Secretary of State's computers, and license numbers broadcast to a four-state area. Eyes were everywhere. Special Agent Waters got mug shots in officers' squad car, and the search continued.

K illen was kept unconscious for the first several days as the burns were assessed and treated. Physicians and nurses came and went, and treatment modalities discussed and implemented.

The burns responded to treatment and medication. Days later, he was taken off the IV morphine. But he was still loaded with oral medication. His wounds had been abraded and sutured where the knives had done their work. But these were the least of the physicians' concerns. Infection from the burns was feared and visitors held at bay.

Every day they changed dressings several times. The pain of dressing changes would often make him pass out. There would be a great inhalation of air, followed by excruciating pain down his torso, relieved only by the darkness that came blessedly swimming toward him.

But the nurses were proud of his fight. They told him over and over they'd never seen anyone fight like him. And his willingness to let them do their jobs—he was admired by the staff. Meanwhile, inside, he seethed at what the animals had done to him. And he seethed at his wife for her complicity because he dimly recalled her flashing past the window of his motel room just before the twins came inside. At times, he would realize he was at that stage in being medicated where he was hovering between reality and hallucination and he would catch himself imagining the torture of those responsible for his pain. Mary Roberta's face was among those whom his angry hands would tear apart, stab, and shoot. Any thought of her made his pain worse, and he found himself wishing he'd never met her. For the first time, he knew real hatred and even though he tried to pray and attempted to forgive her, it always came roaring back and he was enraged at her again.

But slowly the burns healed and medications were decreased. This was at the end of his second week in the hospital.

On the following Friday, they lifted the quarantine.

On Friday night, Katy and Thaddeus brought Killen's two children to see him in the hospital. Mary Roberta was dressing to go and needed someone to watch the kids, so Katy's offer to take the kids over to Springfield to see Killen was perfectly timed. She had jumped right on it.

Parkus was five and too young to visit, Katy decided. He remained in the visitors' waiting room, and Katy read to him while Celena went inside. Celena was eight years old and held back when she saw her dad in ICU. She saw his tears and Celena crept to her dad's bedside.

"Hi, Daddy."

Killen's eyes were open and stared. There were no eyelashes. The hair on his head and eyebrows had been burned away as well.

"Don't be scared. Dad got too close to a fire."

"Does it hurt?"

"It hurts, sweetheart. But they take good care of me and give me medicine, so it doesn't hurt as much."

She moved a step closer to her dad.

"I don't want to kiss you right now."

"That's all right. When I'm better, you can kiss me. For right now I'm just happy happy to see my girl."

"Dad, who did this to you?"

"What makes you think someone did this to me?"

"Because you don't play with fire. And you're not dumb. So someone else must have done it."

"No, I don't play with fire. And neither should you—ever."

"What are all the bandages for on your arms? Did you get burned there too?"

"I did. I got burns all over."

"Are you going to die? Mom said she thought you might die."

"Who did mom say that to?"

"Grandma. She came to stay with us last night."

"Mom was going out?"

"Dad, you know I'm not supposed to discuss mom with you."

"You're not?"

"Of course not, silly. Mom says you're getting divorced, and she needs to have her own life."

"Okay. If Mom says."

"Parkus and I miss you, Dad."

"I miss you guys too. Did Parkus come?"

"He's out in the hall with Mr. Murfee. They won't let him come in. He's too young."

"Well, you tell Parkus how much I love him too. Will you?"

"I will, Dad. But we already know that anyway."

"Okay."

"Dad, Mom says you can't see us after the divorce. Are you going to see us?"

"Sure I am. I'm going to see you every day."

"Good. We want to be with you. Mom's never home anymore."

"I want you with me. I will be home every night with you and your brother."

"Dad, can I touch your hand?"

"Here, let me turn it over. You can touch my palm."

The little girl reached and placed her hand in Killen's hand. She left it there only a moment or two, then withdrew it. She smelled her hand.

"Smell funny?"

"No. It doesn't smell like anything."

"I'm glad."

Celena was then ushered out, leaving Thaddeus alone with Killen.

"I can't lose those little guys, Thad," Killen said, tears rolling down the side of his face.

"I know. We won't let that happen, either."

"What about my drinking? What's a divorce judge going to think when it comes to custody and visitation?"

"It's not good. I mean you've been intoxicated in the presence of the kids."

"And my fight with Mary Roberta?"

"Hell, Killen, you tackled her and knocked her out. That's domestic violence. There isn't a faster way I can think of to lose your kids than domestic violence. You could lose them altogether, you could get supervised visitation, you might have to take a domestic violence course. All kinds of bad stuff comes from that. And you know there's the order of protection. We only got the kids here tonight because the judge entered an order amending the order of protection so the kids can visit you in the hospital. You're in serious trouble, man."

"Will you help me?"

Thaddeus shook his head. He ran his hand through his hair and adjusted the glasses on his nose, thinking of how to phrase his answer.

"Let me say this. I will defend you in the domestic battery case. The divorce case and custody—well, you need a real expert for that. Now, if you haven't got the bucks to hire a good one, I'll bail you out there. Is that fair?"

"Hell, yes, although I'd rather have you speaking for me."

"That wouldn't be wise. I don't know jackshit about divorce and have no business doing one."

Killen shifted his weight in the bed and grimaced.

"Hurts like hell. I might nod off with these pills. Bear with me."

"We've got to get going. The kids are staying with us tonight and Katy wants to get them bedded down."

"At home or your room at the motel?"

"At the motel. Mary Roberta opened an adjoining room where they'll sleep. Don't worry, all doors will be open in case they need something. My guess is, Sarai will probably end up in Celena's bed or vice versa anyway. Should be quite a night."

Killen's eyes fluttered under the influence of the drugs. Still, he fought to stay awake. "So what else is new?"

"Not much. We're just waiting and praying for you, brother."

"Thaddeus, let me tell you something. Just off the record, okay?"

"Okay."

"I want her dead."

"Sure you do. All divorce couples want the other one dead. Don't worry, this too shall pass."

"No. Seriously."

"That's the morphine talking. Don't think about it until you're clean and we can take a look at the other issues too. Don't forget, you're drinking alcoholically and need help there too. This is no time to be thinking of Mary Roberta's punishment. This is the time for you to get well and get your life back together. I promise you, if you do that, the rest of this stuff will take care of itself. You'll get to see the kids, and all the rest of it will come around. For now, close your eyes and don't dwell on her anymore. Can you do that?"

"Yes. But I'm serious."

"Sure you are. For now, just for tonight, let it go, okay?"

"Okay."

"That's a start."

Two weeks later, Killen was released from the hospital with a bottle of Percocet and a tube of wound salve. Thaddeus drove him back to Orbit, and they talked and discussed the divorce lawyer from Jackson City that Thaddeus had hired for Killen.

Things were looking up.

Or so Thaddeus thought.

18

"I'm looking for something I can carry in my purse."

"Is this for self-defense?" asked the clerk.

Barbara Daniels surveyed the fifty feet of the display case in the Gander Mountain outdoor store. There were pistols of all sizes and descriptions; they were even making them in colors now for the women. She looked around to make sure she wasn't being watched. Then she noticed the CCTV cameras strung out above the display cases, and she knew her time there would be anything but private. She would formulate her comments and answers accordingly.

"It's for self-defense."

"Your attacker would be what—carrying a gun, a knife? What is your greatest concern?"

"My attacker would probably have a gun."

"So you maybe want to take some defensive shooting lessons too?"

"That would be a great idea. I don't have the slightest idea how to defend myself with a gun."

"Have there been threats on your life?"

"There have been threats to my family."

The clerk looked solemn. "Well, I don't want to pry, but have you reported them to the police?"

"Not yet."

"Is it a man or woman threatening your family? That will help me understand what kind of gun you could use."

"A woman. A woman is threatening my family."

"Someone you know?"

"Slightly. How about that silver one there? It looks very solid and compact."

The clerk unlocked the case from behind and laid the nickel plated revolver on the felt strip along the top of the display case.

"This is a strong favorite among women. It's a revolver, which means it's much more reliable. It's also a .357 Magnum, which means it has the stopping power of a car head-on at fifty miles per hour. Or so I'm told."

"Is it a purse gun?"

"It is. The holster I would recommend would be the pocket holster. Not everyone likes that, but I do, because you can have it drawn and pointed in under five seconds. We have videos on how to carry and fire, by the way, if you're interested."

"How much are the videos?

"Nineteen ninety-five."

"That sounds about right."

"So is this the gun you'd like to own?"

"It is. And enough bullets to break it in."

"We have a range here in the store. You can buy target loads right there."

"Is there someone there to show me how to load and shoot?"

"There is. For about a hundred dollars, you can buy two hours of instruction. It's invaluable, and I highly recommend."

"Well, let's do what we need to do."

"You can pay for the gun today, and then there's a forty-eight-hour waiting period."

"What's that about?"

The clerk nodded and began packing the gun inside its box.

"Forty-eight hours is a cool-down period. So's people don't come in and buy a gun and then go out and shoot someone the same day."

"I don't like that. I should be able to defend myself now."

"I hear that. But unfortunately, it's the law."

Barbara Daniels' disappointment was evident. Her shoulders slumped, and a dour look crossed her face.

"Well," she asked, "what else do you have for self-defense?"

"Pepper spray?"

"Knives. What about a knife?"

"That wouldn't be my recommendation, not for self-defense. Someone could wrestle a knife away from you."

"Yes, but you could inflict a world of hurt if you got the first jab in, am I right?"

"Oh, we have knives that would stop a grizzly bear if you knew what you were doing. I'm thinking the KA-BAR knife."

"What's the KA-BAR?"

"Lady, I was in the Marines, and if you had to fight hand-to-hand, this was the knife you used."

"Let's see some KA-BAR knives, then. I need something today, not two days."

"Sure. Let me pick up the phone and get someone from that department. Wait one minute, please."

Barbara Daniels turned and placed her back on the gun display case. A knife sounded more appealing by the minute, the more she thought about it. A gun would be too sudden. She wouldn't enjoy it nearly as much as she would feeling the knife stabbing and cutting the bitch.

At that moment, she visualized Mary Roberta Erwin and her smug, beautiful face. And she imagined her husband lying atop her, whispering the words he used to whisper to Barbara back before—back before she put on weight after the second baby and couldn't get it off no matter how much Jazzercise she did; no matter how much speed-walking she did; no matter how much one-on-one training she did at the YWCA. Nothing worked, and now she had lost her man.

She felt seriously threatened for her children, who needed their father's support. What if he ran off? Would she even be able to keep the house?

Hell, no. Her job at the phone company paid minimum wage. There would be no way to keep the house.

No, she had told the truth when she said her family was being threatened.

The KA-BAR knife made more sense by the minute. And so did the gun. She decided she would take the gun, too. There was enough on the card to pay for both, so why not?

And Dave would never know. He had no interest in looking at the bills anymore, not since Mary Roberta had turned his head.

She turned back around.

"I'll take the gun, too."

19

How many red pickups in a fifty-mile radius? Thought Thaddeus. He couldn't say for sure, but just the fact of the divorce filing followed by Killen's disappearance was troubling. Thaddeus had been around the block too many times not to question such apparently random events.

He pulled into the motel parking lot and, just as he did, Mary Roberta's Chevrolet Suburban—red over white—swept by. She didn't look his way and didn't notice him, but then why would she? She had never seen him in the Mustang before and wouldn't make any connection.

So without thinking he turned it around and fell in behind her, two cars back.

They were headed east on Washington Street and five minutes later were downtown and now heading further east and leaving the city limits on the east end. Now there was no separation between the cars, and that was fine; Thaddeus dogged it just a bit, keeping back and allowing the occasional car or truck to move between him and Mary Roberta.

Thirty minutes later they entered the city limits of Jackson City. Thaddeus had no idea whether the private eye routine would pay off, but he had come this far and was determined to keep after her, just to see where she'd be headed, without the kids, in the middle of a weekday afternoon.

It wasn't long until he found out.

The prime dance hall/restaurant/motel in Jackson City was the Blackfeather. At its first turn-in, Mary Roberta switched on her right turn blinker. Thaddeus slowed to allow her to turn in and then he proceeded up to the second turn-in and crept back around. As he arrived perpendicular to the office, he saw Mary Roberta ascending the exterior stairs of the motel. He quickly pulled out his smartphone and began clicking. The snaps would show her climbing the stairs, turning left along the upper walkway, and then stopping at the sixth room left of the stairwell and knocking on the door: room 212. It opened, a man's head appeared, and she went inside.

Thaddeus checked his watch: 2:20 p.m. He located her Suburban and pulled in behind it, one row back. The view afforded him a clear camera angle on the upper room, the walkway, and the stairs. Plus he would have the opportunity to take her picture almost dead-on as she made her way back to her Suburban.

But who was the guy? Thaddeus couldn't see him well enough to judge.

He reviewed the snapshot of the open door and the guy's head. Using his fingers on the smartphone screen, he enlarged the picture. The resolution resolved and the man's face came into focus.

There was no doubt: Dave Daniels. Pipeline welder and pussy hound supreme. Also a married man himself, with a houseful of small kids. That was the sum and substance of what Thaddeus knew about him, which wasn't much. But as far as Thaddeus knew, Dave was together with his wife, who evidently didn't know about the tryst he was having with Mary Roberta, or didn't care, or realized she could do nothing about it. She would be someone for Thaddeus to talk to.

He slouched back in his bucket seat and twiddled the transmission shifter. He pulled the sunglasses from his face and rubbed his eyes. He inhaled and exhaled mightily: but nothing he did would make the time pass any faster.

At 3:40 p.m. the door opened, and she stepped outside. She was adjusting her bluejeans and tucking in her T-shirt. Thaddeus got snaps of those preparations and was glad for them. He continued snapping as she made her way back to the stairwell and as she descended the stairs. Then he lost sight of her behind the parked cars between him and the motel curb. Finally, she emerged at the front of her Suburban, and he was able to take several snaps of her head-on, coming toward the driver's door, keys in hand, cigarette dangling from her free hand. All of this was recorded.

She started up her car and a short blast of white exhaust shot out the tailpipe.

He didn't turn the Mustang's key. He was going to wait.

When she had cleared the parking lot, Thaddeus pulled up to Mary Roberta's vacated parking spot and worked his way forward two more parking lanes. Now he was directly facing the motel's curb where short sidewalks led up to the rooms. He put it in park and waited.

He didn't have long to wait.

Dave Daniels—Thaddeus instantly recognized him—came strolling out of the motel room he had shared with Mary Roberta. He traced her steps along the walkway and down the stairs and, lo and behold, climbed into the car parked beside Thaddeus. It was a beat-up Chevrolet Scottsdale truck with a bashed-in looking toolbox across the bed of the truck. Without looking across at Thaddeus, he backed out.

Thaddeus followed Dave out of the parking lot.

Sure enough, two turns and a red light and they were headed back west, toward Orbit.

All this time, from the motel room door opening to the turn west, Thaddeus was recording the meeting on his cell phone. He forecast it might be useful in some courtroom. It would be helpful in the divorce and just might set Killen free in the pending assault case from having knocked his wife to the floor and injuring her head.

He would definitely share his findings with Killen.

But he would have to be careful when he did. He would need to lay the foundation that she wasn't worth losing sleep over.

20

"**B**arbara? Killen Erwin here. Look, it appears our spouses are out enjoying each other's company tonight. What do you say you and I get together and talk?"

"Where?"

"We could meet here at the motel."

"That would look bad."

"How about the motel lobby? I can send the night clerk into his room for twenty minutes while we meet."

"That sounds better. Or we could meet at the Red Bird restaurant."

"No, too much chance for you getting bad-mouthed."

"Agree. Soon as I said it I realized how dumb it would be. Talk about everyone getting on the phone."

"You'd be the talk of the town, Barb."

She laughed. "I like you, Killen. Did you know I voted for you?"

"Well, thanks for that. Belated, but I appreciate your support."

Thirty minutes later they shook hands inside the Orbit Motel's office and settled into two visitors' chairs. The clerk disappeared as Killen asked.

"So what's up, Killen? Do you kill Dave and Mary Roberta? Or do I get the honors?"

Killen didn't smile.

"We do have an option."

"Divorcing them?"

"That wasn't quite what I had in mind."

"Shooting both of them?" she said and laughed.

"Not exactly."

"So give it up, Killen. I don't have any more guesses. And besides, I'm tired. And I'm old and flabby and so goddamn mad I could strangle the asshole."

"Welcome to the club, Barb. Welcome to the club."

"Thank you.

"So let me bounce a couple ideas off of you. Let's get down to the real deal."

"That's why I'm here."

"Good."

Fifteen minutes later, they stood, and he gave her a hug and walked her out to her beige Toyota. She popped the trunk and withdrew a long, flat box. On its outside was a graphic of the KA-BAR knife she had purchased. She handed it to Killen, and he stuffed it in a pocket.

He watched as she climbed in and then he closed the door. He waved as she drove out of the motel lot and then watched as she rolled up to the highway and clicked on her left turn indicator.

She was headed home. She had told Killen about Dave's videos. They were on his YouTube channel, and they were private. But she had obtained access, and she knew he was filming his trysts. Now to find out where. Killen was guessing room 212 at the Blackfeather. Thaddeus had shown him the video he had made of the Mary Roberta-Dave Daniels afternoon at the Blackfeather.

Now it was his turn.

He spun on his heel and returned to his room.

The night was young, and he had reservations to make at a hotel in New Orleans and two airline tickets to purchase.

He drove to Louisiana, Missouri, and stopped at the four 7-Elevens there. When he was finished, he had $2000 worth of prepaid credit cards—more than enough to reserve a room and buy airfare.

He also picked up a burner phone.

He used it to call the airline and used it a second time to make the hotel reservation in New Orleans.

Then he undressed and went to bed without having a drink.

It was the first sound sleep he'd had in over a year, he decided the next morning over breakfast.

He walked out into the parking lot of the Red Bird Restaurant.

The sunshine was glorious, there was a hint of fall in the air, and troubles were a mile away.

For the first time in a year or more, he smiled.

Really smiled.

He was proud of himself. He wondered if Thaddeus would be proud when he found out.

Maybe yes, maybe no.

But he would find out soon enough.

21

Thaddeus sat down with Katy and coffee. She explained to him what Dr. Maria Coates had told her and what the lab results had said. It was the worst possible result, something he had dreaded and even refused to consider.

Thaddeus was stunned.

Blinding tears came into his eyes, and Thaddeus cried for himself and her. It was the last thing Thaddeus expected, Katy's cancer. There couldn't have been a worse diagnosis for the woman Thaddeus loved. Waves of fear washed over him. For the first time in a long time, Thaddeus knew again what it felt like to be living a life that was totally out of control. Which is something a cancer diagnosis can do in an eye blink. You don't know what it means, you're threatened and scared to death, and you lack all the information you'll need to try to pull yourself together and face what's coming.

Thaddeus rubbed his eyes and made ready to do battle for both of them.

She was standing at the kitchen sink, running water. He came up behind her and wrapped her in his arms. He kissed her neck and held his face against hers. Thaddeus could feel her body relax as he held her, and she sighed. "Thank you, baby," she murmured.

One thing was sure: Katy wouldn't be going through it alone. He would be at her side every step of the way.

"I'm with you in this," Thaddeus said. "You have to know I won't let you down."

"I know, Thad. Thank you."

"Does Turquoise know?"

"Of course not. We don't know what it means yet. We'll tell her when we have to."

"Sure."

At nine a.m. they left the house for the ten o'clock with the oncologist.

~

Dr. Hermann Wolfe was a large man, open in his movements, whose patients thought he might embrace them in a bear hug at any moment. In fact, when he met Katy and asked if he could examine her, he did grasp her across the shoulders and pull her to him.

"Don't worry, Doc," he said to Katy. "I've got this now."

"I'm ready to do this," she said. "Let's go."

He examined her and relayed findings to his assistant, who sat at a keyboard and charted what the doctor was saying.

Then he was done with the physical exam and Katy's history and complaints.

He reviewed yesterday's biopsy and rubbed his chin as he read through the pathologist's report.

"These findings are enlightening but don't tell us everything we need to know. There will be more testing. We can do most of that today. Then we can discuss treatment modalities and decide on a plan for you."

"Okay," Katy said. Her voice sounded small and far away. She was sitting on the end of the examining table, her legs dangling. Thaddeus reached across and took her hand. A little squeeze just to let her know Thaddeus was there.

"So let's do a few things and then I'll see you back in here a couple of hours."

"All right," said Katy.

Three hours later—during which Katy was off in various rooms undergoing tests and films—and they were taken into Dr. Wolfe's office.

"All right. I have reviewed the tests and the films and the radiologist's assessments, and I'm ready to suggest a course of treatment."

"I'm ready," said Katy. "I imagine first there will be a lumpectomy."

"Exactly right, Doctor. I will arrange that. Then I believe we'll do seven or eight weeks of radiation therapy, depending."

"Depending?"

"Depending on results. We'll track things as we move along."

"When will we do the surgery?"

"One week. Time is never our friend in these cases, not at this point. We will act quickly and decisively. Then you will be returned to me."

"Who will do the surgery?"

"Dr. Snopes in our group will be available next Tuesday. Please present yourself at the hospital at six-thirty a.m."

"I'll do that," said Katy.

"His staff will provide you the standard lists of do's and don't's. Just comply and you'll do fine."

Thaddeus needed to ask since Katy didn't. "Will there be a mastectomy? I'm unclear about that."

"There will probably be no need. The course I'm recommending is commonly called breast-conserving therapy. After surgery, the radiation therapy will eliminate any cancer cells that may be present in the remaining breast tissue."

"All right," Thaddeus said. "I just needed to understand."

"Sure, Thaddeus. That's what I'm here for. One more thing you should know. Two studies published in 2002 in the *New England Journal of Medicine* showed that women with small breast cancers—under four centimeters—treated with lumpectomy plus radiation therapy were just as likely to be alive and disease-free twenty years later as women who had

had mastectomies. We've gotten even better since 2002, I might add. Our numbers are better."

Thaddeus plunged ahead again. "What about recurrence?"

"It's important to know that recurrence can still happen with lumpectomy plus radiation. In the study I mentioned, fourteen percent of women had a recurrence in the same breast. However, local recurrences confined to the breast area after lumpectomy can be treated effectively with mastectomy and these women were still disease-free after twenty years."

"All right," Thaddeus said. "Thank you for the numbers."

"Sure. We need to know these things always."

Thaddeus looked at Katy. He reached across to her and took her hand in his. She was sweating but hiding it well. "Anything you want to ask?" Thaddeus said.

She shook her head. "I think that about covers it. I'll be ready in one week."

"Great," said Dr. Wolfe. "I'll see you then."

"You'll be at the hospital?"

He smiled. "With you, Doctor, I'll be in the surgical suite as well."

"Well, that is wonderful. Thank you."

"Hey," he said, "if the shoe were on the other foot, you'd do the same for me, yes?"

"Yes."

Then they were finished, and they found their way out into the bright August sunshine.

They found a Starbucks and got drinks and headed home.

"You know what?" she said, halfway there.

"Hmm?"

"I'd like to get lunch with you before we go home. Just the two of us."

"All right."

"Then I'd like you to take me home and just hold me."

"Can do."

"Just get up on the bed with me and hold me for a half hour."

"Definitely."

"All right, then. After that, I'm good to go."

"I know you are. I love you, Katy."

"Me too. You're my guy."

"Always."

22

K illen was represented by Joseph Bostow, III, the attorney hired for him by Thaddeus. He was a recent honors graduate of Saint Louis University School of Law. Mary Roberta was represented by Elizabeth Melendez, a svelte, serious woman in her fifties. Melendez was known as the woman you went to if you needed a hatchet job done on your husband. Her divorce practice had bought her a farm worth in excess of one million dollars, a small plane for getting around central Illinois, and a reputation as a fierce negotiator and courtroom combatant who didn't know the meaning of "quit."

Judge Veinne listened to the testimony of Mr. and Mrs. Erwin, sitting with her hands folded before her at times and furiously making notes at other times. It seemed to Killen that the notes were made only during Mary Roberta's testimony. While he testified, he felt the judge's eyes upon him and knew she couldn't be making notes too.

Then the judge entered the divorce case's temporary findings and orders.

Killen was ordered to pay spousal maintenance of fifteen hundred per month. Child support was ordered in the same amount. Temporary use of the marital home to the wife. All income from motel operations to wife. All income from any new law practice or employment to husband up to seventy-five-hundred split fifty-fifty above that. Each party kept his or her motor vehicle. All utilities at marital residence paid by the husband. Temporary care, custody, and control of the children of the marriage to wife. No allowance for visitation, based on husband's demonstrated propensity for domestic violence.

"What about supervised visitation?" Killen said, making a last-ditch plea to the judge when she finished and asked if there were anything further. "I haven't hurt my kids."

"We disagree, Your Honor," said Melendez. "It's foolish to think the kids—at least the daughter—don't know their dad viciously attacked their mom, causing a severe brain injury. They're lucky to still have her in their lives. With his track record, I can't see any manner of visitation until and if he completes domestic violence counseling. If—"

"Court agrees, counsel," Judge Veinne interrupted. "No visitation on a temporary basis, Mr. Erwin. You will receive a written order setting out the where's and how's of your domestic violence counseling. When and if that is completed, let the court know and we'll revisit the temporary visitation issue. Right now, I'm looking at supervised but really can't predict. That is all."

"You bitch," he hissed when Mary Roberta strode by with her smiling attorney. "This isn't the end of it."

"I heard that," said the lawyer. "Watch your mouth, Killen."

"Your slut client thinks she won here today. Tell her for me it's temporary. She better damn well enjoy it while she can."

Melendez stopped walking. She pointed her finger at Killen.

"You better damn well watch your mouth. One more word and I'm hauling your ass back in here for violating the Stay Away order. It applies in here, too, Killen. Now back the hell off!"

Killen looked enraged, but he said nothing further. He stuffed his hands into his coat pockets, searching for his keys. Then, without a word to his attorney, he stormed out of the courtroom, the courtroom he had once owned as District Attorney.

Clearly he owned it no more.

23

J udge Wren presided over the arraignment of Killen Erwin. He began by explaining the crime of aggravated domestic battery:

"Aggravated domestic battery is a Class Two felony. Any sentence that includes probation or conditional discharge must also include a condition requiring the defendant to be incarcerated for a minimum of sixty days. If the defendant has one or more prior convictions for aggravated domestic battery, the judge must sentence the defendant to a minimum of three years in prison. Are you getting my drift here, Mr. Erwin?"

Killen's eyes searched the floor between the defendant's table and the judge's perch. He really could think of nothing to say. So Thaddeus, standing beside him, spoke up.

"Your Honor, I have impressed on my client the importance of the Stay Away order and the importance of this never happening again. He understands that a second transgression is a mandatory term of three years in prison without parole. It won't happen again, Judge."

"By your forthrightness am I to assume there will be a plea, counsel?"

"No plea, Your Honor. It's my client's position that his wife was as much at fault as he."

"You're saying your client believes she injured herself?"

"Your Honor, at this point we're not saying anything on the record except that my client pleads not guilty."

"Very well. Is that your plea, Mr. Erwin? A plea of not guilty?"

Killen looked up. "It is, Your Honor."

"We move that conditions of release stay as they are as well, Your Honor."

Special Prosecutor Eleanor Rammelskamp had drawn the short straw again and was prosecuting Erwin on the aggravated domestic battery charge. She pulled herself up to her full height and said she had no objection to the conditions of release remaining unchanged. She also reminded the court that she had obtained a Stay Away order that required Mr. Erwin to stay at least five-hundred-feet away from his wife and children.

"We would ask for a modification of the Stay Away order. Mr. Erwin has committed no acts of violence against or in the presence of his children. The Special Prosecutor obtained the original Stay Away order without Mr. Erwin's presence, and we would move that it be modified to allow him to visit his children, now that he can be heard. Arrangements will be made that would allow a third party to pick up and return the children to their home without Mr. Erwin coming within five-hundred-feet of his wife. Nobody, I might add, wants to stay away from Mary Roberta Erwin more than Killen Erwin at this point, Your Honor. So we would move that he be allowed ordinary visitation with his children, consisting of every other weekend and Wednesday nights, plus alternate holidays and alternate birthdays. Thank you."

"Counsel?" said the judge to Eleanor Rammelskamp. "Your position?"

"No, no, no! The defendant has demonstrated his propensity for violence, as evidenced by the injury sustained by his wife. The children were in fact in the house with their parents the night it happened and, except for the fact they were sleeping, they would have witnessed the brutal assault of this defendant on his estranged wife. We would respond to the defendant's motion by strenuously objecting to any such order of visitation. Please, judge, let the civil proceedings handle that matter inasmuch as the defendant will certainly be required to undergo domestic violence counseling before the civil authorities allow him around his children again. The state would ask the court not to interrupt that civil process."

Judge Wren nodded and turned his attention back to Thaddeus. "Counsel, that makes sense to me, that the civil court be allowed to handle such things as visitation of the defendant with his children. Truth be told, I'm not even convinced this court has jurisdiction over the issue of child visitation, so I'm going to pass. The court will not amend the Stay Away order. Defendant is reminded that he is not to come within five-hundred-feet of his wife and children while that order of protection is in effect. Is there anything else, counsel?"

"No, Your Honor," both attorneys said.

"We're in recess."

Killen immediately turned to Thaddeus. "What the hell, man! I can't even visit my kids at all? What the hell is going on here? She started the damn fight; she's the one who opened the motel door and gave the twins a shot at me; she's the one sleeping around; she's the one driving my truck when Johnny died—and yet I'm the one paying the price? What the hell kind of justice is this, Thaddeus?"

Thaddeus shook his head. He grimaced and placed a hand on Killen's shoulder. "I couldn't agree more. Except the part about the fight. She's the one who was gravely injured, so the law presumes you were at fault. The court's assumption is that she didn't injure herself. When you laid hands on her that night, brother, you opened the door to all this bad stuff raining down on you. Lesson learned? Stay the hell away from your wife. Could that be any clearer?"

"Thad, you're not hearing me! Those kids need their father. Now more than ever! God only knows what kind of crap she's feeding them about how she got injured. Didn't you notice in the hospital how slow Celena was to warm up to me?"

"No, I didn't. I thought she was scared by the fact her dad was in the hospital all bandaged up. I didn't think her hanging back was about you at all."

"Then you didn't see what I saw. Which is only normal since

she's not your kid, and you don't know her like I do. No, she was brainwashed. I'm never going to see my kids again, Thaddeus, am I?"

It was a statement more than a question. Thaddeus went about packing up his briefcase and trying not to argue with his client. What more could he say to him? He had never seen Killen so out of control before. No matter what Thaddeus said, Killen wouldn't see the truth that lay at the bottom of it all: he had caused Mary Roberta's injury. Nothing else mattered to the system, including whether or not she was brainwashing his kids against him.

"In a domestic situation, Killen, all bets are off once you lay a hand on your spouse."

"She was taunting me. She was having sex with men right in front of me. Who wouldn't have lost it? She's damn lucky I didn't kill her. She sure as hell had it coming."

"Not so loud, please! You can't be saying that crap, Killen. Promise me you won't say that to anybody else. She might deserve a lot, but she doesn't deserve to be killed. Bottom line: your wife is a slut, and your rage has put you in a damn hard spot. Now it's up to you to climb out of that hole—both of them—and get your life back on track. Threatening and whining isn't going to get it done. Not this time, buddy. Nor is drinking. You need an A.A. meeting like yesterday. If you want, I'll take you."

"I don't have a drinking problem, Thad. I have a wife problem. She's got her hooks in me. She's going to get my house, the motel I paid for, half my ponies and farm, and she's going to get my kids. All because she spread her legs for me. Hell, she deserves none of it, but the court is going to reward her for sleeping around. It just isn't fair, brother. You and I both know it, too!"

"All right, all right. She's a loser, and you're the good guy. What else can I say? One, leave her alone. Two, get the hell to an A.A. meeting. Three, straighten out your own life and leave your kids out of it for awhile. You're not even taking care of yourself, how can you take care of little kids?"

Ignoring his lawyer, Killen added, "Plus, she caused me to lose my job. Now I have no job, no income, and mouths to feed, including twenty-two horses. What the hell am I supposed to do? I've got sixty-five-hundred in the bank and no more coming in."

"I don't know. I can't make a loan because that would be a conflict of interest. I don't know what you're going to do, Killen. But you're a resourceful guy, so you'll figure it out. Hell, sell some horses. Sell all of them. Go from there."

"I can't. There's a restraining order in the divorce that prohibits me from selling assets. She hasn't missed a trick. I'm done. I'm finished."

"No, you're just starting over. But you won't listen to me. We're done here, Killen."

"Yes, we are. You go on out. I'm going to sit here and clear my mind. There must be a move I can make."

"A.A., one. Get her to agree to a horse sale, two. Take care of you and leave the kids alone, three. There're your moves."

"Sure, Thaddeus. But I'm not you. Those are your moves, not mine."

"Fine. Whatever. Later, Killen."

"Later."

Thaddeus had lost his patience with Killen. He hadn't had anything else to offer him. He rejected the help that Thaddeus suggested for his drinking problem. He dismissed the idea of selling the horses by seeking his wife's cooperation. He refused working through his domestic violence issues so he could visit with his kids. So Thaddeus had just said, "Later, Killen," and let it go at that.

He would forever regret that he hadn't done more.

But there it was. He hadn't.

Thaddeus and Rammelskamp met on three different occasions in an attempt to reach a plea agreement on the domestic violence charges. Thaddeus shared with Ms. Rammelskamp that Killen wasn't doing well, and that closure to the case would help reduce hostilities and help Thaddeus steer his client into counseling and treatment.

Finally, the charge was reduced from Aggravated Domestic Battery to Domestic Battery and that was when Killen agreed to plead guilty.

Probation was ordered, three years. Plus domestic abuse counseling.

Killen shut his eyes and swallowed hard.

Domestic abuse was something he knew all about. They had just charged the wrong person.

She was as guilty as he was, in his mind.

Maybe more so.

The figure was seen leaving the Blackfeather Motel, room 212, at 4:50 a.m. Friday morning. It was September 10.

By ten o'clock, the Blackfeather was swarming with police and detectives and crime scene investigators. The maids had made a terrible discovery. The motel manager was making his rounds from room 212 to office to parking lot where a crowd had gathered, all the time wringing his hands and trying to disperse the crowd so the event would draw as little attention as possible.

By ten-thirty the body was removed on a stretcher. The figure was totally covered by a white sheet that was turning red with blood smears.

"Who is it?" the manager asked Lamar Hunt, Detective One, of the Jackson City Police Department. Hunt was an oily man with a great smile who seldom showed it. Now and again he would smile, but that was only when he was trying to set a witness or perp at ease and get them to talk. This wasn't one of those times, and so his face remained blank.

Hunt looked the manager up and down and evidently decided he had a right to know.

"Her name is Mary Erwin. Mary Roberta Erwin. Was she a guest of the motel?"

"There was no one registered by that name. Two-twelve was registered to David Daniels of Orbit."

"We'll be speaking with Mr. Daniels this morning. Orbit PD is rounding him up for questioning."

"What do I tell my insurance company?"

"Seriously?" said Detective Hunt. "Tell them your security people were on the premises and you were doing everything you could to make the premises safe. I imagine her family will end up suing you. That's what usually happens in these public inn cases."

"Oh, my God. Sued for what? Oh, my God."

"Would you state that name again," asked a news reporter who had listened in on the conversation.

"Mary Roberta Erwin."

"Thought so," said the reporter. "If I'm not mistaken, she's the wife of the Hickam County District Attorney, who just resigned. Name of Killen Erwin."

"Sure, I know him," said Detective Hunt. "Met him and talked to him. How were they getting along?"

"They weren't," said the reporter. They were separated, and he was facing domestic battery charges for assaulting her."

"All right. Michelle, make a call to the Orbit PD. Have them round up Killen Erwin and hold him for questioning too. We'll be there around noon."

Michelle—a robust woman in her mid-thirties—nodded that she had heard the order. She went to her unmarked car and made the call.

Thirty minutes later, Killen Erwin was confronted at his farm, asked to step down from his tractor, and taken to the police department, where he was placed in an interrogation room and told to wait.

"I want to call my lawyer," he said.

"You are a lawyer," said the Officer Dunleavy, who had brought him in.

"My lawyer. I have the right to call him."

"Use your cell phone. Knock yourself out, Killen. Tell him this time you've gone too far."

"What is this about?"

"You haven't heard? Your wife was murdered last night."

Killen Erwin turned white. "My God!"

"'Subject said, "My God" on being told his wife was dead.' I'll be sure that gets in your booking report."

"Am I being booked?"

"Not yet. Personally, I would book you, but the dicks just want to meet and talk. From my vantage point, who else had a motive to see her dead? Make your call, Killen, and stop talking to the police. You should know better."

"Right. Some privacy, please."

"Knock yourself out," said the officer, and he closed the door.

"Thaddeus," Killen said into the phone, "it's Killen. I've been brought in for questioning. You aren't even going to begin to believe this!"

26

"Questioning about what?" Thaddeus asked. He was working out of Chicago. The call caught him riding in the backseat of his Escalade, returning to the office from a ten o'clock court hearing.

"The officer told me that Mary Roberta was found murdered."

"Go slow. What happened?"

"I don't know. Sheriff Altiman got me aside for a minute when they were booking me. He said the Jackson City cops want me charged with murder."

"Okay, we can't talk about that. No telephone."

"Agree."

Thaddeus looked out the window of his car. The light changed to green.

Thaddeus said, "You remember my admonition? Under no circumstances are you to talk to the police?"

"I haven't."

"Remember, people convict themselves with their big mouths. Remember our rule?"

"No talking. Listen, I didn't do it, Thaddeus. You have to know that."

"I know, I know. You don't have that in you. You might be mad and crazy right now, but a killer you're not."

"Thirty seconds," the jailer said to Killen, who was using the pay phone outside the cells. "Is that your lawyer?"

"Yes."

"Tell him they're bringing over a complaint charging you with murder. They're going to initial you this afternoon."

"Based on what? They've got nothing to tie me to this case."

The jailer smiled. "Not what I heard. It's all over dispatch. They found bloody pants in your motel room."

Killen turned pale and pounded his fist against the wall. "When can you get down here? They're going to have me appear for initial appearance this afternoon."

Thaddeus sighed. "I'm turning this car around right now. Ask Judge Wren to hold off until I get there. It's eleven-thirty now; I can be there by four, four-thirty."

"Thank you, Thad."

Thaddeus looked out the smoked window. He shook his head. This wasn't going anything like what he had wanted for Killen. Or Mary Roberta, either, for that matter. The woman was no damn good, Thaddeus thought, but she sure didn't deserve to die for her faults. No one deserved to die for their faults, in his view. And worse, now Killen was looking at a possible conviction for first-degree murder on this latest. Compounded by his plea on the domestic battery charge he'd never get out of prison. Thaddeus felt a burning in his stomach.

"JT," he told the driver, "let's hit a Mickey D's. I need a shake and a Big Mac."

JT nodded. "Got it."

Thaddeus punched in the number of the Hickam County District Attorney—Killen's old number.

"Imelda, Thaddeus here. Is the new DA around?"

"He's over at the jail, Thaddeus. My God, what's going to happen to Killen?"

"Hard to say. I'm coming down is the reason I'm calling. Ask your boss to hold off on the initial hearing until I hit town. Probably around four."

"Will do. Thaddeus, do you think he did it?"

"Come on, Ima. You know I can't discuss that with you."

"I'm just so worried," she said. "A lot of us just feel horrible about what's happened to Killen. Lots of people in the courthouse still believe in him and want him back in office. Is there a chance he might run again?"

"Hard to say, Ima. Probably not. If we can set him free on the two felonies he's looking at now, we'll be lucky. It's too early to tell, though."

"I'll have Mr. Stoops hold off on the initial until four. I'll call Judge Wren's chambers, too."

"Good. You saved me a call, Ima. Thanks."

"See you at four."

"You'll be in court?"

"Oh, Thaddeus, we'll all be there. We'll be there to support Killen. He needs his friends now."

"He sure does. So thanks for the vote of confidence. Sit on the defense side of the courtroom, okay?"

"Of course. It'll piss off my boss, but I don't care."

"So Stoops is going to handle it?"

"Maybe. I think they're deciding that right now. I know he called Eleanor Rammelskamp a while ago, and they talked about a Special Prosecutor in this case too. But I don't know yet."

"Sounds fun. See you at four."

"Okay."

Thaddeus felt his stomach flip-flop.

"JT, burger and shake."

"I see the golden arches next corner, boss."

"Excellent. You da man."

Thaddeus sat back and closed his eyes. He would need to call his office and clear his calendar. He made the call, and Albert said he would handle Thaddeus' calendar. Thaddeus drummed his fingers on the leather seat. Then he opened his iPad. His car had WIFI, and he used it to log into the Illinois statutes.

It was time to read about murder.

Again.

27

A t four-fifteen p.m., Thaddeus walked into the Hickam County Circuit Court in Orbit. He had left JT, his driver, with the Escalade. When last seen, the driver was commandeering a courthouse lawn bench and accepting a game of chess against a retired farmer.

Thaddeus' heart fell when he saw Eleanor Rammelskamp enter the courtroom. He had been hoping for the new DA, the youngest DA in Illinois, Iggie Stoops. That guy he could have knocked around. But oh, no, instead they send one of the state's top prosecutors, Eleanor Rammelskamp. She walked right in front of Thaddeus without so much as a word. With a great clamor and scraping of chairs she rearranged the furniture around the prosecutors' table so that it fit with her idea of courtroom decor. Then she plopped her massive document case on the floor beside her chair and opened it. Withdrawing two books, she arranged those before her and crossed her hands. Abruptly remembering one more preparation, she again stuck her hand in the document case and this time came up with a thin buff folder. Thaddeus guessed it contained the Information—the charging document—that would accuse Killen Erwin of First Degree Murder.

Judge Wren from Quincy walked in next with no fanfare, as the defendant's appearance was mandatory, and everyone seemed to be almost working together and respecting each other's agenda enough to make the whole thing work. Thaddeus kept looking off to the side at the prisoners' dock with its bars and locked gate but so far no Killen. Thaddeus hadn't had the chance to drop by the jail, but he felt that wasn't needed anyway. Killen was a pro and knew the ropes. Surely he understood now more than ever to keep his mouth shut.

Then there was a commotion in the dock and Killen stepped inside the small cage from an outside entrance. He wore the orange jumpsuit, wrist manacles, leg irons, and waist chain of the truly damned. Escape risk? Security risk?

Hardly. They were simply processing him as he deserved to be processed, in their eyes: one more for the grinder. The people working the system all knew that it was all but inevitable; Killen would be charged, tried, and convicted and could expect to spend the rest of his life in one of Illinois' godforsaken prisons, among the worst in the nation.

With one reservation. Extra security around the courthouse and inside the City of Orbit was in place. Mikey and Markey hadn't yet been brought to justice, and some feared that they would seize the opportunity to gain access to Killen when he appeared in court. They had been known to do that previously in their brother's case and any opportunity for a repeat performance was squelched. Their efforts to ensure the defendant's safety even included dressing him in body armor just in case.

The judge mounted the bench and zipped his robe, bottom to top. He adjusted the necktie knot and pressed his glasses up on his nose. Then he coughed into his sleeve and switched on the mike.

He said, "The court calls the case of People of the State of Illinois v. Killen Erwin, Number 15534-2015." The words were muffled and didn't rattle about inside the ancient courtroom as usual. Then it occurred to Thaddeus why. He turned and looked over his shoulder. Every seat was taken. Citizens, press, police, family—everyone had turned out in full force even though the case had appeared on no calendar. Sure enough, sitting directly behind Thaddeus, was the court-house gang that had snuck away from their work details, led by Imelda Sanchez, Killen's secretary.

As the judge finished, the deputies led Killen from dock to counsel table and indicated he should sit beside Thaddeus. As if he didn't already know.

Thaddeus and Killen didn't bother looking at each other or acknowledging each other in any way. It would have made no difference if they had. What was done was done and what remained to be done was before them. No amount of small talk or pale greeting was going to change that, so they passed.

The judge continued.

"For the record, the state is here today represented by Eleanor Rammelskamp, and the defendant is represented today by Thaddeus Murfee. Lady and gentleman, do I have that right for the record?"

"Yes, Your Honor."

"Yes, Your Honor."

"And the defendant is present in person. Sir, would you state your name for the record?"

"Killen Erwin."

"And Mr. Erwin are you under the influence of any drugs or alcohol as you sit here today?"

"No, Sir."

"Our task before us will be brief. We are here to provide the defendant with the charges against him and to consider conditions of release. Counsel for the state, have charging documents been prepared?"

"Just an hour ago, Your Honor," said Rammelskamp. "Permission to hand the Information to the Clerk?"

"Granted. Let the record reflect that the Special Prosecutor is giving the Information to the Clerk of the Court. The Clerk will pass it to the court for review."

The Clerk passed the Information to the judge, who read it.

"Counsel, please distribute to the defendant and his attorney," the judge continued, evidently satisfied with what he had read.

Thaddeus briefly looked over his copy of the Information. It was signed by the Special Prosecutor and charged Killen Erwin with the crime of First Degree Murder, as well as lesser included offenses.

"Counsel, have you had a chance to review the Information?"

"I have, Your Honor," said Thaddeus.

"And has your client had the chance to review it?"

It was the time-honored question required by law. Everyone who answered it positively committed perjury, and nobody cared. In fact, it was encouraged in the interest of moving things along.

"He has, Your Honor, and we would waive the reading of the Information."

"Very well. Mr. Erwin, do you understand the charges against you here today?"

"Objection," said Thaddeus sharply, "that question seeks to confirm the defendant's competency to stand trial. Mr. Erwin hasn't been examined yet by the proper medical personnel. At this point the opinion of the accused of his competency is irrelevant. Moreover, the question seeks to abridge the defendant's Fifth Amendment right against self-incrimination."

"Counsel, are you saying Mr. Erwin is incompetent?"

"No, sir. But neither am I saying he's competent, and neither is he saying he's competent. Whether he understands the charges against him is irrelevant. You can ask, Did he read the charges? And whether he has any questions about the charges, but his understanding is an issue in the case, one that I'm unprepared to take up at this time with the court."

The case called for hardball. Thaddeus was batting.

"Very well, Counsel, the court will withdraw the question. Now the matter of conditions of release. You may be heard, Mr. Murfee."

"May it please the court. Whether the defendant is a flight risk is the first question the court is required to address. So please let me sketch out what we know about Mr. Erwin. His connections with the community are multiple and deep. A resident, a property owner, a husband and father, a community volunteer, a member of Rotary, of the Moose, of the Orbit Community Schools School Board, and as a past District Attorney and private attorney Killen Erwin is a solid, stable member of this community with connections as plentiful as you can have.

"When considering granting bail, Your Honor may consider several factors, including whether or not the crime charged involved violence; the nature of the offense charged; and, whether the accused was on bail pending trial when he was arrested for the current charge.

"Obviously the defendant was not on bail pending trial, and obviously the crime charged involved violence. However, bail should be set where there is insufficient evidence to show a probability of my client's guilt. So far, Your Honor, there has been no connection made between my client and the act in question. None. To hold defendant without bail at this point would be a gross injustice. Defendant requests that bail be set at a reasonable amount."

The judge looked at the Special Prosecutor. "Ms. Rammel-skamp? I'm sure you would like to be heard."

"Thank you, Your Honor. Judge, I've just been handed a note stating that a pair of bloody jeans has been found in defendant's motel room. In all honesty, we don't know yet whose blood it is. But until we do, it would only make good sense to hold the defendant without bail, as there is a high probability of defendant's guilt if the blood is that of his wife.

Making this determination will take seventy-two hours for the Illinois Crime Lab, so the state asks that defendant be held without bail pending the results of that testing, at which time defense counsel can revisit the issue if desired. Thank you."

Thaddeus was caught completely off-guard. He'd had no opportunity to talk to Killen and was unable to formulate any argument in response to the state's avowal to the court. It had happened only once before, but now it was happening again: he was speechless.

"Counsel?" said the judge to Thaddeus. "Reply?"

"Without knowing—there has been no showing—Your Honor, without knowing the source of the blood we would still ask that bail be set. My client has previously appeared at all times and places on the first offense, and he will do so for this one."

The judge looked at the attorneys and considered their points; then he was ready to rule.

"Bail will not be set at this time. Pending the state's testing of the bloody jeans, the defense may renew its motion at that time. Ms. Special Prosecutor, I want you to immediately turn over to the defendant all reports of testing on the pants. Do you understand me?"

"Completely, Your Honor."

"Then we're done here. Court stands in recess. The defendant is remanded to the custody of the Hickam County Sheriff."

Killen rose stiffly and quietly, body armor yet in place while restraints were reattached to his wrists and ankles. He sighed loudly and shook his head. But no one gave his discomfort a second thought. Any attacks by the twins had been thwarted, the initial appearance had been held, and the authorities were relieved it was concluded without incident.

Thaddeus went out the back of the court to avoid the press. He double-timed down the stairs and walked out on the courthouse landing.

"JT!" He called to his driver. "Let's put away the chessboard and hit the road."

JT apologized to the farmer with whom he had been moving pieces around the checkered board. The farmer, a seventyish man in OshKosh overalls and a blue feed cap, waved off his new friend.

"You'll be back," the farmer said. "I took a picture of the board with my phone. We'll get her set back up next time you come through. I'll be waiting."

Thaddeus shook his head.

It was a new age in Orbit.

28

F ollowing the Initial Appearance, Thaddeus and JT drove out to the Red Bird Inn. There were three decent places to eat in Orbit, and the other two were right down-town where the media would likely accost Thaddeus. So the duo opted for the west end of town and the Red Bird. They were hungry and needed to sit and let the road-weary take a breather. They ordered coffee. JT ordered a pork tenderloin sandwich with mashed potatoes and gravy and Thaddeus ordered the same but with fries.

Coffee arrived, and JT stirred in cream and sugar. Thaddeus stirred in cream.

"So, did you get bail?" said JT.

"Afraid not. Police found bloody pants at Killen's motel room."

"It looks like he did it?"

"Well, a man named Henry Thoreau said, years ago, 'Some

evidence is very strong; like when there's a trout in the milk.'"

"So the cops caught a trout?"

"If it's Mary Roberta's blood, they've hooked something big."

"Weren't you telling me he put her in the hospital a while back?"

Thaddeus quit stirring.

"I did tell you that."

"He hit her head? Or she hit her head?"

"He knocked her down, and she hit her head—so the story goes."

JT thumped the table with his fist, not hard, but enough to emphasize his point: "So maybe the blood on the pants is from before? Is that possible?"

Thaddeus set his mug down.

"JT, how would you like to move up in my law practice?"

"You serious?"

"As serious as a heart attack. I'm thinking we send you to paralegal school."

"I don't know. I barely graduated high school."

"Maybe so, but you have something important. You have the ability to analyze. You just proved that."

"Could I get paid while I go?"

"You bet. I would just want your commitment you would work for me at least a year after you graduate."

"Hell, yes, Thaddeus. Done."

"I'm going to throw down this tenderloin, and then we're going over to the jail. I've got to see a man about a pair of pants."

"Got it. I won't dilly dally."

The sandwiches were served, with potatoes, and both men ate in silence.

Thaddeus had moved way down the defense road.

～

"So, Killen, tell me about the pants they found."

It was just after six p.m., and they were sitting in the attorney's conference room at the jail. Sheriff Altiman had gone out of his way to provide coffee and had told Thaddeus to take all the time he needed. He also confided that the entire police force was pulling for Killen. Almost no one believed he murdered his wife. And those that did he also confided, thought she had it coming.

Killen's hands shook. "Jesus," he muttered. "This is astonishing! My wife's dead! And they seriously think I had something to do with it? Jesus!"

Thaddeus nodded slowly. "They're serious enough to prosecute you, Kills. And right now I need to make a quick appraisal of their case. We're coming in for bail in a day or two now, and I want to be ready this time. Where were you last night?"

"At home."

"Any witnesses?"

"I was doing legal research. Most of the time there aren't witnesses to legal research."

"No need for sarcasm. I've got to ask."

Killen lifted the Styrofoam cup of coffee to his mouth, and it sloshed over the edge.

"Man, I'm coming unglued. I haven't been this scared since my first bar exam. Tell me something good, Thaddeus. Who is with my kids?"

"Mary Roberta's mom. JT and I already checked on them. They're just fine. Now, what about the bloody pants?"

Killen took a swig of his coffee.

"I was wearing those pants the night she hit her head on the floor. They just haven't been washed yet. You know how it is when guys live alone, and certain hygienic chores go wanting?"

"You're saying you weren't washing your stuff."

"That I am."

"So they've got bloody pants but they were from the fight you had with Mary Roberta in your house?"

"Yep. I was nowhere near that motel room last night."

"How can we prove that?"

Killen smiled.

"Like I said, legal research."

"We can prove you weren't at the motel by legal research? What the hell are you saying, Kills?"

"Last night, I was doing legal research. My search queries will show up on the other end of the Internet. Westlaw will have a record of all of my searches and the date and time they were done."

"Very interesting. So you're saying you were researching all night?"

"Since early this morning. Very early."

"What in God's name for?"

"Mainly for my political aspirations. Looking to see if I could run for office again. I do this when I can't sleep."

"And Westlaw's records will prove this?"

"Yes."

"What time parameters?"

"Let's see. I began around three or four and finished around eight this morning. Do we know what time she checked into the motel?"

"We don't even know if she was the registered guest or if she was a visitor there."

"Well, I'm sure your investigator will need to find that out."

"I'm sure he will."

"Who are you using?"

Thaddeus smiled. "Believe it or not, I called Christine. She's going to pitch in and help me this time."

"Christine Susmann? How could I be so lucky!"

"I need the help. You're facing life without parole since it's a murder committed with a prior violent offense. That's your natural life going by while you count dust mites, pal."

"I hear that. How can I ever repay you guys?"

"By telling us the truth. If you killed her, I need to know. If you didn't kill her, I need to know. Either way, I'm not pulling out. But I need the truth. Some lawyers never want the truth. I'm not one of those."

Killen favored Thaddeus with a blank look. Thaddeus had expected something more defensive, like a shout of innocence. Instead, he got low key.

"I have no idea who killed her, but it wasn't me."

"Well, let's talk about who else might have wanted her dead. My immediate thought is Dave Daniels' wife."

"Mine too. I would say Barb Daniels is at the top of my list."

"All right, who else?"

"Maybe Dave himself."

Thaddeus shook his head. "Dave was tapping that. I can't see him killing her. What makes you put him on the list of suspects?"

"Who knows? She made me crazy. Maybe she was pulling the plug on him too, and he lost it. I'm telling you; her sex makes men crazy. You screw her once, and you're ruined for any other woman."

"I don't get that at all, but I'll put Dave on the list. Now, who else?"

"Maybe one of her earlier flames. I can think of about five of Dave's predecessors who might want her dead."

"Would that include you?"

"Ha-ha. Funny boy, sneaking back around to me. Yes, I wanted her dead, I mean, who wouldn't? She was taking my kids away, she was screwing every swinging dick that came along, she was about to ruin me financially in the divorce, she was probably driving when Johnny was killed, and she ran off to pin it on me, she had humiliated me dozens of times, she had caused me to lose my job: hell yes, I wanted her dead. But did I kill her? No, I did not. I applaud whoever did it, but it's not a crime to applaud. Not in this state."

"Yes, well let's keep that between you and me. So who do I follow up with first?"

"Well, first we need a time of death, to see how that comports with my legal research alibi."

"So noted."

"Then we want motel registration data. And we want motel security video. And we want motel employee statements."

"Agree. My investigator can handle that."

"Then we need statements from Barbara and Dave Daniels."

At that moment, Sheriff Altiman stuck his head in the door.

"Guys, I don't want to disturb you, but you will want to know this. The Special Prosecutor decided you two would try to point the finger of blame at someone else. So she decided to go proactive and rule everyone out. So she gets a search warrant for Barbara and Dave Daniels' house. And guess what?"

"What?"

"What?"

"It just came over the radio. Pretty exciting stuff: Wells Waters did the search, and he's saying he found a bloody T-shirt at their house."

"You must be kidding!" Thaddeus exclaimed. "What if the pants are Mary Roberta's blood, and the T-shirt is Mary Roberta's blood? The plot thickens."

Killen shook his head and grinned. "Or they could argue that one of us held her down while the other one stabbed her."

"This is getting deep in here," said the Sheriff. "I'll butt out, but I thought you'd like to know."

"Hey," said Thaddeus, "not my circus, not my monkey."

Sheriff Altiman laughed, and Killen threw back his head and joined in.

The mood had definitely lightened.

29

P eter Quinze was the investigator Thaddeus flew down from Chicago. He put him up in the room next to him at the motel and began assigning various aspects of the case to him.

Peter was a graduate of the University of Illinois at Chicago. His graduate degree was a master's in forensic science. He had retired from the Chicago PD after twenty years of service, with a gold medal and a letter of commendation. Then he had opened his own forensics/investigation office. Thaddeus, upon meeting him and using him on the Glander Peaks case, had made Quinze an offer he couldn't refuse and hired him to work full-time in Thaddeus' law practice.

Peter Quinze was tall for a Latino—six feet—dark with mostly black hair he wore in a short Afro. Mostly black hair, because it was streaked with a shock of white that ran straight back to the center of his head. Many police associates started calling him "Rocky" after the Beatles' raccoon when Peter's hair changed and he resembled a striped raccoon, and the name had stuck.

"Rocky," Thaddeus told him on the second night after the investigator was moved in, "I need you to analyze these films from the motel. The state turned them over to us in their discovery response, and I'm certain there's key info there, but I just don't have time to get to them. They go on for hours and days. Our murder date is September ten so maybe you can focus down there and see what turns up. Also, I'm not saying other dates and times won't be relevant as well. They might be, so an exhaustive review is required."

"Sure enough, Boss," said Rocky. "You got an office for me?"

"There's a room right off my office at the bank. I want you to set up in there."

"Perfect. I've got my paraphernalia and gear stowed in my room so I'll start moving in."

"Sounds good. Let's do the videos out of the gate."

"Roger that."

"Oh, here's another chore. Killen says he was using Westlaw on the night of Mary Roberta's murder. I need you to get a log of his searches, times, etc. You know the drill."

"We're proving he was online using the research service?"

"Exactly. We might just have an alibi right there if the times are right."

"Will do. I'll get a subpoena out for those records today."

"Thanks. And welcome aboard."

"Hey. One thing I've noticed about Orbit."

"What's that?"

"Dude, are there any other Latinos around this town? I do not see any brown skins."

"Not after sundown," Thaddeus laughed.

"Tain't funny, dude. Seriously."

"Oh, we're serious? I don't know about Latinos in Hickam County. But I do know there are no blacks living anyplace in the entire county."

"Why's that?"

"Who knows?"

"Jesus. I'm staying inside after sundown."

～

Once he was moved into his new digs, Rocky began watching video. From seven a.m. until six p.m. he watched, four days in a row. Locations were flagged and notes made. He viewed September the tenth at least a dozen times and on Friday night called Thaddeus into his office.

"Look here," said the investigator, "I've isolated this cut."

He clicked his mouse, and the screen came to life as the video rolled.

9.10.2014/4:44 a.m. A lone figure wearing pants, dark shoes, turtleneck shirt, hat, and long coat, was picked up by the video camera. The shot was approximately twenty-five yards into the parking lot from the stairwell leading up to room 212. The figure was diminutive in stature, maybe five-five or - six and moved gracefully. The figure looked neither right nor left, though that was hard to tell, as he or she was swathed in the wine-red coat and hat and dark glasses, and had pulled a red bandana up around mouth and nose while approaching. There was a brief instant where the face was somewhat revealed, but it was from too great a distance and in such poor light that the features weren't particularized. On it came, up to the stairs.

9.10.2014/4:45 a.m. From the far end of the walkway on the second level, exterior, the camera there picked up the figure coming head-on. At room 212 the figure turned the doorknob and boldly went inside.

9.10.2014/4:49 a.m. The figure reappeared, walked back the way it had come, passing the stairwell and walking another twenty feet before turning left. Then, within a matter of seconds, it reappeared and came back toward the camera until even with the stairwell, where he or she turned left, descended the stairs, and was picked up again by the downstairs camera. This time the view was from the rear and gave no clues about identity: same hat,same coat, same dark trousers and turtleneck. Same slight frame and stature.

9.10.2014/4:50 a.m. In a matter of twenty steps, the figure walked out of view of the camera and wasn't picked up again by any of the parking lot cameras. Why that was, was anyone's guess. Rocky had visited the parking area and motel and had carefully examined the camera setup and taken pictures of the setup for use with the jury. But he was at a loss to explain why the lot cameras didn't show the figure getting inside any car. Totally at a loss.

"Maybe she ducked down behind a car or truck, boss, I don't know," said Rocky.

Thaddeus stood upright and took the single visitor's chair in the investigator's office.

"Maybe someone was waiting just out of range of the motel camera, and she climbed inside their vehicle, got down, and was driven away."

"You're saying maybe two people were involved?"

"Why not? It helps explain things."

"I don't know. Usually, these lovers' quarrel type crimes are the work of one guy. Or one woman. It's usually not a twosome."

"Agreed. So, we just don't know. But now we know what the DA knows. Which is nothing. I mean, is there anything from that entire video that allows you to follow up on the perp's identity?"

"I'm not done with my frame-by-frame analysis, but speaking preliminarily, I'd say not. There's nothing that gives up ID."

"So the CCTV isn't going to convict my client."

"It sure doesn't look like it, boss."

"And what we have is six minutes of video. Any other? Day before? Earlier day of?"

"Nada, except we do have Dave Daniels and Mary Roberta checking into the room earlier that night."

"Dave wearing what?"

"Jeans and a rugby shirt. Horizontal stripes, red and blue."

"And when he was leaving?"

"Same thing, jeans and rugby shirt."

"What time did he leave?"

"Four-thirty-six."

"And eight minutes later the killer shows up?"

"Yep."

"Isn't that pretty damn coincidental?"

"Think of this: if it was Dave all along, why would he leave and come back?"

"To change clothes and make it look like someone else."

"Entirely possible. But I doubt it."

"Why doubt it?"

"From what I know about the guy, he's not that smart. Good looking, woman-magnet, but not all that bright."

"How can you be so sure?"

Rocky smiled. "I've already got everyone's high school records. All grades. Dave was a special needs kid."

"As in?"

"Lack of motivation to learn. He was a goof-off, always causing a ruckus in the classroom, talking back to authority, getting lousy grades."

"So you're saying he probably wouldn't have been bright enough to leave and come back."

"I doubt it. Plus there's the issue of motivation. You usually don't murder someone else's wife when you're screwing her. It just doesn't work that way."

"Here's something else. If Dave found out the day of the murder that he had probably videotaped it, why didn't he go online and destroy the video?"

"Because he knew it exonerated him. He knew he was innocent. Simple as that."

Thaddeus shook his head.

"Okay, Rocky. Good work, man. Good work."

"Oh, and I've heard from Westlaw. They're going to make the log available to us on their website. Turns out they get hit with subpoenas all the time."

"When will we know something?"

"Probably Monday or Tuesday. I'll catch up to you as soon as I have it."

"Good work. Thanks."

"Oh, Thaddeus one last thing. Almost forgot."

"Yes?"

"Illinois Crime Lab. Report just came in. The bloody pants? Guess whose blood?"

"Mary Roberta Erwin's."

"Bingo."

"No bail. Analyze their report and let's go over it with Chris in the morning."

"I'm on it."

"Is there any reason to do our own blood testing?"

Rocky smiled. His perfect white teeth glinted in the jittering neon light.

"None."

"I thought not. Okay, good night."

30

"So what time did you check into the Blackfeather?" Christine Susmann asked Dave Daniels.

Thaddeus had rented office space in the First National Bank of Orbit. It was an upstairs suite, with room for a reception-ist, lawyer one and lawyer two offices, a conference room, and a paralegal/secretary workspace outside each lawyer's office. She was meeting that day in the conference room, a windowless inner office in the bank building that was furnished with the mandatory conference table and eight comfortable chairs. Dave sat across from Christine, his arms folded across his chest. Every few minutes he would pat the cigarette pack in his shirt pocket and give Christine a dour look indicating he needed a nicotine jolt. She had ignored his silent pleas and plowed ahead.

"What I'm asking is, were you there a day or two before the murder? Or had you just checked in sometime that night?"

"We checked in together. No, that's not right. She waited in my truck while I got the room. We'd been dancing at

Harley's Dive in Springfield and were headed back to Orbit when things heated up between us and she made me get a room in Jackson City."

"Why the Blackfeather?"

"We'd been there before. We had a special room that was ours."

"Such as?"

"Room 212. That's the temperature where water boils. It was for when things heat up."

Christine nodded. "What do you mean, 'things heat up'?"

"Kissing, grab-ass that turned into something serious."

"Would it be fair to say, Mr. Daniels, that your relationship with Mary Roberta was based on a common sexual desire?"

"Yeah, I guess so. I mean we didn't have a whole hell of a lot in common."

"Tell me about that. What would someone need to be interested in if they were to have something in common with you?"

"Saint Louis Rams. Truck pulling contests. Bass fishing. Deer hunting."

"What about those Rams? You and Mary Roberta ever watch them?"

"No."

"And the truck pulls. I'll bet she bugged you all the time to take her to a truck pull."

"Not hardly. She didn't even know I liked that stuff."

"Did she own her own bass boat? Her own rod and reel?"

"Nope. We never fished together."

"Did you ever take her out in your boat?"

"No. My wife woulda found out about that."

"Well, deer hunting then. She probably hid out in your deer stand with you? Maybe carried her own shotgun and nailed one or two?"

"Please. You're insulting me now."

"Well, let's just say I'd be mighty surprised to find a stuffed deer head mounted on the wall of her house."

"I would be just as surprised."

"So what other things did you two enjoy together?"

"Drinking. Dancing."

"Drinking, dancing, and screwing? Is that about the sum and substance of your relationship with Mary Roberta?"

"I guess."

"Well, don't guess, please. If I'm missing something now's the time to speak up. While the recorder's running."

Dave shot a look at the digital recorder between them.

"You gonna use this in court?"

Christine smiled. "Only if you try to change your story."

"We about done here?"

"Just a little more. Did you kill her?"

"Of course not."

"Do you know who did?"

"The law says Killen Erwin."

"Do you have any evidence he did it?"

"I don't, no."

"Tell me about the bloody shirt at your house. Where did that come from?"

Dave's face flushed. He patted his shirt pocket. Nicotine was severely required.

"I have no clue where that shirt came from."

"Can you prove you didn't bring it into the house?"

"No."

"Well, here's what I see. You were the last person to see Mary Roberta alive. Outside the killer, of course. So you are connected to the scene of the death by, one, being there with her, and, two, by having a T-shirt that probably is going to prove to have her blood on it. Now, the police have already played their ace card by indicting Killen for the murder. Which means they can't come after you. But if Killen walks, do they then come after you? Or, third possibility, do you think your wife might have killed Mary Roberta and brought the shirt home herself?"

"Barb won't even let me kill the mice we catch in the winter. She definitely wouldn't stab anyone to death."

"Have you ever cleaned a deer?"

"I've butchered a few deer, yes."

"Very bloody, I assume."

"Yes."

"So you would have less compunction about butchering a human being than, say, your wife would, just based on your experience in such things, correct?"

"Probably correct. But like I said, I'm sure she didn't do it."

"If you're sure, then where oh where did the bloody shirt come from?"

"Maybe Killen put it there?"

"Really? Did Killen have a key to your house?"

"No."

"Has he ever even been to your house?"

"Not that I know of."

"What time did you leave the motel yesterday morning?"

"Four-thirty. I had to drive to Quincy for my job."

"You're sure about the time?"

"Yeah, I've got the alarm set on my cell phone. Want me to show you?"

"No, I believe you. So you left before Mary? How was she going to get home?"

"That was the thing. We always left her car at the Black-feather whenever we went out. That was where we always met up. So her car was already there."

"So anyone who saw her driving home wouldn't know she'd been with you. Cute."

"Hey, it was what it was."

"What about the funeral? You planning on going?"

"You know, you and I was doing all right until that bullshit. There's no need for that."

"Just curious. I've always wondered how a married lover sends off a married lover. Do you go? Don't you? I don't know; I don't know. Oh, Dave, you amaze me, guys like you. And gals like her. Never a dull moment."

"Are we done here?"

"You know what? We are done here. Thanks for coming in."

She turned off the recorder.

"I didn't do it, you know."

"I know."

"You don't believe me, though."

She smiled. "You know what? I never believe anybody. So don't take it personally, okay?"

"Bitch."

"I know, Dave, I know."

31

The lumpectomy surgery left Katy exhausted and emotionally wrung out. She was released from the hospital the day after, with a drain in place. It consisted of a tube inserted into the breast at the location where the tumor had been, and on the distal end was a bulb that had had the air squeezed out of it so that it could evacuate the fluid from the excision site.

She required Thaddeus' help, so several times a day he would remove the bulb from the end of the drain and empty it, deflate the bulb and then reattach it.

This process continued the first-week post-surgery. Then the two Murfees went to see Dr. Snopes for the first visit post. They were shown into an examining room where Dr. Snopes, quiet, soft-spoken scientist, and surgeon proceeded to examine the wound site and ask his questions.

"And who handles wound care?" he asked the husband and wife.

"Thaddeus has been in complete control."

Dr. Snopes smiled. "Well, Thaddeus, you've done a fine job. The wound site is clean and free of infection, and the surgical site feels like pretty much normal tissue. I think we can remove the drain today and allow the wound to close. Katy, you're looking just fine."

"When do we start the chemo?" she asked.

"No chemo. Radiation."

"Thank God," said Katy.

Thaddeus smiled, relieved she wouldn't have to do chemotherapy.

"Radiation will begin in three weeks—thirty days after surgery so the breast can heal and everything return to normal. We'll do seven weeks, and you'll have a session every day. The sessions can leave you sore, tender, nauseated and similar complaints. But after that, you're finished."

Tears came into Katy's eyes. "How can I ever thank you enough?"

"You know how? Find a charity—maybe the American Cancer Society—and make a donation. I'm quite serious. Money is required to defeat cancer. Your help will be important to others who follow you."

"Done," said Thaddeus. "I'll take care of that tonight."

"Good for you two," said Dr. Snopes.

Thaddeus and Katy returned to the black Escalade used to move them around Chicago. The driver, John Thomas Kinsey, was leaning against the front driver's door, engaged in a conversation with another driver. They were animated and laughing. Two steps away, on the sidewalk, stood the two XFBI agents that followed Thaddeus and Katy wherever they went inside the city. It was necessary because of the law practice and because of Thaddeus' history that would make some people want him dead.

"JT!" shouted Thaddeus, "Let's lock and load."

"Well?" said John Thomas. "How did it go?"

"Piece of cake," said Katy, "just like you predicted."

"See what I said?" John Thomas exclaimed. "My Holly had that same thing. One month and then the radiation and you're done. You're lucky you caught it in time, Mrs. M."

Both Katy and Thaddeus smiled as they climbed in the back seat.

"Don't we know it," said Thaddeus. "We know how lucky we are."

"Where to?" John Thomas said into the rearview.

"Home for both of us," said Katy. "Enough excitement for one day."

32

Two weeks before trial, the state's DNA tests came back. The blood lifted from both the pants and T-shirt was Mary Roberta's. In a way, the finding was helpful to the defense, Thaddeus thought, because the state was now facing a situation where the clothes that were arguably at the scene of the murder were found in possession of two different individuals, each of whom had a compelling motive for seeing Mary Roberta dead.

Which raised an interesting question, one Thaddeus and Christine had to work through. They were seated in Thaddeus' office on the second floor of the bank building late Friday night after the others had gone home for the weekend. Christine had been to the motel and changed into jeans and a T-shirt she had picked up at a Santana concert, and she was drinking a coffee purchased from the local McDonald's "coffee bar" and making faces with each swallow.

"This stuff's rank," she said and set the twelve ounce paper cup aside.

"We have our own coffee maker in the paralegal room. Why not use that?"

"Who knows? Let's just say the McDonald's sign looked friendly out here in the middle of nowhere."

"Now don't tell me you've outgrown your hometown?" Thaddeus mused. "Anyway, we have before us an interesting development."

"Right. Clothing with Mary Roberta's blood has been found in the possession of the two most likely people to kill her. The question begs: were they working in concert?"

"Or is this a setup," said Thaddeus.

"Setup by who?"

"Maybe by Killen. Maybe by Barbara Daniels."

"Okay, let's take them one at a time. If Killen offed his wife, he possibly came away with her blood on his clothes. We're looking at a situation where logic would lead to the conclusion that he shucked the pants at the motel and then somehow, for some baffling reason, he then took the shirt he was wearing over to Barbara Daniels' house and (a) planted it there, or (b) gave it to her and she knowingly received it. Logically, he has no reason to plant it there unless he's trying to point the finger at her. But if he's doing that he is the world's dumbest murderer, because he kept the bloody pants in his room at the motel. So that doesn't fly. So we're left with the situation where he kept the pants and turned the shirt over to Barb. This is nuts. It makes no sense."

Thaddeus leaned back in his executive chair and shut his eyes.

"You're right. It makes no sense. So let's leave off the whodunnit scenario and suppose that they both done it. By the way, there's also a third possibility."

"Which is?"

"The bloody pants are from the fight he had with his wife where she hit her head on the floor. And the shirt is from the murder scene where Barb Daniels cut the throat of Mary Roberta."

Christine nodded vigorously. "That crossed my mind. Question it raises, though, is why Barb Daniels, who just killed Mary Roberta, would come back home with the T-shirt at all. The search warrant says it was found in a lawn mower basket. She was trying to hide it. But why not ditch it along the way? Why home?"

"So there might be complicity between Killen and Barbara."

Thaddeus looked out the single window in the small office at the light traffic going by on Washington Street. Finally, he nodded and spoke.

"You want to know how we're going to be sure there's a game going on between these two?"

"How?"

"If the knife used to slice her throat is recovered in the possession of Killen. That would place both him and her at the scene of the murder. Logically speaking."

"Yes, it would."

"But they searched Killen's room at the motel and no knife."

"And they searched his car and no knife."

"Which means if we assume Killen was the murderer, that he discarded the knife elsewhere. In which case, it likely won't be found."

"Keeping in mind that the search of Ms. Daniels' home yielded no knife either. Same logic; she got rid of it, and it won't be found."

"One other possibility," Thaddeus said, turning back around in his chair. "Might not even be a knife we're looking for. Might be a razor, might be a razor blade—hell, it might even be a shard of glass that was used and then discarded right at the scene after the killer broke it to smithereens."

"Not an easy case," said Christine.

On Monday, the defense sent the fabric samples to its own DNA lab. The samples were from the pants and the shirt. Four days later the results came back, at a cost of three thousand dollars for the testing: Mary Roberta's blood was confirmed on both the pants and the shirt. There was no possible way to determine the age of the blood samples. The lab couldn't help by saying the sample from the pants was six months old and the sample from the shirt was only three months old, spreading the samples between the fight where she hit her head on the floor six months ago and the murder where her throat was cut three months ago. That kind of testing was unavailable. At least not according to the lab chosen by Thaddeus.

The night before jury selection began, Thaddeus and Christine had decided on a shotgun-approach defense strategy. The jurors they sought would be people who were uncomfortable with ambiguity, because it was ambiguity—reasonable doubt—that the two lawyers agreed would be spread around the courtroom like manure in Killen's pasture—just to see what might grow up out of it. They expected enough different interpretations of the evidence to take root and spring up that the jury would find itself hopelessly deadlocked among several different interpretations of the state's case.

Jury selection went about as expected, with the twelve jurors filling the box being from among the registered voters of the county and representing all manner, shapes, and sizes (mentally and emotionally speaking) of people. There was a chiropractor who missed being at his office adjusting sprained backs. There was a nurse, a schoolteacher, a barber, and three construction workers, and a student and a postal employee. As voir dire proceeded, the panel evinced varying degrees of interest in participating as jurors. They ran the gamut from disinterested to courtroom junkie (the schoolteacher, a middle-aged man without much hair who taught civics to freshmen) and everything in between. Thaddeus and Christine, with Killen's input, made their notes about each prospect and proceeded to accept/reject with as much logic, shored up by gut feeling, as they could muster. Rocky also helped by running down all the data he could get on the panel members by speaking with the Clerk of the Circuit Court, Fletcher Mannfred. Mannfred knew everyone on the panel. He was the chairperson of the Hickam County Democratic Party, and it was his job to know everyone. Moreover, he was naturally inclined to side with Killen in the very ugly murder case, and quickly shared with Rocky everything he knew. At each break in the court action, Rocky would join the two attorneys and Killen at counsel table and provide updates on the new jurors brought into the box since the last break. It was a game of musical jurors as first one side and then the other accepted and rejected. As Christine said, the end result was going to be twelve people who represented the lesser of two evils for both the prosecution and defense. This was because the excellent candidates were booted off by the lawyers who knew they would likely help the other side. "This jury is vanilla," said Christine. "And that's what you always get in a murder case where there are so many opportunities for the lawyers to kick people off. Vanilla and not very interesting."

"Except we have Staunton Galloway, juror number four," Thaddeus reminded her. "He's the guy who's going to reject the state's case because he was married when his wife cheated on him. Thank Mannfred for that nugget of information. When I make eye contact with the jury, it's always got to include Galloway."

Christine nodded her agreement. The attorneys had decided to split the trial duties between them. Thaddeus would take on cross-examination of the state's witnesses. Christine would take on direct examination of the defense witnesses—which were very few and would depend on how the state's case came in.

Eleanor Rammelskamp had the benefit of Wells Waters, the chief investigator, who had access to all the usual police and FBI background information on the jury panel. So when she struck particular jurors, and those strikes surprised Thaddeus, he knew that she was relying on data only she was privy to and that the deck she was playing with was fuller than his. Which was unnerving. He could only hope that

Mannfred's insider information would make up the difference and hold the line.

The final jury accepted on the afternoon of the third day, were jurors each side thought could be manipulated to accept its version of the facts and logical suppositions.

The courtroom was packed with gawkers and press, and Thaddeus could feel the nervous anticipation of everyone in attendance like electricity in the air. He considered that phenomenon and realized that everyone who entered had skin in the game: they were either strongly for Killen or strongly against Killen.

After lunch, just after sitting back down at counsel table, Thaddeus was elbowed by Christine.

"See that guy behind Rammelskamp? Don't look now!"

"Then how am I supposed to see him?" Thaddeus hissed back.

"It's Dave Daniels. What's that asshole doing here?"

Thaddeus spread his hands. "My guess? He was the last one to see Mary Roberta alive. Rammelskamp has to immediately rule him out as a suspect, so she goes in headfirst and qualifies him as one of the good guys. He's waiting to be first in line to testify just as soon as we get this jury picked. I'm turning around now—"

Thaddeus broke off and turned his head to the right. As he did, he saw Dave Daniels, who he knew from back in the day when Thaddeus was living and practicing in Orbit. Same old Dave, Thaddeus thought. Then Dave looked back, and Thaddeus saw what he was wearing to court.

"Check it out. Your guy is wearing a white dinner jacket."

Christine's shoulder shook with laughter. "You've got to be kidding."

"No, look. It's sad, really."

"Sad why?"

"I don't know. Because the guy is trying so hard to be the guy Rammelskamp needs him to be. I know what it's like not to have the money to dress right. I get it, Chris."

"There was a time," she said. "I have to admit, I have seen you down, sir."

Thaddeus snuck another look. Then he was jolted. Dave had flipped him off. Surreptitiously, seen only by Thaddeus, but there you were.

"Son of a bitch just gave me the finger! Forget all the decent things I was saying about him."

"What, he flipped you off?"

"He did. And he mouthed something to me, too. He's wearing his crazy face."

"He's just scared."

"I don't know. If he killed Mary Roberta, he knows this is the most important afternoon of his life coming up. Probably scared shitless."

"I'm thinking he did it, Thaddeus. I'm thinking he did it, wearing the T-shirt, and left it in Barb's clothes basket on purpose."

"Naw, he's not that stupid."

"Hey, I talked to the guy just yesterday. He *is* that stupid."

～

At the afternoon break, Rammelskamp abruptly stood up and asked Judge Wren if counsel could meet in his chambers during the break. She wanted to discuss an evidence issue that had just developed. Judge Wren agreed and gave the jury a thirty-minute break instead of the standard fifteen. In single file the lawyers entered the judge's chambers: Christine, Rammelskamp, Thaddeus, and then came Killen and Wells Waters, both of whom had a right to listen in. Judge Wren shucked the robe and loosened the red necktie and unbuttoned the top button of his white shirt. He was wearing black Docker's pants and black tennis shoes—comfortable and unseen by the onlookers and jury. He sat behind his desk, clasped his hands behind his head and rocked back, proceeding to give each attendee the once-over as he got ready for the first real problem of the trial. Everyone knew it would be an issue because all trials had sudden evidentiary issues that were supposedly unforeseeable but which always attempted to stack the deck in favor of the presenting party.

Thaddeus took a deep breath and got ready for the onslaught from Rammelskamp. Before it came, however, a knock came at the judge's door, and the judge's secretary said there was someone in the outer office with a package for Special Agent Waters. He went to see and returned carrying a manila evidence bag sealed with red crime lab tape. Thaddeus had seen enough such packages to immediately recognize the item, and it sent a shiver up his spine.

Waters sat back down, balancing the bag in his lap like a baby.

Judge Wren launched right in, once everyone was seated, and the court reporter had her tripod and keyboard in place.

"Back on the record in *People v. Erwin*," the judge said. "Ms. Rammelskamp?"

At that point, Agent Waters began peeling crime lab tape with his fingernail. Oh no, thought Thaddeus, here comes a blow for justice!

"Your Honor," Rammelskamp began, "no one hates this more than I because it looks like the state has sandbagged, but we just got this evidence back from the crime lab last night. It is the smoking gun."

"Go on," said the judge, checking the clock on the wall. "We've chewed up five minutes just getting ready to get ready. Please show us what it is."

Agent Waters, delight etching the smile lines on his face, reached inside the manila bag and proudly withdrew and held up for all to see a Marine KA-BAR knife. Its blade was black, and its cutting edge glinted in the afternoon light.

"Your Honor, this knife's blade has been confirmed micro-scopcally as the knife that slit Mary Roberta Erwin's throat. But that's not all. The crime lab has also located on the knife handle a partial print. We believe, and our expert will testify, that the partial fingerprint matches the fingerprint of Killen Erwin, the defendant."

"Objection—"

"But wait, I'm not finished. DNA testing also found a drop of blood on the knife that matches the blood of Mary Roberta Erwin. So, we have the knife used, the victim's blood, and the perpetrator's partial print. A crucial piece of evidence and one that justice cries out be shown to the jury."

"Judge," cried Thaddeus, "we object! This knife has never been listed in any disclosure documents and is a complete surprise. Further, the defense hasn't been given the opportunity to have the knife and the fingerprint examined by its own lab, much less the DNA. Defendant objects to the use of this knife by the prosecution and requests an order banning it from being shown to the jury or testified about by any witness. I mean, hello, where has this knife been hiding all this time?"

"This knife was found four days ago by a maintenance worker at the Blackfeather Motel. His name is Arturo Sandoval, and he will be called as the state's witness to testify regarding the circumstances of the find. He will testify that the knife was found behind the Coca-Cola machine on the second floor of the motel during routine maintenance on the machine that required it be moved away from the wall. Mr. Sandoval wasn't the repairman, but he was assisting, and he found the knife. Knowing there had been a slaying and that the manner of death was a slashed throat, Mr. Sandoval did a very smart thing: he didn't touch the knife and stood watch over it until the crime scene investigators arrived. It was then bagged and tagged, transported by one officer to the crime lab, where it was tested and examined, and now is brought to us this morning by the same officer."

"But they've known about this for days now!" said Thaddeus. "And they're just now getting around to telling us about it?

This amounts to withholding evidence, Your Honor, and
that violates the *Illinois Rules of Criminal Procedure*. Here we
are within hours of opening statements to the jury and the
state just happens to have found the murder weapon! The
court must deny the use of this knife to protect the defendant's right to due process. Not only that, the whole thing
stinks."

"Counsel," said Judge Wren, "I don't think 'it stinks' is a legal
predicate for anything, but I get the gist of your argument.
So here's what the court is inclined to do. Today is Wednesday. I'm going to order that the knife be turned over to the
defense for testing of its own. That will give the defense
until Monday to do the testing it deems necessary. I will
instruct the jury that something has come up that makes it
possible for them to go home and take a few days off from
work since they have been granted leave from work by law
anyway. I'm sure they won't mind a paid holiday. Then
Monday they will return, and we will start right up with
opening statements. Any objections?"

"Well, the state objects," said Rammelskamp, going for the
kill. "The state feels the momentum of the case going its way
and doesn't want to interrupt the flow of evidence and testimony for something that doesn't need to be done. The
defense is fully capable of cross-examining the state's
witnesses regarding their lab findings and making any arguments it wants from that. Further testing isn't going to
change any of this."

"Hold on," said Thaddeus. "Is this for real? Counsel is seriously suggesting the defense doesn't need to test its theories
of proof? Now I've heard everything! Judge, the defense
needs—demands—the opportunity to test. My guess is the

fingerprint evidence alone is inconclusive and without that glue the rest of it doesn't stick to my client. So we are especially right in demanding the chance to test and dispute."

"The court agrees, counsel. We will recess until nine o'clock Monday morning. The state will turn over the knife to defense counsel no later than four p.m. today. Anything further? Hearing nothing, we'll return to the courtroom and dismiss the jury with the admonition."

"Judge, one more thing," Christine said. "The defense moves for a continuance of the trial to use the chance to appeal the court's ruling. Allowing the knife into evidence is prejudicial, inflammatory, and violates defendant's due process, which is a constitutional argument and which deserves to be studied and ruled on by the court of appeals. As it is, Your Honor is clearly attempting to placate both lawyers here without considering doing justice for the defendant."

"Counsel!" roared the judge, "how dare you accuse me of placating lawyers! Another comment like that and you'll find yourself spending twenty-four hours in jail considering your behavior before a judge of this Circuit. An apology is required on the record. You have ten seconds."

Christine smiled and waved her hand through the air. "Judge, how can I apologize for something that's as plain as the nose on your face? You are seeking to appease rather than make sure justice is done. And sending me to jail isn't going to cure that. In fact, if you decide to send me to jail I must insist on the right to appeal that contempt citation before the punishment is levied. I am asking the court to allow the cooler heads at the Court of Appeals to hear this mess before it goes any further."

The judge slapped his hand with all his power against his desk.

"Enough!" he bellowed. "Ms. Clerk, go out into the court-room and bring the bailiff in here. This attorney is going to jail!"

The Clerk headed for the door.

"Now hold on, Your Honor," said Thaddeus. "To jail my co-counsel is to deprive the defendant of counsel of his choice. I would ask the court to rethink this and continue the contempt citation until after the trial is over, so my client gets the attorneys of his choosing."

The judge sat back. The look on his face said he couldn't argue with that logic. He nodded and pointed a finger at Christine. "Counsel," he said to her, "the court's finding of contempt is final. But punishment will be levied after the close of all the evidence, and the jury retires to deliberate. You can thank your co-counsel Mr. Murfee that you're not walking over to the jail right this minute."

"Thank you, counsel," said Christine with what could only be described as a smirk. "And thank you, Judge, for allowing my client to have his lawyer available during a murder trial when the entire rest of his life is on the line. That's thoughtful."

"Counsel," said the judge much more evenly, his eyes narrowed at the attorney, "That is contemptuous as well. Now there are two counts of contempt against you. One more and you will go to jail for the remainder of this trial. I promise you that. So what, do you want to try for number three?"

Christine dropped her eyes to the legal pad before her. She began making large, lazy circles with her pen.

"All right, we're done here. We're in recess another fifteen minutes."

The defense reassembled around Killen at counsel table while his jailers hovered nearby.

"My God," Killen whispered to Christine, "you've grown up, girl!"

Christine smiled. "We need to knock his dick in the dirt right out of the gate. It's a start."

"All right," said Thaddeus, "so we're doing good lawyer/bad lawyer. I just wish I had known that beforehand."

Christine smiled and smacked him on the arm. "Too bad you never served. You'd have been a damn good soldier."

"So what the hell?" said Killen. "A knife? With my print on it? Where's that coming from?"

"Did you recognize the knife, Kills?" Thaddeus asked.

"It looked like my knife. I use it at competitions to dig the shit out of my ponies' hooves. But how they got their hands on it is anybody's guess. It was in the barn when last seen."

"Do you keep the barn locked?"

"On the highway side. On the back end, no. We have too many workers coming and going to keep it locked. It would be a nightmare managing all those keys."

"So the cops—or someone else—could have gone inside the barn and taken out the knife without you even knowing."

"I suppose so, but why?"

Thaddeus smiled. "Well, evidently to cut the throat of your wife, if what the Special Prosecutor says is true about it being the tool that caused the marks on Mary Roberta's throat. We don't know that, but I'm guessing they aren't lying."

"Who would want to do that?"

"Someone who wanted it to look like you killed your wife. Maybe Barb Daniels? Maybe Dave? Who the hell knows at this point?"

"Son of a bitch," said Killen. "I'm being framed one bit of evidence at a time."

"Well, there's still the T-Shirt at Barb Daniels' house," said Christine. "That keeps the ambiguity angle in play."

"Not with the knife it doesn't," said Thaddeus. "Juries always want to see the murder weapon in these cases. And once they have that and once it's connected to the defendant, the trial is all but over."

"So tell us," said Christine, "did you or did you not throw that knife behind that Coke machine, Killen?"

"I did not! I swear it! It might be my knife, and it might have her blood on it, and it might even have my partial print, but *I didn't put it there*, I swear to God! You guys have got to believe me!"

The two lawyers traded a look that alarmed Killen.

"What?" he said. "You don't believe me? Am I going to have to get someone else to defend me? Someone who believes me?"

Thaddeus leaned close. "What the fucking hell does it matter whether we believe you or not? Do you honestly think it matters to us whether you killed the woman or not? You get the same defense whether you did it or didn't do it. Don't be so quick to sell us short, friend!"

"I'm sorry. I'm just thrown for a loop here."

"Aren't we all? I've gotta pee," said Christine. "Murder weapons always make me need to pee."

"Thanks for sharing with us, Chris," Thaddeus said. "Anyone else need to go?"

33

It turned out that Thaddeus did need to urinate. But he was able to hold it until the court dismissed the jury and recessed until Monday. Then he told the others to wait for him and hurried to the restroom.

Thaddeus unzipped and bellied up to the urinal. The restroom door opened and closed behind him. He was just far enough to the right of the mirror that he couldn't see who had entered the room. He was standing with his fly open, guiding his stream of urine with his right hand when the blow caught him across the back of the head.

Then he was on the floor of the restroom, staring at row upon row of receding tiles. He noticed the perspective, how the tiles looked smaller the further away they reached. All this in two seconds, right before the steel-toed boot caught him across the forehead. Then the lights went out.

～

A day later, his eyes opened. Of their own accord; he wasn't in charge of opening them. In fact, he wasn't in charge of anything.

His eyes saw Katy sitting beside him. She was holding his hand. It slowly registered on his brain who she was and what she was doing.

Crying.

"Hey, baby, what you crying about," he meant to say, but it came out all consonants and stutters. His tongue found what was left of his front teeth and discovered two missing. And it felt cracks along the upper teeth, right side. Beyond that were lips so swollen they couldn't be closed even when he concentrated. Other parts of his body began sending pain signals to his brain as his mental process picked up.

"What happened to me?" he managed to ask.

"In a nutshell, broken ribs, teeth kicked out plus four teeth broken, broken clavicle, pissing blood, hand stomped and two fingers broken. Your nose is also broken, reset and packed. Plus there is a severe concussion based on EKG's and based on eye reflexes. I've mixed up the fractures with the kicking and stomping, but it's the best we can do. You were unconscious when he worked you over, and so you're no help at all."

"I forgot. Who did it?"

"That's what we're all wondering. Did you get run over by a bus in the restroom?"

"Honestly? I don't remember a thing."

"Do you remember being in court yesterday afternoon?"

"Vaguely. We were picking the jury?"

"That's what Chris told me. She's gone to get coffee, by the way. She'll be here in a minute."

"So who did this to me?"

"We seriously don't know. The police department wants us to call them the minute you wake up. They have lots of questions for you."

"Lotta good it's gonna do. I don't know jack. Who found me?"

"Don McIlhenny the bailiff. Chris became worried when you didn't come back into the courtroom, and she sent the bailiff. He found you and immediately called 911 on his shoulder mike and the EMT's came running. You've been unconscious since then."

"Who's my doc?"

"You have several doctors. You've been examined by a neurologist, a maxillofacial surgeon, an orthopedic surgeon, and an internist who was interested in finding why you are passing blood in your urine."

"What's wrong with my face? I can't feel it."

"The jaw surgeon had to put two screws in your jaw. I'm guessing the local is still working. You only came out of surgery maybe two hours ago. But it couldn't wait because you would have been in horrible pain if you'd been awake."

Thaddeus felt himself sink back into the bed. His first reaction had been to rise up as if to get dressed and leave, but then he realized he was days—weeks?—from leaving. He closed his eyes and moaned. She still had his hand in hers and wouldn't let go.

Then he heard her say, "He just woke up, Chris. He doesn't remember anything."

He opened his eyes again. "Chris. You're looking great."

She wasn't going to joke. "Who the fuck did this?" She hissed. "I'm all over them!"

"I don't know. I can't remember jack."

"You can't. Okay. Well, was it Dave Daniels? You said he flipped you off in court."

"I don't remember saying that. I don't know who it was. It could have been Dave, I suppose, but I don't remember anything about Dave. Sorry."

"I know it was that bastard!" Christine exclaimed. "I am going to fuck him up!"

"No, Chris," said Katy, "you're not going to do anything except go home to Chicago and take care of your practice until Thad's ready to go back to court."

"I'm in court?"

"You're in trial," Christine said. "*People v. Killen.*"

"Sure. Got it."

"We just picked our jury."

"That I remember. Dallas somebody is on the jury. The guy whose wife cheated on him. Or something like that."

"Yes, something like that."

Katy said, "Chris, let's let him rest now. You should go."

"Running me off, eh?"

"Yes, I am. He just needs to rest now. He's said enough for one day."

"Talk to me outside?"

"Be right there," Katy said. She carefully placed Thaddeus' hand beside him on the bed. She patted it and then went out into the hall with Christine.

"Okay, girlfriend," Christine began, "is he ever going to remember who did this?"

"His neurologist says that depends. Sometimes he'll get it back, sometimes he won't. They honestly don't have a clue; you want the truth. Usually, this kind of trauma and concussion resolves only with time."

"So that means I don't get to go over Dave Daniels. At least not yet."

"No, not yet. Not ever, you must know."

"I know, I know. But it just proves to me the guy is capable of extreme violence. If I wasn't certain before, I am now. He killed Mary Roberta, and that's all there is to it."

"If you say so. But can we please leave Thaddeus out of this until he's cleared to go back to the office? Which I hope he never does, incidentally. I'm fed up with this law practice bullshit."

"And you just had your surgery. How's that going?"

"Surgery, radiation, I'm all clear and cancer-free. Have been for several months. Thaddeus was an absolute doll to me during all that." Tears came into her eyes and Christine reached around her shoulder and pulled Katy close.

"Hey, the big guy's gonna be all right. Thad's a fighter. He'll be kicking ass and taking names before you know it."

"I know. I hope I know, I mean. I mean I don't know what I know. I'm scared!"

She started sobbing in earnest then, her face against Christine's navy blazer, crying shamelessly in the hallway with the door to Thaddeus' room closed. Then she straightened herself up and said, "There. That's enough for now. I've got to get back in there and watch him."

"Where is Sarai? Turquoise?"

"Turquoise moved back in with us from her dorm. Until we're all back under one roof."

"Is she here, in Orbit?"

"Yes, XFBI brought both of them down until the threat could be adequately assessed."

Christine nodded knowingly. "Because no one knew if this was a one-time/one-guy restroom assault or if it was coming from somewhere else and might be a threat to you and kids too. Got it."

"So you need to watch your step, too."

"Always, lady. I'm Dave Daniels' worst nightmare come true if he fucks with me. I'd just as soon bury that asshole."

Katy laughed. "Your language."

"What about my language?"

She laughed again. "It's so—so—Christine, that's what it is."

"Back at you, doll. Well, later. I'm flying out in about thirty minutes."

"Say hello to the kids in Chicago. We'll all get together soon."

"You've got it."

34

One week later, he was still sleeping in four-hour cycles: sleep-pain-medicate-sleep. The days and nights became a blur, and he lost all sense of time. Sometimes when he woke up, Katy was there. Sometimes he was alone. Sometimes Christine was there, often reading to him. The old Thaddeus, who had wanted an English major in his life, was being drawn out by the stories and poems she read. Katy read too, and that first weekend Turquoise came down from Chicago and she read. The idea was to reach his mind, to engage him, to bring the familiar into his consciousness so he might reconnect with his thought patterns. His neurologist recommended this to family and friends, and they were doing everything they could to make it work. Albert flew the Lear down from Chicago on Sunday morning, read law cases to him all day, and flew back to Chicago that night as he had taken over the practice and was needed back.

Judge Wren had continued the trial indefinitely; the Illinois Bureau of Investigation was all over the incident and had interviewed everyone in the courtroom that day, including the jurors and the deputies and the bailiffs. And Thaddeus, for the most part, slept through it all.

One week after, Christine arrived back in Orbit and went straight to the hospital. She found Katy there with Thad; a group of nurses and doctors were conferring outside his door.

"When does he get out of here?" she said to the group.

"Who are you?" asked one of the doctors in her lab coat.

"I'm his best friend and law partner, Christine Susmann."

"Chris!" said the same doctor. "It's Irlynn Adams. We went to school together from first grade all the way through high school!"

"OMG, Irlynn! How are you, girl!"

"Just moved back to Orbit. My new husband wanted a small town practice, and I told him I knew just the place."

"So you're married. He's a doctor too?"

"Yep. Radiologist."

"And you're treating Thad?"

"I am. I'm his internist. I'm in charge of his treatment. You married?"

Christine's face tightened. "I was married to Sonny Susmann. You remember him, our class too. He was murdered."

"Oh, no!"

"Yeah, a couple of years now."

"I'm sorry."

"Thanks."

"Well, we were just talking about Thaddeus. I think I'm ready to try him at home. He'll be discharged tomorrow."

"Restrictions?"

"Tell the truth, he can do whatever he feels capable of. First he'll want to get the dental reconstruction going. He complains every minute about his bite. Someone keeps bringing in Whataburger's, and he can't chew well. So he bitches. But his real restriction is the brain injury. He still has no recall of the incident, and he's having trouble with abstractions. I'm prescribing voc rehab."

"Oh, no. We were right in the middle of an important case."

"I know. Killen Erwin. Judge Wren called me about it, and I told him about Thaddeus. It looks like it's being continued one month at a time."

"Okay. Yes, I got that minute entry."

"So, how long you staying?"

"I'll be here until Thaddeus is up and around and hitting on all cylinders. I brought my youngest with me. We're looking for a place."

"To buy?"

"Yes. I have to be here for Thad. I wouldn't have it any other way. I put all my junk on hold back in Chicago. Plus I have my elves handling the rest of it."

"Well, I have other patients to visit. Hey, here's an idea. It would help for you to talk law stuff with Thaddeus. Get him engaged. See if that helps brings him back into his normal thought processes."

"I can do that. And will."

"Thanks, Christine."

"We'll talk again, I'm sure."

Christine went into the room and found Katy there, reading a *People* magazine to Thaddeus. His eyes were closed, but they opened when Christine whispered hello to Katy.

"Hey," Christine said. She walked up to his bedside and peered down, smiling.

"Hey, yourself." He reached and took her hand. "Thanks for coming. Are we in trial yet?"

"No, honey, we're not in trial," said Christine. Katy, sitting back, smiled sadly.

"Well, I've been thinking about our case."

"Sounds good," Christine replied. "What have you been thinking?"

"I've been thinking Killen probably did it. Killen probably murdered Mary Roberta."

"And why do you say that? The bloody pants?"

"That, and he must have hated her. Cheating like she was. Divorcing him. Taking away his kids. Who wouldn't want her dead?"

The hospital room became silent. Katy looked at Christine, who backed off and took the other visitors' chair. She pulled it up to his bedside. The two women's eyes met, and Katy gave a slight nod, seen only by Christine.

"So what else are you thinking?" Christine asked.

"Lots of stuff. I'm thinking I should be back at the office getting ready for trial."

"That will come. What else?"

"I'm wondering how to get Killen out of it. What if we point the finger at Dave Daniels?"

"We could do that. Why do you say Dave?"

"He was the last one with her. And that would explain where the bloody T-shirt came from--Dave himself."

"Why would Dave want his girlfriend dead?"

Thaddeus moved uncomfortably in his bed. His back hurt and his kidneys ached. Trying to get comfortable, he pulled loose the IV drip from the back of his hand.

"That'll bring someone," said Katy.

Sure enough, in less than five minutes a nurse came breezing into the room, all smiles and a chipper voice for Thaddeus.

"Hey!" she cried. "You trying to disengage and get out of here?"

"Yep. I'm going home today."

"Well, that's not what the doctors say. Let me replace your IV, Thad. Give me that hand, please."

The nurse went about the task and Thaddeus watched. His lips moved as she worked, but no words could be heard.

"What did you say?" Katy said to him.

"I said, 'Then put the damn thing back in,' if you must know. It looks like I'm stuck here. No pun intended."

"Nicely played," said Christine. "I like your pun."

"Dr. Adams said you'll be going home this week. But you're probably not going back to the office right away. Do you need to talk to Chris about that?"

Thaddeus nodded. "What about it, Chris? When do we go back to court with Killen?"

"In about a month. All else being equal."

"What all else?"

"You thinking clearly."

There, Christine had said it. The pink elephant was addressed.

"I know," he said. "Things are pretty scrambled. And I still don't know who did this to me."

"Visualize Dave's face in that bathroom. Can you see him there?"

"I've tried that. I really can't put his face there. The truth is, I can't even remember what Dave looks like. I even forget your face, Chris, when you're not here." His eyes filled with tears and he held out his hand to Katy. She pulled a tissue from the box on his table and pressed it into his hand. He wiped his eyes and blew his nose. "Damn!"

"I don't understand," said Katy. "Why isn't everyone pointing the finger at Barb Daniels? She had more motive than anyone. Mary Roberta was trying to take her husband away! Good grief, who had more motive than her?"

"We could do that," Thaddeus said. "I've thought of her, too. It seems that she, she—"

The women waited.

"—she—I lost what I was going to say. Oh, it seems that she was up there with Killen, as far as motive. Maybe they did it together, given the dual motives and the cops finding the pants and shirt with them." Thaddeus looked at Christine. He hoped that what he was saying made sense. He was rapidly learning to read the looks on people's faces when he said something to them—learning to read whether he'd just made sense or not. He knew that he wanted to talk about the case, but he wasn't certain he was holding up his end of the conversation. He felt frightened and was hesitant; he hadn't been unsure of his legal acumen for several years now, and he didn't like the new feeling of sometimes being at a loss when it came to applying logic to facts. He hated it, in fact, and was growing depressed with it by the hour. When were his thoughts going to straighten out? He wondered. Was this how it was going to be from now on? Reading faces? Hoping he said the right thing, rather than being certain he was on the logic path as he had always been? A shudder traveled down his body, and Katy noticed.

"Need a blanket?"

Again with the tears. Using the same wad of tissue, he again swiped it across his eyes.

"This is ridiculous," he said with a laugh through tears. "I can't control my tears, and I can't control my thoughts."

"Dr. Adams said you would have emotional ups and downs," Katy reminded him. "I wouldn't be too concerned about it. Not yet. Try to remember, you received a significant concussive event to the brain. It's going to take time; it would with anybody, not just you."

He blew his nose and nodded.

"Don't do that!" Cried Katy. "Your nose was broken. Don't blow!"

"Forgot."

Christine opened her purse and produced a sheaf of papers.

"Got something, boss," she said to him.

"What's that?"

"Our witness list. I want to leave it with you and have you consider my notes beside each person's name."

"Sure."

"Here's another slant. You'll see I have a person named 'Suspect X.'"

"Who's that?"

"We don't know. Suspect X is a person who did the crime whose identity is unknown to us. Whose existence is unknown to us. A person who randomly selected Mary Roberta to murder. Or maybe it was a robbery. Some such."

"What about her purse? Anything missing?"

"Unknown."

"We know she'd had sexual intercourse, recently. Autopsy finding."

Christine smiled and shot a glance at Katy, who returned the smile.

"That's what the report says, yes."

"Do we have lab reports?"

"We have DNA," said Christine slowly. She was hesitant because this was old ground. They had discussed the DNA testing before Thaddeus was attacked. Dave's DNA was found in the sperm inside of Mary Roberta. And in her stomach contents. "Do you remember what the report said?"

Thaddeus drew his fingers along the bars on the side of his bed. He hesitated.

Then he said, "Not really. I don't think we have the DNA report yet. Do we?"

"We do. Dave's DNA was found inside Mary Roberta's vagina."

"Oh, sure. I guess that slipped my mind."

"Well," Katy interrupted. "That's probably enough for one session, you two. Dr. Murfee is going to have to shut you down and let Thaddeus get some rest."

"I need a hit on the pain pump too," said Thaddeus. "And that puts me out, so I'm sorry."

"No, no, no," Christine said. "Please don't apologize. I'll be back tomorrow, and we can pick up right where we left off."

"Sounds good," Thaddeus said. He grasped the small button that would drip a minute quantity of pain medication into his IV, and he pressed it. Immediately a general sense of well-being and a feeling of warmth spread through his mind and body. His eyes fluttered shut.

The women nodded their goodbyes and Christine exited the room.

Katy remained behind, watching Thaddeus' breathing resolve into slow and shallow respirations. She moved her chair back beside him and took his hand in hers.

"Sleep, baby," she whispered. "I'll be right here watching over you."

She swore she saw a small smile play at the corners of his mouth.

Tears washed across her own eyes, and she fought back the sobs that wanted to come out. As a doctor, she knew he was struggling and knew it would be a long, arduous path to get back a reasonable degree of mental power. As a wife, she felt paralyzed, unsure what to do, uncertain where to turn for help. For the first time in her life, she didn't have quick and sensible answers for their predicament.

She honestly did not know what came next.

35

Katy had purchased an old Victorian sprawl of a house one block off the Orbit town square. She had had the floors taken down to hardwood and re-done and had replaced most of the kitchen appliances. All while Thaddeus was in the hospital.

Upon discharge, Thaddeus had improved to the point he no longer required pain meds. The cast was off the fractured fingers; the jaw ached only at night and only when he inadvertently rolled over and slept on it; the clavicle was on the mend, and the teeth had temporary crowns. There would be a need for dental implants for those teeth that were kicked out. There would be a need for crowns for the front teeth that had been fractured and left as stubs.

Katy drove him home, where Sarai was waiting with her sitter. She ran to her dad and flung herself against him, wrapping her arms around his waist and holding tight.

"I missed you, honey," she said.

He laughed. "I missed you too, honey."

"Let Daddy come in where we can take care of him," Katy
said.

They went into the kitchen and sat at the round maple table
with its captain's chairs. Katy made coffee and passed a cup
to Thaddeus, with half and half. He tried a sip.

"Yee-ouch!" He cried, touching his hand to his teeth. "Temperature sensitive."

"I'm sorry. I should have thought of that. But you weren't
having trouble with ice at the hospital. But hot is a no-no."

"I'll let it cool down and try again. The sooner I can get
crowns the happier I'll be."

36

Christine followed Dave Daniels. She got to know his watering holes, times and places. She studied his fornication game. She saw that most nights he struck out—going home alone. But on the third night she watched, he scored with a frowzy young woman in a green sequined dress. They left Brownie's Dew-Drop-In on the east end of town just after eleven. Christine followed them to the Black-feather, where they checked into room 212.

What was it with room 212? She wondered. Every tryst required room 212, and that was where Mary Roberta was found butchered. *Did he keep whips in there? Knives? What was the attraction?*

Then there was the matter of the videos. Killen had told her what Barbara Daniels knew about Dave's video collection. Tryst after tryst on video, on YouTube, private but, while she didn't know the password, she knew they were there. He had drunkenly passed out and left his laptop on at his cheap Ikea desk beside the washer-dryer combo. A frame depicting a blurry man and another figure in bed was frozen on the screen. Barbara had leaned around Dave and clicked the PLAY arrow. What she saw had revolted her: Dave and another woman. Barbara studied the setup. YouTube. She then went to bed and never mentioned the video to Dave. But she did tell Killen, who told Christine.

So Christine followed up.

The next afternoon at one o'clock she checked into the Blackfeather and requested room 212. The clerk asked why that particular room and she replied it was because she had spent a beautiful night there with a man named Dave and she wanted to re-enter the dream. The young woman shrugged and said, "Whatever," and accepted the $100 bill Christine insisted she take rather than a credit card. Then she handed over the key and, without a word, went back to reading *Us*.

Christine climbed the stairs and turned left. Down to 212, slipping the key into the doorknob and twisting and the door creaking open.

She hurried inside and allowed the door to shut behind her.

She started with the bed. She stripped off the bedspread and sheets and stashed them in a corner. Then came the mattress pad. She held it up to the light and examined it for stains. Nothing. She opened her purse, withdrew a small, powerful flashlight, and proceeded to examine the mattress. She turned the flashlight switch, and it went to ultraviolet. She examined the mattress with the new light. Again, nothing.

So she stepped back, reached down from the side, and flipped the mattress over.

She tried the ultraviolet again.

It fluoresced. The all-but-invisible streaks in the material were visualized. Blood stains.

"Sons of bitches didn't replace the mattress," Christine whispered, and, as she did, she had the strong feeling she was being watched.

She then began a detailed examination of the walls, headboard, and electrical outlets. Nothing was seen or felt. Facing the foot of the bed and installed on the wall on that end was an HVAC vent. She bent and looked inside with her light.

"Bingo!" She cried.

Using a dime, she unscrewed the vent cover.

There, its lid raised, was a tablet, its camera lens aimed at the bed. The unit was turned on and, she guessed, recording. She seized the tablet, shut it down, replaced the vent cover, and stuck the tablet in her purse. She had found what she was looking for. Or had she?

Into the bathroom, she went next. Again the examination of the walls, towel bars, bathtub-shower metal and HVAC vents—two of them. Nothing turned up, so she replaced the vent covers and turned out the light. She was done in there.

Back to the main room where she retraced her earlier search. Nothing more was found.

She drove back to Orbit.

There, she entered the office space she was sharing with Thaddeus. Christine switched on the tablet. She suspected that in doing so she had energized the video lens and software again, but now she didn't care. Whoever had placed the tablet in the wall probably knew by now the tablet had been discovered and removed.

She searched the tablet and found no video files. Which led her to believe the video was being streamed to some server. Barbara had mentioned the video she watched being on YouTube.

She sat back in her chair and buzzed Adrienne Hanley, the receptionist.

"Ades, would you come in here, please?"

Two minutes later she was joined by Adrienne, a junior college student who worked days for Thaddeus and attended school in the evening and on weekends. She was tall, wispy blonde hair, with sparkling green eyes and a firm smile. She was tops on the phone and knew how to handle all of the many personalities that called the office seeking Thaddeus and Christine. Plus, Adrienne was totally plugged into electronics and social media. Exactly what Christine needed.

"Okay," said Christine. "I found this tablet hidden away in a particular room."

Adrienne gave Christine a sideways look. "Was that thing in the room where Mary Roberta was found?"

"God, am I that obvious?"

"It only stands to reason. You and Thad are looking for the real killer since it wasn't Mr. Erwin."

"If you were shooting videos in that room, where would you send the feed?"

"That's easy. Instagram."

"Which is what?"

"Serious? Only the website where everyone posts their video. That or YouTube, YouTube is public by default, but you can set your videos to private. So maybe Instagram, as long as the video is less than fifteen seconds because that's the limit on Instagram. If the video is longer, then you would want to post it on YouTube and set it to private. Yes, YouTube."

Christine opened the browser on her laptop and read the Google (YouTube) privacy policy. Indeed, information was private, subject to "enforceable governmental process."

"We need a subpoena," said Christine. "Is Bat around today?"

"He's back in Chicago. Flew up this morning. Can I help out?"

"Do you know how to prepare a subpoena?"

"Yes, no. I can learn. Just give me a chance and I'll do it."

"That's the spirit. All right, here's what we need."

An hour later the subpoena was printed out and walked across the street, where the Clerk of the Court's signature was obtained, making the subpoena an official court order. It was then sent out for service on the YouTube custodian of records.

Christine had a hunch. She requested all videos be made available from accounts held by David S. Daniels of Orbit, Illinois.

It was a long shot, the name; surely there were many others. But none in Orbit.

So Christine liked the odds.

Besides which, the whole undertaking was free and by the time Daniels came to know about the subpoena the whole thing would be over.

Seven days later, the videos were made available on a private YouTube server to Christine Susmann, in response to the court-ordered subpoena.

Immediately the phone rang. "Eleanor Rammelskamp," said Adrienne over the intercom, "and she sounds hot."

Christine picked up the line.

"I demand copies without delay! I saw the certificate of compliance with the subpoena filed by YouTube."

"Relax, girl," Christine told her. "You'll get copies."

"When? When will I get them?"

"When I've had a chance to look them over."

"That's not good enough. This is a first-degree murder case. I will have an order from Judge Wren by five o'clock if I don't have the records by then."

"Hey," said Christine, her voice low and powerful. "Knock yourself out, chickadee. I told you you'd get a copy. If you want to go whine to the judge, go for it. But I said I'd make the videos directly available to you. In fact, I was planning on putting them in my cloud account and sharing with you."

"How long would that take?"

"You could have them in oh—checking my calendar—probably, let's see. Five minutes. How's that, girlfriend? Five minutes quick enough? Just give your email to Adrienne and we'll make it happen. So long, now."

Christine buzzed Adrienne, and she took down the prosecutor's email address.

Then she downloaded the files into cloud storage and shared the folder to Eleanor Rammelskamp.

"Done," said Christine. "Now let's see what we've hooked."

~

Thaddeus was ensconced in his home office, where high-speed cable took him online, and network access was provided both for his Chicago practice and his Orbit office. Christine messaged him:

CHRISTINE: Check out this cloud link. Get back to me, please.

Thaddeus clicked the link, found the video files, and was immediately overwhelmed by their number.

THADDEUS: What am I looking for?

CHRISTINE: Date of MR's murder, September 10.

Thaddeus found the video file dated September 10. He clicked, and the video sprang to life on his screen.

It was a bunch of nothing. Just a static view of the bed in 212. The ambient light was dim, and his eyes eventually decided there were two figures in the bed. No movement; evidently sleeping.

He found he could click and drag the video cursor left to right and acquire a high-speed review of the recording. Finally, something happened. A man sat up on the left-hand side of the bed, stood upright, stretched, and began pulling on his pants and shirt. It was still very dark in the room, and his features were indiscernible. Five minutes later, the outside door to the room opened—Thaddeus could tell by the sudden influx of exterior lighting—and the man wasn't seen again.

Thaddeus again fast-forwarded through the video. Meanwhile, the solo body lay in the bed—turning over now and then. At one point she came up on one elbow, reached for the clock radio and studied its digital time, then replaced it on the bedside table, following which she flopped back on the bed, and there was again no movement for the next several minutes. Then a figure entered the room from left to right.

Thaddeus watched carefully. The angle of the recording device caught the figure just above the waist and just as low as the knees, maybe a few inches higher, just about the level of the foot of the bed. A knife blade darted up and down in the quickening morning light. The blade itself was dark, as Thaddeus could make it out, perhaps even black. The figure went around to the right-hand side of the bed, where the sleeping woman lay unmoving, and Thaddeus watched in horror as the knife plunged downward several times and then was seen being drawn from below the event horizon to above. The entire length of the blade was smeared with blood this time. Then the visitor departed.

Curiously, the visitor was not wearing gloves. Thaddeus noticed—he thought—a diamond ring on the assailant's left ring finger. He backed up the video and watched that portion again: several times the ring flashed as the knife came upright in the video before plunging down again. He was sure of it: there was a ring, and it could probably be identified insofar as cut and karat weight with the appropriate analysis of the recording.

THADDEUS: Where did this come from?

CHRISTINE: YouTube.

THADDEUS: Subpoena?

CHRISTINE: On David S. Daniels' account.

THADDEUS: Good work. What turned you onto that?

CHRISTINE: Barb told Killen about some videos of Dave's that she had discovered. I rented room 212 at the Blackfeather. Looked around, found a tablet in a vent. It was videotaping.

THADDEUS: How did the cops miss this?

CHRISTINE: Unknown.

THADDEUS: What kind of device did you find?

CHRISTINE: iPad.

THADDEUS: Have you had it dusted?

CHRISTINE: I shipped it to my lab in Chicago. Initial report is no prints. DNA testing is underway.

THADDEUS: What about video analysis?

CHRISTINE: You noticed the ring too? Left hand? That could be a prize-winner.

THADDEUS: Yes, especially since Killen doesn't wear rings.

CHRISTINE: Exactly. Video analysis is on the menu. We'll get a computerized enhancement and make some judgments.

THADDEUS: What else showed up on the videos? I haven't watched any others.

CHRISTINE: Lots of different women. Dave was evidently keeping a library of his conquests.

THADDEUS: Whose rings? Barbara Daniels'?

CHRISTINE: I'm guessing. Second guess would be Dave wearing rings to make us think it was Barbara.

THADDEUS: I watched the exterior view of the figure approaching the motel. Not big enough to be Dave.

CHRISTINE: Agree. Assuming that figure was the killer.

THADDEUS: Pretty sound assumption, no?

CHRISTINE: Or another woman who was pissed at Mary Roberta.

THADDEUS: Yes, another put-upon wife.

CHRISTINE: The net widens.

He replayed the murder video. Then, twice more.

THADDEUS: I don't think we need to turn it over to the Special Prosecutor. At least not yet.

CHRISTINE: Your thinking?

THADDEUS: Until we have our analysis complete, we don't know if it's evidence of our crime or not.

CHRISTINE: You're still pissed about her sandbagging you on the knife, am I right?

THADDEUS: Honestly? I had forgotten all about that. Memory loss.

CHRISTINE: Yes, she delayed turning over the knife and testing to us until the trial was underway.

THADDEUS: What happened?

CHRISTINE: We've had the knife tested. Turns out it's the murder weapon.

THADDEUS: DNA?

CHRISTINE: Only Mary Roberta's.

THADDEUS: Doesn't make sense. The assailant wasn't wearing gloves.

CHRISTINE: Sometimes you don't get DNA. That's the way the cookie crumbles. Not every contact is positive for DNA.

THADDEUS: I should have known that. I'm struggling here, Chris.

CHRISTINE: Relax, I'm not. Besides, I see you getting better every day.

THADDEUS: Really? That's encouraging.

CHRISTINE: I wouldn't say so if it weren't true. Everyday I'm seeing more of the old Thaddeus coming around.

THADDEUS: Thank God.

CHRISTINE: We also know there's a partial print on the handle of the knife. A partial print belonging to Killen Erwin.

THADDEUS: Does it positively link to him?

CHRISTINE: No, that's the good part. It's only a partial. What there is of it, definitely matches that part of Killen's fingerprint. But it's not enough to say definitely. I'm going to come by later, and I'll show you the report.

THADDEUS: Thanks, Chris. Like always, I'll be right here. They won't let me drive yet.

CHRISTINE: Why's that?

THADDEUS: I don't know. I'm just not released to drive yet.

CHRISTINE: That'll happen too. Keep the faith, little brother.

THADDEUS: Thanks, Chris.

CHRISTINE: Later.

Thaddeus stood up from his desk and walked over to the office window that looked over the backyard. It was early March, and the snow was a foot deep across the backyard of the old barn of a house. The window where he stood was drafty but clean; Katy had done what she could to bring the place up to speed. New storm windows were indicated next, he decided, as the heat transfer was very apparent around the window's edges. He leaned and breathed steam onto the glass. With his right index finger, he then drew a ? some three inches high, and said, "That's me. A big question mark."

Then he decided he didn't want to go down the self-pity

road, and he abruptly backed away from the window and sat back down at his desk.

He wrote:

What if the rings are Barbara Daniels' rings? If they are, the finger of blame definitely shifts away from Killen.

Katy interrupted his thoughts, bringing a carafe of coffee and placing it on his desk without a word.

"Help me think through something, please," he said. He realized that since being discharged from the hospital he began conversations with Katy and Christine quite often with that phrase, "Help me think through..." or "Help me with my thinking..." or "Check my thinking about this...." He no longer felt a hundred percent certain about the validity of his thoughts and it drove him crazy. He had gone from total self-sufficiency to a man afraid to make judgments without the input of others around him. It was maddening and made him sad as well.

And the worst part? He still had no idea who had done this to him. None.

"Help you think about what?" Katy said in her sweet voice. "Tell me what's on your mind."

"Well, we've got this video of the murder."

"You do? Amazing! Where'd you get that?"

"Christine. You know her. Anyway, the video shows a diamond ring clearly on the assailant's left ring finger. So I'm thinking 'wedding ring.'"

"Sure. That sounds right."

"And then I'm thinking, 'Barbara Daniels' wedding ring.'"

"Sounds logical."

He poured a cup of coffee and followed it with a small hit of half and half. Then he stirred, wondering if he should tell her the part, and then deciding he had to.

"Okay, so what if—and I'm just tossing this out there—what if someone else was wearing rings just like Barb Daniels' rings? Someone trying to throw us off."

"Why on earth would anyone do that?"

"I don't—to try to make us think it was Barb when it really wasn't. Does that sound logical?"

"Uh, not logical, no. But it does sound possible. I mean, stranger things have happened."

"So, don't pursue it?"

"Sure, pursue it, but I wouldn't toss it in front of a jury as my working hypothesis, no. You would need to connect it up to do that."

"Agree. We'd need the same ring or look-alike in someone else's possession."

"Exactly. You're halfway there right now. Does that make sense?"

He looked at her. Now she was asking him if she made sense. He wondered whether she was doing that to bolster his confidence or if she really valued his opinion or both or neither.

Life had become hard since the beating and injury.

"By the way, Dr. Santini's office called. "Your crowns are ready."

"Thank God! I finally get rid of these temporaries. They feel like I've got Chiclets where my teeth used to be."

"I knew you'd like that."

"I like it. I like it. When do I go in?"

"Tomorrow at ten-thirty. I've got it on your calendar."

"Okay. Well, thanks for listening."

"You're welcome."

Katy left, and Thaddeus turned back to his computer.

He called up the return on the search warrant from Killen's room. He wanted to look to see if they had found—

What was it?

To see if they had found—

He had lost the train of thought.

Back up. He had been talking to Katy about his teeth. But before that, about the rings on the killer's hand. So he wanted to go to Killen's search warrant return and see whether they had seized any rings.

He reviewed the list of items seized.

They had not seized any rings.

But why would they? Rings wouldn't be something the cops would know to be after. They hadn't seen the video and seen the rings the killer was wearing, so they would be clueless.

THADDEUS: We need pictures of Barbara Daniels' rings for the lab. They'll do video enhancements and compare frames to the stills.

CHRISTINE: All right. I'll send a photographer. I'm sure she'll cooperate as she won't want it to look like she has anything to hide. What else?

THADDEUS: We need to get inside Killen's room. I just need to be sure he's not sandbagging us.

CHRISTINE: Like wearing rings when he did the cutting.

THADDEUS: I'm thinking a lack of evidence would be a good thing. For starters, the cops didn't find any rings according to their search warrant return. That helps our case. Now we search and find no rings, and you and I can sleep better at night. What do we do, break in? Or just tell him we need access to his room?

CHRISTINE: I'm one step ahead of you. I paid off the front desk. They're letting me in his room tonight.

THADDEUS: I can be there.

CHRISTINE: No need. I might need you to defend me on burglary charges if I get caught.

THADDEUS: So don't get caught. And find those rings.

CHRISTINE: Done. And you know what's cool?

THADDEUS: What?

CHRISTINE: We were both thinking alike. About the rings being in Killen's room, I mean. Your thinking is looking excellent.

THADDEUS: You have no idea how much I've wanted to hear that.

CHRISTINE: I'll be by later tonight.

THADDEUS: I'll be waiting. Take care.

Thaddeus called Rocky and directed him to the online videos. It was time to let a real pro study the latest find.

It was time for confirmation.

37

C hristine, usually perspicuous and alert to her surroundings, missed that Special Agent Wells Waters was following her when she left her office.

She had the key, and she had Killen's room number, so she drove straight to the motel where he'd been living, The Erwin Motel on the west end of Orbit.

It was an excellent layout: the motel was set back fifty yards off the highway, one road going up, one coming out, and beyond that and to the left was the barn where he kept his horses and beyond that and even further left was the house where Mary Roberta and the kids had been living. Christine knew that since the murder, the kids had been living with Killen's in-laws—Mary Roberta's mother, Mary Aseline Kittenforge. All reports had it that the children were still bereft, but that their grandmother had set aside her partying ways in favor of giving the children the best care possible. She had even hired two nannies. Killen was worried sick about them and brought it up every time Christine visited, but, as she told him, it is what it is.

She turned on her right blinker and turned onto the motel road. Agent Waters went on by. He would go out to the Y and then turn around and come back so she wouldn't notice him.

The room had been tossed. The cops, search warrant in hand, had been there before her. This was known, of course, but Christine wasn't looking for the obvious items the cops were. She was looking only for rings. She sat on the bed—which had been stripped of sheets and blanket—and considered the setup. Against one wall was a three drawer cabinet with a flat screen TV and box perched on top. On another wall was a guitar case. On the third wall was a love-seat, tan in color, with a console capable of holding two drinks. Plus it had a console cover that, she knew, would lift up and that, she knew, had already been perused several times, at least, by the police. The fourth wall was occupied by the bed where she sat.

Leading off the guitar wall was a doorway to the bathroom. An open closet with hangers was on the other side of that doorway. Several suits and dress shirts still in plastic from the cleaners hung from the single closet bar. Down below were four pairs of shoes and one pair of work boots, scuff-out ropers that obviously fit the barn better than fit the office.

She drew a deep breath and shut her eyes. Where would she hide an engagement and wedding ring in the room?

She wouldn't.

She would hide them in the barn.

So she went back outside and drove up to the barn. She tried the door to the front office. Locked. She walked all the way around back to the far end. Locked. Plus, there was a nondescript four-door tan sedan with a man inside back in the motel parking lot. She was able to make out his profile, and it occurred to her that he might be watching her.

She thought better of jimmying the lock and decided to leave.

She would call Thaddeus.

～

"Did he ever say anything to you that might indicate where he would hide something out at the farm or motel?"

She was on her cell phone at her new house. Thaddeus was in his home office, reviewing video.

Thaddeus ran his hand through his hair. "I'm trying, Chris, but honestly I cannot remember anything being said."

"Anything unusual happen out there during the times you were out helping with the horses?"

Thaddeus stiffened in his chair and looked at the ceiling.

"Only thing that happened this time down was my back problem at the barn. My back went out, and we went to the ER."

"What else?"

Thaddeus shrugged. "I can't say. They gave me a script for muscle relaxants, and I took them. Three days later I was fine."

"That's it?"

"Honestly, that's all I can come up with."

"I've just got a strong feeling the rings are there somewhere."

"The rings on the woman's left hand?"

"I'm not entirely convinced that left hand belongs to a woman."

"You think it was Killen?"

"Don't know. But I don't want to leave any stone unturned. You know me."

Thaddeus smiled. "I know I would hate to have you after *me*."

She smiled. "Never going to happen, little brother. You and I are legal soul mates."

"I like that. Legal soul mates."

She shook her head. "But that doesn't mean we're going to see things the same way. I'm thinking Killen right now, and you're thinking one of the Daniels. We're covering all the bases, and that's what counts."

"All right. Let's meet in the morning and hash it over."

"I'll be there."

Thaddeus put down the cell phone and sat back and probed his new teeth with his tongue. The Novocain was all but worn off. No pain. He could feel his lips again.

And he could chew.

"Katy, what's for supper?" He called.

She came into his home office all smiles.

"Corn on the cob."

"You're the best. I'm starving for corn on the cob."

"Bon appétit."

38

The neuropsychologist selected to study Thaddeus' brain injury was Tanya Willis, Ed.D. of Springfield. The referral was made by Thaddeus' treating internist Dr. Adams of Orbit. Dr. Willis was a warm, confident woman who wore wire-frame glasses and spoke with a slight lisp. Thaddeus had visited with her twice, the second time being for a battery of written tests. Now, on the third visit, he and Katy were summoned for test results.

Dr. Willis took them into her office, complete with Native American wall hangings of rugs and fabrics. Her desk was cluttered with files, some with red tabs, some with green tabs, and some with beige tabs. Thaddeus noted, when she picked up his file and glanced it over, his own tab was red. He wondered what that meant, but it didn't take long to find out.

"So, thanks for coming in," the doctor smiled. "I see you have water and if there's anything else we can get you please just speak up."

"Thank you," Katy said. "So why are we here?"

"Well, we have some results back on your husband's tests. Thaddeus, before I get into that, can you just update me on how you're feeling?"

"Feeling great. Anxious to get back to the office. The state bar office has me on temporary disability but if you give me a clean bill of health I can get that removed and go back to work."

"And that's very doable. Can you tell me about your thoughts, your memory?"

He spread his hands. "I remember nothing about what happened to me. I've put two and two together, and I think I know what happened, but truth be told, I have no memory to confirm what I'm thinking."

"What are you thinking?"

"I think Dave Daniels attacked me from behind, put me on the ground, and proceeded to kick the living hell out of me. That's who I think did it."

"Why do you think that?"

"He was in the courtroom. My client had killed his lover— well, let me back up. His lover, Mary Roberta Erwin, was dead and her husband, my client, was charged with her death. I think Dave became enraged at me for defending his lover's alleged killer. That makes the most sense to me."

"But no recall?"

"None."

"Okay. Now, I have been asked to perform several assessments of you. The first thing I did was interview you. That took right at two hours. Next, I administered a battery of tests designed to measure your ability to think. Part of it is IQ testing, part of it is other stuff. The key test I administered was the WAIS-IV, to determine your level of intellectual functioning. Results from that are excellent. You are performing intellectually on a level with your peers, maybe much higher, so that's good."

Thaddeus smiled and looked at Katy. "Great," he said.

"And I have also done a neurological assessment, which is a far more extensive form of assessment. You spent an entire day on this testing—that was day two of your second visit here."

"Tell us what that kind of testing is for, please," Katy asked.

"NA is used to determine all of the cognitive strengths and deficits of a person. It's usually done with people who have suffered some brain damage, such as strokes or injury."

"What tests were done on Thad?"

"I tested Thaddeus for higher cognitive abilities—what some might call executive functioning. This cognitive type of testing is sensitive to the frontal lobes and frontal circuitry. Tests are proven to measure such things as assessing, planning, abstraction, concept formation, organization, reasoning, inhibition, mental flexibility, initiation, and problem-solving."

"You did all that to me?"

The doctor smiled and held up one finger. "Also, the frontal lobes can also play a role in memory by utilizing strategies for the recall of the information. Many frontal lobe skills are often needed for competitive employability. And yes, you and I together tested for these things."

"So how do I stack up?" Thaddeus asked.

"Bottom line: there are some deficits. How long-term they might be is anyone's guess."

"In what regard are they deficits?"

"Thaddeus is having trouble with planning and reasoning, for the most part. Those are the spikes—downward spikes, if you will."

His heart fell. "Planning and reasoning? I shouldn't be practicing law if I can't reason, should I?"

"It's a close call. What I am going to recommend for you is support staff. You'll need legal assistants and secretaries who are educated in how to help you. And you'll need a support attorney to bounce things off of, to run things by, to strategize with—all of this being done before you unilaterally take action on a case. If you can work with your staff on this basis and allow me to continue work with you too, then I can release you back to work."

"Sold!' Said Thaddeus. "How do we start?"

She nodded. "First thing is for me to come and spend an afternoon with your staff, meet with them. I need to educate them in your deficits and train them in ways to support you."

"When can we do that?"

"In about ten days. I can do it on a Saturday if you can get your staff in on a weekend."

"Done. I'm sure there'll be no problem."

"Let's shoot for—not this Saturday, but the next? April eighth?"

"Done. We'll have everybody together then. Do you need my driver to bring you from Springfield to Orbit? Happy to do that."

"No, I've got a brand new Volvo that I want to get out on the road. It's only sixty-some miles, I think."

"Sixty-five as the crow flies," he said. He was excited and smiling.

On the way home, Katy and Thaddeus discussed Christine.

"If only," said Katy.

"I know," said Thaddeus. "I'd give anything if she'd throw in with me. Just like the old days."

"Well, she's in on the Killen case, bless her heart."

"She's really stood by me. I can't even begin to thank her."

Katy looked out the window. She turned down the radio.

"Tell me something," she said. "You two adore each other. Are you not in practice together because you don't want anybody else as good as you? Or is it her? Does she not want to be encumbered with a partner?"

"I don't know. It's not me. I'm totally good with Christine. We've always worked well together, and she's usually a step or two ahead of me, which is great. What I can't come up with, she does. And vice versa."

"Do you think you should talk to her?"

"Yes, especially in light of what Dr. Willis wants for me."

"That's what I'm thinking. I mean Albert is great—"

"Albert is so overwhelmed with his case load I can't ask him to supervise me too. No, I need someone I can partner with on my cases. At least until I'm fully recovered. And I couldn't do any better than Christine. In fact, it would help me heal to know Christine was in it with me."

"Do you want to talk to her?"

"I don't know. I could, but—"

"But you'd rather I spoke to her and gave her the medical view?"

"Yes, if you would. I feel like she'd say okay to me just out of pity. I'd like her to hear the real truth about my condition from you so she fully understands what she'd be getting herself into. I'm not exactly the prize at this point. More like the booby prize."

She looked over and saw tears in his eyes. She placed her left arm around him as he drove.

"I can't even imagine what you feel. I'm sorry it happened to you."

He said, through his tears, "God, I can't even tell you how frustrating it is to lose my train of thought, or to come up with something real off the wall and not realize it until I say it aloud to someone and get that kind of blank look people give when you're not making sense."

39

D r. Willis met with the staff on Saturday morning.

Present were Billy A. Tattinger—Christine's paralegal who was once Thaddeus' paralegal—Adrienne Hanley, Rocky, Christine Susmann, and Thaddeus. JT was lurking down the street at the Starbucks, but Dr. Willis would just mention a few things to him later after the meeting.

She began.

"Your boss has had a severe closed head injury. As with all concussions, there has been brain injury. Thaddeus' damage is somewhere on the scale between high-moderate to severe, if I tried to put it in terms that would give you a handle on where he's at."

"Will he recover?" asked Adrienne Hanley.

"More or less. He might have a full recovery, he might have less. Only time will tell. But in the meantime, he needs your help in some unique ways."

"We can do that," said Adrienne. "Whatever it takes."

"You're all experienced legal assistants. You all know what commonly happens around a law office, and you all know what instructions lawyers are likely to pass out to their staff. Which brings us to Thaddeus. I'm going to ask you to be extra careful when he tells you to do something or asks you a question."

Dr. Willis went on to explain how the staff could best interact with Thaddeus and how they could best assist him. Thaddeus sat and listened to the doctor go on and he tried to concentrate. At times, he felt as if he were in a dream or a lecture hall listening to the needs of someone he'd never met. At times, he realized he actually had never met the new Thaddeus. It was extremely difficult to see oneself when suffering organic brain deficit, he decided. So there was new territory to discover within, and he would try as much as he could not to lash out against this incredible staff that was standing by him. He felt misty-eyed when he thought about it and resolved that he would do everything he could to reward his staff for their loyalty and allegiance to Thaddeus and the office.

Christine was another matter altogether. He wanted her with him, and it caused his heart to thump in his chest when he considered that one day she would have to return to Chicago and leave him here alone. Or leave him in Chicago alone. Whatever and wherever. The time would come, and he would have to stand and deliver from his own two feet. Would he be able when the time came? He honestly did not know. And he realized that he would be living with this ambiguity for some time to come. Acceptance, that was the key for him. He vowed to work on his acceptance, the serenity to accept the things he couldn't change but the courage to change the things he could. It worked for him, this approach, and he loosened his grip on life two clicks.

He went through the rest of the day with spirits uplifted after the staff had left to resume their weekend and after Dr. Willis had gone her way too. Killen's trial was back on the calendar; Thaddeus and Christine had just two weeks until opening statements would be given. So Thaddeus decided to sit down and write out his statement just like in days gone by when he was new, and opening statements and closing arguments were best tested first in ballpoint and a legal pad. He wrote on through that afternoon, leaving the office just after four p.m. to go home to Katy. Turquoise would be down for Saturday night, and Thaddeus was looking forward to reconnecting with his older daughter.

JT had put together a new swing set for Sarai in the backyard. The little girl was hanging on to the glider for dear life as she zoomed up and back, up and back, five minutes then ten. Thaddeus watched as he pulled up and parked. Thank God for JT, too, he thought. The guy was an odd duck but, like the rest of them, he was loyal almost to a fault. So Thaddeus took great care with his requests for JT.

He found Katy in the kitchen at the table overlooking the backyard. She was sitting there staring out at Sarai and didn't turn even though she heard him come inside.

He encircled her from behind with his arms and smelled her hair. Sweet and clean. Just like her soul, he thought, and he loved her then more than he had ever loved anything. She was perfect for him, and he said a silent prayer of thanksgiving for her.

"Hey," she said, her voice soft and, to his keen ear, dispirited.

"Hey," he said back. "Everything okay?"

She turned then and looked up at him. Tears glistened in her eyes and streaked her face.

"Hey, hey," he said, "what is it, Kates?" Kates—his special name for her.

"I'm maybe imagining things, but probably not. I felt another lump."

Thaddeus felt mentally staggered as if hit with a board.

"You mean—you mean—"

"Uh-huh. This time it's the right side of my neck."

"Let me feel."

She loosened his right hand from around her and placed his index finger on the side of her throat. Sure enough, he felt a swelling there. But it was slight. Could it mean all that much? His mind raced.

"I don't feel much at all," he said.

"That's just it. I'm being very careful and palpating every day. Several times a day, ever since my radiation. This swollen lymph gland is new. It might mean nothing and it might mean something."

"So you're going to Chicago day after tomorrow to get it checked out? JT will drive you."

"Yes, I've already called Maria Coates. She can work me in at one-fifteen. So I'll need to leave early."

"How did you get hold of her? It's Saturday."

"Called her service and she called me right back. She's moving some things around for me. God love her."

"I think I should go with you."

"No, she'll just needle biopsy it and that will be that. I'll have JT bring me back down here after. Sarai can hang out after school with you. You can pick her up Monday afternoon?"

"Of course. Whatever you need, Kates."

"Okay."

She stood up from the table.

"Now, that delicious smell coming from the stove is Katy's Marvelous Vegetable Soup. Turquoise's favorite."

"What time is she pulling in?"

"She said it would be after seven. They had volleyball practice this morning and then she had to hit the library."

"Hold on, are we done talking about the swollen lymph gland? I mean, I'm scared. Aren't you? I don't want to be an alarmist, but hey."

She turned and threw her arms around his neck.

"If it is something, they'll take care of it just like last time. A little surgery, little radiation, who knows? I have a world of confidence in my Chicago team."

"I don't know."

"Let's just enjoy the weekend with our girls and let Monday take care of Monday."

"If you say so. Roger that."

"Roger that. You've been hanging out with cops too much."

"It's Rocky. Everything is 'roger this' and 'roger that.' Too much time in the police uniform."

"I'm just glad you have Rocky. I only wish his name wasn't Rocky."

"I know."

"Why not Peter? This is the United States, you know."

"Peter."

She smiled. "Speaking of, tonight's your lucky night, big boy."

His heart jumped.

"I'm in. All the way in."

"I know. You always have been."

40

I t was the Friday before the trial was to start on Monday, and a bombshell had just exploded in Thaddeus' office. Not a real bomb but the effect was the same, jarring and jolting everyone within the radius of the lab report that had just been delivered.

While Thaddeus was in the hospital, the Marine KA-BAR knife found behind the soft drink machine at the motel had been turned over to Christine. This was done pursuant to the judge's order that last day of trial before Thaddeus was assaulted.

She had sent the knife out to their Chicago Lab, DNA Research Institute. Now it was back, along with the report. At four forty-five the UPS courier brought the mailing envelope upstairs and handed it off to Adrienne, who took it right into Christine, as it was addressed to the attorney.

She pulled the zip tab and opened the sleeve. There, on two pages was the DNA report.

She read it, dropped it on her desk, cursed silently, and picked it up again.

At the door beyond hers, she knocked.

"Thaddeus?"

"Come in!"

She pushed the door open and approached his desk. She was holding the DNA report in front of her like a dirty diaper.

"You're not gonna believe it."

"What's this?"

"The DNA Research Institute workup on the knife."

"Short version?"

"Killen Erwin's DNA was found on the knife. By our lab!"

"We're hosed."

"We are."

She flounced down in a visitors' chair and leaned forward, rubbing her hands at her temples.

"Shit shit shit!" She cried.

"Double that and raise you one," he said. "So now what?"

"We have a duty to turn it over to the state."

"Do we?" He asked.

"You know better than that. Of course we do."

"Do we have to do it tonight?"

"We could always mail it to her."

"That would suck. Judge Wren would eviscerate us."

"He would. So let's scan and email and hope to hell she doesn't check her email before Monday."

"We're going to have a shit weekend."

"We are."

"Thanks, Chris, for having DNA testing done on the murder weapon. Jeesh!"

"You would have done the same thing. Besides, you were in the hospital, and I didn't exactly have the chance to run it by you."

"Seriously, I'm not blaming you," he said. "You did what was indicated. I would have done the same thing, you're right."

"No, the old Thaddeus was too smart to take that chance. I screwed the pooch on this one."

"You sure as hell did," he said with a smile. "Well, there goes my happy weekend."

"I was just going to head out to Chicago. I've got to get home and check in on Jamie."

"Sure. Have a happy weekend anyway. And say hello to Jamie."

"Will do."

"I'll give it to Adrienne to scan and email. She's the only one still around."

"Okay."

"Have a lousy weekend, Thad."

"You too, Chris. We deserve it."

"We do."

41

J udge Wren sent a clear message to the litigants: things would now move along on *his* schedule. When Thaddeus and Christine and Killen took their seats at counsel table, Judge Wren proclaimed he was limiting opening statements to the jury to thirty minutes for each attorney. Thaddeus would be giving the opening statement for Killen, and the judge's announcement immediately caused a neuronal shutdown, as Thaddeus had been preparing over the weekend for his opening statement with the help of a one hour alarm. Now the judge had cut that time in half, so Thaddeus would have to improvise.

And improvisation is not something that comes easily to many victims of traumatic brain injury.

Thaddeus, sitting at the far right end of the defense table, felt a knee collide with his left knee. It was Christine tagging him. "Easy," she whispered. "You can do this opening statement in your sleep."

His muscles in his neck and shoulders gave way to her

soothing words. His mind slowed, and he began looking over his notes, deciding where one sentence could work in place of an entire paragraph or page. Thaddeus had been down the opening statement road before and had once too often had the prosecutor jump on his *opening* statement in the prosecutor's *closing* argument and point out all the things the defense had promised that it hadn't delivered. Thaddeus began thinking, then, that the judge's ruling was perhaps a good thing. It would rein him in and guide him to promising less in the way of proof.

There was another part of Judge Wren's thirty-minute rule that caught Thaddeus' notice, too. The judge was sending a message to the attorneys that he was there not to waste time but to use it expediently. As a trial lawyer, Thaddeus knew that long, going-nowhere examinations of witnesses would be shut down earlier than usual. He knew that long, almost pointless sidebar discussions would be frowned on—at first —and then denied if abused with too many requests to join the judge for a private discussion at the bench.

He leaned forward and caught Killen's eye. Killen was to Christine's left and looked almost childishly small—in part because he was barely over five feet and in part because the enormity of the proceedings seemed to downsize him, like such proceedings always did to everyone. He saw Thaddeus looking his way and made a weak attempt at a smile of acknowledgment, but it came across as a look of panic at where he was and what he was facing. Thaddeus, looking toward Killen and away from the jury, gave him a strong smile, and a slight nod and Killen seemed to relax.

Thaddeus sat back and opened his tablet to a clean page and set himself ready to listen.

Eleanor Rammelskamp went first. As was his practice, Thaddeus never took his eyes from the jury as the prosecutor told the jury what she expected the evidence to be. He listened and analyzed carefully, ready to object on a moment's notice if her opening became argument. Telling the jury what to expect—that was the purpose of an opening statement. But arguing to the jury was the strict domain of closing argument and was anathema to opening statements.

He watched the jury's reaction to her. He noted which jurors responded to her positively: a nod of the head, a slight smile, uncrossed arms indicating an openness to what she was saying—none of it escaped the young lawyer. Likewise, Christine was there with him, hanging on every word and making notes as the open rambled along.

Rammelskamp's opening statement was logical and slightly understated. She didn't want to come across as strident—that would be reserved for later, the sudden eruption, at the point where it would best interrupt the defense's case. Logic prevailed, and soon the flow of facts she was stacking up piece by piece began to sound compelling. Thaddeus wondered how the jury could find things other than how she described them. He found himself almost voting her way right at the start, and if he were feeling that way, then the jury must be all but in her pocket just ten minutes into her presentation.

But he managed to set all that aside and just listen to her descriptions of what she expected her witnesses to say and her evidence to show.

She planted her feet firmly and leaned forward to the jury.

"The only reason you're here is because of the rage and jealousy of that man there—" pointing at Killen Erwin, seated to Christine's left—"that man who let his heart get the best of him. Because his wife was a cheat. Some even said she was a slut. But you know what? We don't get to execute people for being cheats and sluts in America, that's not—"

"Objection! Argumentative."

"Sustained. Please stick to your factual presentation, counsel."

Thaddeus could see several crestfallen jurors who had wanted to hear more of Rammelskamp's argument. They were joined with her and ready to carry her banner into the fray. Thaddeus realized it was going to be up to him to gently turn the jury from Rammelskamp. And he further realized that it was going to take every bit of cunning in his mind to win them back over.

But there was the rub. Was his mind even still capable of cunning? Of compelling abstraction? Or would his arguments and legal constructs fall short, impressing no one on the jury, garnering no votes for acquittal? He felt a bead of sweat pop out on his forehead and again, just at the right moment, Christine's knee came crashing against his.

She would control him in the trial in just this manner. Kicking him when he needed reminding that he wasn't alone. She would also be standing in the gap for Killen when it was her turn with a witness. He was very, very grateful she was there with him. Even more, he was grateful she was on his side.

"So that's what I expect the state's case to prove," Rammelskamp was saying, "and now I want to suggest what the defendant is going to do. First, it will be smoke and mirrors. You will be introduced to half-truths that the defense will try to get you to accept as whole truths. You will be exposed to a witness or two—maybe three, if the defendant testifies —who will flat out lie to you. That's what I expect the defendant's case to be: half-truths and lies.

"So here's what you do. Keep your eye on the shell in the shell game. Do not let Mr. Murfee's sleight-of-hand confuse you. He is a magician in the courtroom and has made quite a name for himself by presenting cases perfectly camouflaged with false logic and a winning smile. And oh yes, he does have a winning smile. A charming man. As well, his co-counsel Christine Susmann is every bit as charming but even colder at the bone. You will probably see her seek to reach down inside my witnesses and turn them inside-out. That's her *modus operandi,* and she is very tough and very strong-willed. It will be a fight for me, but I'll do my best to uphold my side of things, even if I am outnumbered two to one."

Thaddeus fought down a smile. When the other side began attacking him, the lawyer, he knew they were running scared. It was a happy moment for him, and the attack did some heavy lifting in restoring his self-confidence. That was who he was, he reminded himself, cunning and wholesome and able to speak truth to power when the poor and downtrodden fought to survive.

As the prosecution's opening sped down the tracks, Thaddeus kept an eye on juror number four, Staunton Galloway. Don Gaffney, the bailiff, had pointed him out to Thaddeus as the guy who would reject the state's case because he was married when his wife cheated on him. Even now, Thaddeus was able to capture the juror's eye and the man all but nodded to Thaddeus. Thaddeus finally broke off eye contact, ending the moment with just a hint of a smile.

It was coming back to Thaddeus, some of it in a rush, some of it less quickly, what had transpired during jury selection those many months ago. The court clerk had given Thaddeus a list of ninety names composing the first pool of jurors. Thaddeus had turned the list over to Rocky—Peter—who cranked up his laptop in the attorneys' conference room and went to work. The Internet coughed up a wealth of information about who in those ninety names had been divorced or was in the process of divorce. Those people would very likely have a grudge for the life partner and would more quickly understand how a fight could break out where a wife went down and hit her head. To Thaddeus, such physical abuse would never be acceptable. But it wasn't up to him; this was a trial, and he would have to set aside his feelings and defend his client even when he held strong disagreements with his actions. So he was looking for the jurors who had suffered at the hands of a cheating spouse. They would understand the taunting that could break out between a couple and drive one of them to violence. They would be much more capable of forgiving a one-time incident when portrayed against the backdrop of Mary Roberta's incessant cheating on her husband. They would be much less likely to hold it against Killen.

So Thaddeus had asked the prospective jurors very personal questions: Have you or anyone in your immediate family been involved in a divorce? In a custody lawsuit? Have you ever had your spouse go outside the marriage for love and physical comfort? Have you ever cheated or been in love with someone not your spouse? Have you ever been the lover of a married man or woman? Have you been the other woman or the other man? These questions efficiently drove right to the heart of the jury pool and helped Thaddeus locate those jurors whom he would consider acceptable to his side. They were embarrassing questions, but Thaddeus made it clear he was not looking to embarrass but to defend. It was his job to ask, he explained, so please forgive him.

Which is where Rocky had fit in. By the time the judge had seated the first twelve jurors in the jury box, Rocky was back to Thaddeus with the goods on nine of those twelve. The nine jurors ran the gamut of people who had sued or been sued for divorce, to people who had been called as witnesses in divorce cases, and to Jennifer Hedwin, who was a pharmacist's assistant at the CVS in Jackson City and who had answered no to all the divorce questions. But Rocky had found her maiden name and had located her on the Internet in a case involving her parents' divorce when she was thirteen. Thaddeus asked Jennifer Hedwin if she thought all people involved in divorce should be scorned for their failure or if they were simply good people who had made poor choices. She answered that there were times when married couples would fight and even strike out with their fists but that the combatants were ordinarily good, decent people who sometimes just lost control. Rammelskamp sent her packing with her next juror strike, and young Jennifer Hedwin went back to the CVS and doling out pills and potions. Which was fine with Thaddeus, because it turned out Rocky had learned Ms. Hedwin's husband was a Detective One with the Springfield Police Department. Hers was the exact profile Rammelskamp would have wanted on her jury, but she hadn't done her homework.

The pharmacy tech's vacant seat was then filled by Staunton Galloway whose wife was a rounder. Galloway had run his own filling station for twenty years, meaning he rarely got home before midnight, which was when the graveyard crew relieved him. He would drag home to bed, reach across and find an empty pillow. According to Fletcher Mannfred, Staunton had tried to drown his sorrows beneath the draft beer spout at the local Elks Club until Mrs. Galloway divorced him. Mr. Galloway had then gotten sober and had never shown any interest in any woman since. He had been burned, fatally, on the topic of marriage. But, best of all, he kept it to himself and when it came time to answer whether he had ever been divorced he answered yes but when the questions were posed about fidelity in marriage he had looked down at his feet and given up no response.

Thaddeus felt sure Galloway had felt the same feelings Killen had felt. Both men's wives had cheated out in the open, right under their noses, making no attempt to hide their sins or atone for them. They were, as Killen had once told Thaddeus, "rotten to the core." If there was any juror on the panel who might hang the jury and refuse to vote guilty no matter how compelling the state's evidence, Thaddeus felt it was Galloway. His ace in the hole. His point man.

He watched Galloway as Rammelskamp began describing how the pieces fit together. Though she admitted there was no eyewitness, there was video of *some*body and video of *some*thing—though who was underneath the hat and sunglasses she couldn't prove absolutely. Galloway sat back in his chair during this portion of her presentation, pulling away, face turned to the side, refusing to even listen. Even when she spoke about the bloody pants he wouldn't return her eye contact. The closest he came to acknowledging her was when she mentioned the partial fingerprint on the KA-BAR knife that might be Killen's, but the evidence wasn't conclusive—not on that point. But then she brought up the DNA that, thanks to the defense team, connected the defendant to the knife. "That's right, the defense team helped find the defendant's DNA on the murder weapon." Thaddeus could almost reach out and touch the horror manifested in Galloway's eyes at this. An inconclusive fingerprint, to the cuckolded juror, was the same as a whopper. It meant nothing and couldn't be trusted. But the DNA made it a whole new game. Now Galloway wouldn't return Thaddeus' look.

Then it was Thaddeus' turn, and he felt his heart speed up as it always did the first time he stood to address a jury. Any jury, it didn't matter.

"Ladies and gentlemen," he began, "my name is Thaddeus Murfee, and my co-counsel at the table is Christine Susmann. It is our job to defend Killen Erwin against these serious but confabulated charges. Confabulated, as in untrue.

"As you know, it is our job to defend our client zealously. Our ethics require this. So at times during the trial there may be verbal battles but please remember the parties are only doing their jobs. Some of you might be offended by how I do my defense work and if you are, I am sorry and apologize now going in. Just remember that my shortcomings are not the shortcomings of Killen and please don't hold my faults against him. Now let me introduce Killen Erwin."

Thaddeus opened his hand—as opposed to the prosecution's closed-hand pointing—and waved it to indicate that

Killen should stand. He did stand up and faced the jury, hands clasped before him and a forced smile on his face, exactly like Christine had practiced with him. "Smiling," she told him, "means you're an undeserving ass-kisser. But forced smiling—that means you're trying to be pleasant in a difficult situation—which they'll empathize with and wind up supporting you. So let them know it's forced. They'll love you even more for it."

Thaddeus continued. "Now one thing you'll notice about Killen: he's fairly short. All of five-six. Killen at one time rode thoroughbreds, meaning he's braver than I'll ever be. And meaning he turned what some men develop into a complex into a positive. He made money, and lots of it, because he was small and lightweight. And that's been the story of his life. But it's also the reason his wife cheated on him, taunting him that he was less than a man because of his size. Even his performance in bed was made fun of by her, always referring to his size. That should about say it all, as to who she was. But as for Killen, the evidence will show he never once went outside the marriage for female companionship and shared love. No, he hung in there. He hung in because he loved Mary Roberta, and he clung to the hope she would see the error of her ways and rejoin him in the marriage with fidelity.

"Now why do I mention his diminutive stature? Because there is a video recording of the killer in this case. And she is also about five-six, according to our expert. Same size as Killen. That similarity between Killen and the disguised killer is what Ms. Rammelskamp is hanging her hat on. She wants you to believe they're one and the same. But we'll show you why we think the killer is someone else.

"Now, what's this case about?"

Thaddeus looked down at his notes and counted to five.

"The state wants you to believe this was a crime of passion. A case of a husband hating his wife. But, ladies and gentlemen, that is not this case." He was looking directly at Galloway when he said, "No, this case is about revenge. The revenge of one wife on another who has taken away the first one's husband. There's the motive for the murder."

He watched Galloway lean forward in his seat and begin nodding as he spoke from there on, and Thaddeus knew he had a chance at regaining his ally. Then he played his hole card.

"The DNA on the knife was mentioned. But what counsel failed to mention is that Killen Erwin owned the same knife, and it was stolen from him before the murder."

A collective gasp went up around the courtroom. Every eye of every juror was fastened on him, waiting.

"That's right. Killen Erwin's knife was stolen and, of course, it had his DNA on it. It might even have a fingerprint or two though the work gloves worn at the horse farm ordinarily would have prevented fingerprints. The DNA would be the sweat through the gloves as Killen labored. Or directly from his skin as he put the knife up or sharpened it or whatever. So we say yes, that's Killen Erwin's knife, and we also say the real mystery for you to solve is who removed the knife from Killen's barn and who plunged it into the throat of Killen's wife and who discarded it behind the soft drink machine. These are the real truths about the knife."

He stopped and let that soak in. He had gone so far as to

claim the knife was Killen's own, though he had no way of proving that. But it had to be done, given Killen's DNA on the knife. Besides, it fit with the theory of the defense: that someone else had killed Mary Roberta and that person was now trying to frame Killen.

He finally drew a deep breath and continued, looking from juror to juror as he spoke.

"So what is this case really about? Who is the real victim here?" Thaddeus' eyes came to rest on Vicki Nielsen, who Thaddeus knew was a recently divorced mother of four. She labored by day in a grocery checkout line and on weekends on an industrial cleaning crew. She was glued on Thaddeus when he said, "This case is about the little ones, the children of the marriage. They only wanted their mother home with them. But she refused to give them that. They wanted stability in their little lives, but she refused to give them that. They wanted her full attention, but she turned her attention outside the marriage to strange men. She refused to give her own kids her full attention. Yes, this case is about those children and is about you voting to return their loving father to them to take care of them in peace. Thank you for your attention."

The judge called for a fifteen-minute break before the start of testimony. As the courtroom emptied, Thaddeus and Christine stayed in place at the defense table. His opener had elicited a powerful response from the jury. The prosecution would get a running start over the next few days, but Rammelskamp now knew Thaddeus was back.

"Thank you, Thaddeus," Killen said as he got up to return to the holding cell with the ever-present deputies.

Thaddeus looked at him and then he looked at Christine.

"Don't thank me yet," he said.

When he was gone, Christine reached behind Thaddeus and squeezed his shoulder.

"Welcome back," she said.

It was enough.

42

The break ended just as Thaddeus finished reviewing his notes on Special Agent Wells Waters. He knew the non-guilt witnesses would be called first. These were the witnesses who wouldn't try to implicate Killen in the homicide but would, rather, be called to set the stage. They would give the location of the motel, the stairs, the room layout, and all the rest of the minutiae that would be used later on by what Thaddeus called the guilt witnesses: those who connected Killen to the murder.

The first witness called by Rammelskamp was a heavyset woman named Arlita Aguilar. She took the stand and gave the judge a terrified look. He responded with a stern look, and Thaddeus could almost see the woman deliquesce into the Naugahyde of the witness chair. Her worst fears had come true: appearing in an American courtroom while in the country illegally.

Aguilar testified that she worked the four a.m. to one p.m. cleaning shift. Her usual supervisor was Willy Peters, who had that day off, and so she was working unsupervised with her daughter, eighteen-year-old Nancy Aguilar. Typically, mother and daughter worked as a team, she said, which was common in the commercial cleaning industry.

They started that day in the lobby of the motel, running the vacuum, washing windows, emptying trash containers, cleaning up the Breakfast Xpress area, making the Continental Breakfast coffees and putting out the Danish and doughnuts and fruit. During that time, they went several times to the supply room, which was an unmarked room that was positioned in the center of the motel, between the west and east wings, on the first floor.

Once breakfast was in place and the office chores completed, they moved to the checkout rooms—those rooms where the guests were gone. They worked along and finished cleaning the downstairs bedrooms by about ten-thirty a.m. They took their morning break, drinking Mountain Dews and eating Pringles out of the guest vending machines on the first floor between the two halves of the motel. Ten minutes later they took the freight elevator to the second floor, their cleaning cart between them in the car.

Starting at the far end of the second floor was their usual routine, and then working back toward the stairwell at the center of the motel.

"Did anything unusual happen that morning on the western end of the second floor?" Rammelskamp asked.

"Unusual happen? We find a dead woman."

"In what room?"

"Two-twelve."

"Tell us what you saw."

"I use my passkey and push the door open with my back. I go the bathroom for towels and washcloths. They come out first. But I don't get there."

"Why not?"

"I see the woman sleeping in the bed, and I tell her, 'my goodness, I'm sorry. I did not know you was here.'"

"What happened next."

"Then I see her neck. It was all blood, and it was all over her pillow and run down."

Rammelskamp then took her through a description of the woman. Her first reaction was to withdraw back outside, but then she returned inside and called the front desk. She told the manager what she'd found. Within four or five minutes, she heard sirens drawing nearer. Then the police arrived and told her to wait outside. She did, with her daughter. Did her daughter see the body? No, the mother wouldn't let her go inside.

Then Rammelskamp shifted gears.

"Now, let's talk about that morning around four-thirty or five while you're loading up your breakfast cart from the supply room. Did you happen to notice any people coming or going in the parking lot."

"Yes, people come and go all day long."

"Do you recall anything or anyone specifically between four-thirty and five in the morning?"

"Yes, I see a woman wearing a hat and sunglasses come down the stairs."

"Can you tell us what she looked like?"

"I could not see her front. Her back was what I see when she climbed down the stairs. I'm back inside between the two buildings and I only see her back."

"So you can't describe her?"

"No, ma'am."

"Are you sure it was a woman you saw?"

"I thought it was a woman because she was small, about my height."

"How tall are you?"

"Five-four."

"Think carefully about this next question before you answer, okay?"

"Okay."

"Would it be possible that the person you thought was a woman was actually a small man?"

Aguilar's face became a study in puzzlement. It was obvious that this part of her testimony hadn't been polished up by the prosecutor in the days leading up to the trial.

"Could it be a man? Do you mean maybe a boy?"

"Or a small man?"

"I guess it could be. I mean I see men that little."

"At the very least, wouldn't it be fair to say you couldn't tell if it was a man or a woman?"

Ms. Aguilar chose that moment to roll her arm over and examine her elbow. Clearly, she was thinking.

"I think it was a woman. She walk like a woman, move her hips like a woman."

"But it might have been a man?"

"Objection! Asked and answered."

"Sustained. Move along, counsel."

Rammelskamp stood at the podium and toyed with her yellow pad, appearing to be going back over her notes. But Thaddeus knew the real truth: her first witness had failed to draw blood. In fact, she had opened a relatively large hole in the state's case, giving Thaddeus the opportunity to make the case for a mysterious third person—a woman—who had perpetrated the crime. Inside he was deliriously happy. How Rammelskamp would have walked into a gaffe of this magnitude was something he couldn't understand. She was the pro, the gunslinger, hand-picked by the powers-that-be to send Killen Erwin to prison for life. She had just lost the storyline of her case, and her momentum had come to an abrupt halt. Worse, she had told the jury during opening statement that she would present a witness who saw a man leaving the motel wearing a coat and hat, so his features were hidden. A suspicious man, she had said, leaving the motel at about the time the murder occurred.

"That is all, Your Honor," said Rammelskamp, closing out her direct exam of the witness.

Thaddeus stood and walked to the podium. He smiled at the woman and kept both hands in sight so she could see he wasn't flipping pages of notes. He wanted her comfortable for this.

"This person you saw, the one who walked like a woman—did you happen to notice whether she was wearing any jewelry?"

"No, no jewels. She had her wedding rings on her left hand like American women wear."

"American women wear? What's that mean?"

The witness smiled at long last. "In Mexico we don't wear wedding rings. It's our custom. So I notice American women's rings. They are very lovely to look at."

"Describe this woman's rings."

"I just see a diamond flash when she reached to pull down her hat."

There it was. She—it was more a she than a he—attempted to better cover her face by pulling down her hat. And the rings were seen at that moment. What would have been a clear view.

But there was one more matter.

"How far would you say you were from the woman when you saw her rings?"

"Me to you."

"About twenty feet?"

"Six or seven meters."

Thaddeus held up his left hand. "Can you describe what you see on my hand?"

"A gold ring."

"So your vision is good."

"The man at the eye doctor tells me I'm perfect both eyes."

"Well, good for you. That is all, Mrs. Aguilar. I thank you."

"Okay."

Rammelskamp said she had no re-direct, and the judge told her to call her next witness.

43

Thaddeus expected Rammelskamp to call the custodian's daughter next, to corroborate some of what her mother had said, but instead she went with the first responding officer. She was going to get the jury up to the morning break with descriptions of blood and gore running through their minds.

He was a stout, confident looking patrolman who was wearing the under-the-shirt body armor that made police officers look like baseball umpires with all their chest and abdomen protection. Rowdy Conners was his name, and he was a Patrolman II, according to the state's witness list.

He lowered himself into the witness chair, adjusted his utility belt and body armor, and swiped a hand over his short hair. His sunglasses hung from his chest pocket, beside two ballpoint pens.

"Comfortable?" said Rammelskamp.

"Yes, ma'am," said the state's first of many professional

witnesses. These were the pay-to-play witnesses, the ones who had attended testifying school.

She took him through his name, training, assignment, experience, arms qualifications, commendations, and all the rest of it. Five minutes later, the jury had a pretty good idea who Rowdy Conners was, and he was a pretty good guy, all in all.

"Take us through what happened when you arrived on-scene, officer."

"I knew backup was just moments behind. The manager met me in the lot and directed me to room 212. I hurried up the stairs, hoping the victim was still alive, and I could employ first aid."

"Was she?"

"Not at all. She was on her back, and she was clearly deceased."

"How so, clearly?"

"Her throat had been cut open from ear to ear. There was massive blood loss. There were other wounds in her throat too. She had stab wounds on other parts of her body as well. Her eyes were open, dilated and glazed; there were no breath sounds."

"What did you do?"

"I backed out of the room and returned to my squad car for crime scene tape. I put tape across the door to the room and then began taping the upstairs walk and the staircase. You never know in these cases, and I wanted the dicks to have a prime scene."

"Dicks? Detectives?"

He turned red. "Excuse me, yes."

"Did you notice whether her purse was still in the room?"

"Objection! Assumes facts not in evidence. No showing yet she even had a purse."

"Sustained."

Thaddeus knew the prosecutor was trying to circle back around to the room and get in some more about the blood and the gore. But he didn't want her back in there and was ready to fight her on it.

"Was anything taken from the room?"

"Objection! Foundation."

"Sustained."

Sustained because the officer didn't know what was in there to begin with. If Rammelskamp wanted to go there—to an inventory of the room's contents—she would first need to show the cop had prior information as to the room's contents when last seen by the staff. She didn't have that.

So, she decided to leave it alone.

Thaddeus drew a deep breath. Beside him, Christine whispered, "Rookie."

She meant the prosecutor. She was fumbling and stumbling. Both defense attorneys clearly recognized such.

"What happened next?"

"Just about all duty officers in my section hit the scene with their lights and sirens. Then came the d-detectives, and I turned the scene over to them."

"Were you done there?"

"No, it was still my job to keep people away. So I did that. I blocked anyone coming upstairs. Some upstairs guests wanted to go downstairs. The detectives told me to keep them in their rooms for questioning, which I did."

"Now I'm going to show you a thirty-by-forty blowup marked State's Exhibit Seventeen. Would you look at that and tell me what that picture is?"

The prosecutor held the blowup so the jury couldn't see the image. It wasn't their turn and wouldn't be until she got it admitted into evidence.

"That's a photograph of the victim."

"Is this photograph a true and accurate depiction of what you observed of the victim upon entering room two-twelve that morning?"

"Yes."

"Your Honor, State moves "State's Seventeen" into evidence."

"Counsel?"

Thaddeus shook his head. He'd seen the photograph too many times to count in preparing for trial. One thing about murder cases was always inevitable: the State would get at least two photographs of the bloody, dead body of the deceased in front of the jury. Two seemed to be the standard in most Illinois trial courts and he figured this one wouldn't be any different. But he didn't have to like it. Photographs of human death always arouse emotions in the living. And photographs of violent human death always cause the same response in jury members, the desire to punish the wrong-doer. Whether drunk drivers or negligent doctors or killers with knives, the emotions were always aroused, and the jury began, at that exact moment of seeing, the hunt for someone to punish. Thaddeus knew it had always been that way, and when the pictures of Mary Roberta Erwin were placed on the tripod stand before them, this time would be no different. Their view of Killen Erwin would change and they would begin thinking in terms of punishing him, forsaking what the judge had told them was their role at this point, which was to keep an open mind until all the evidence was in, including the Defendant's evidence. Thaddeus could even foresee the new frown on Galloway's face as the pictures carried the day for the State. For a moment, he felt it all slipping away.

"No objection."

"Seventeen is admitted into evidence," the Judge said.

Rammelskamp then continued.

"Now what does this mark here on the victim represent?"

"That's the wound where her throat was cut ear to ear."

"And this down here?"

"That's a stab wound in her neck. So are the others nearby."

"And is this pool of blood consistent with what you saw that morning?"

"It is."

She then introduced "State's Eighteen," another thirty-by-forty blowup that represented the victim in death, but from a different angle. The questions and answers were essentially the same as with Seventeen.

Then Rammelskamp appeared to have shot her wad. She had run out of questions for the witness.

"What else did you do that morning?"

"That's about it."

"Nothing further, Your Honor."

Thaddeus stood and launched right in.

"Officer, did you see any women around the scene wearing coats and hats?"

"No."

"Did you see any women wearing wedding rings? Engagement rings?"

The police officer looked at the judge, who nodded. "Please answer."

"I don't know. I wasn't looking at rings."

"Isn't it true that you left the scene without having the slightest idea who had murdered that woman?"

"Yes. It wasn't my job to locate suspects, though."

"And isn't it true the detectives later left the scene without the slightest idea who had murdered that woman?"

He knew the question was inappropriate, but the witness gave him a platform, and he used it to present his view of the case.

"Objection!" Cried Rammelskamp. "Foundation."

"Sustained. Counsel, are we through here?"

"We are, Your Honor," said Thaddeus. "Nothing further."

"May the witness be excused?"

"Yes," said both attorneys.

"Very well, we'll take our morning break. Everyone back here in fifteen minutes and please remember the admonition, ladies and gentlemen of the jury. No newspapers, radios, TV and no discussion of the case. Not with anyone."

The red light on the TV camera blinked out. They were in recess.

"Nicely done," said Christine. She stood and stretched forward and backward.

Killen stood and allowed himself to be moved away by the deputies. "Hey, you guys don't have to grab me and steer me. I know the drill now. First the cage, then the table, then the cage. I've got it, okay?"

"Sure, Mr. Erwin. We're just doing our job."

"I know that. I'm just restless. I'm ready to get this rodeo over with."

"Who's up next?" Thaddeus said to Christine.

"Special Agent Waters. He'll be the bridge between the two crime scene witnesses and the detectives. This case is all but over, though. That stuff about it being a woman and not a man and the stuff about the woman's wedding rings. Jeesh!"

"I know," Thaddeus replied. "But you know what? This is

almost too easy, too good. I'm a little apprehensive about that."

"Relax, Thad," she said. "No reason some of them can't be home-runs."

"Guess not."

44

Next up was Alexi Conroy, a member of the three-person Jackson City crime scene team that had processed the crime scene at the motel. Lexi—as she preferred to be called—explained to the jury what she and her team had done at the scene. One did hair and fiber; one did trace and transfer; one did blood spatter and fluids. Rammelskamp essentially used Conroy to introduce the crime scene report into evidence. She evidently believed the thing spoke for itself and that there were no issues regarding crime scene investigation. This kept the direct testimony quite short, surprising Thaddeus that it was over so soon.

But he quickly regained his place, hurrying to the podium for his turn.

On cross-examination, Thaddeus asked, "You have reviewed the entire crime scene report for the day in question?"

Lexi nodded and smiled, responding, like all professional witnesses must, directly to the jury. "I have reviewed the entire report. The people whose findings and notes are included are people who report directly to me."

"For the record, we are referring to State's Exhibit one-hundred-twenty-two, correct?"

"That is correct."

"And regarding hair and fiber, how was the crime scene searched for hair and fiber?"

"Visually and by vacuum. The tech visualized the bed where the body was found and literally using a magnifying lens attempted to visualize rogue hair and fiber. The same was done in the area where the killer would have had to be standing, on the right-hand side of the bed."

"And then you say the tech used a vacuum?"

"Yes, a handheld vac like you might carry in your car. That is used to lift hair and fiber from surfaces. It is then opened and its contents reviewed in the crime lab."

"So it was very thorough for hair and fiber?"

"Yes, it was."

"Now please look over there and tell the jury about the hair and fiber at the scene that came from my client, Killen Erwin."

Again with the warm smile. "That would be impossible. There was no hair and fiber linked to your client, Mr. Murfee."

Thaddeus acted surprised. "Nothing? Does this indicate to you he was never at the scene?"

"No, it indicates to me that whoever did this probably knew

what they were doing. They were careful. Same could be said for trace and transfer. There were no fingerprints, and there was no DNA that linked your client."

"And you know this how?"

"We took hair samples from your client's hairbrush when we searched his motel room. That DNA has been compared to all of the DNA we identified from motel room 212."

"And none of it belonged to Killen Erwin?"

"No, sir."

"Doesn't that indicate to you he wasn't there?"

"No, it indicates to me that whoever did this probably knew what they were doing."

"Tell the jury about trace and transfer evidence, please."

"Trace materials include human hair, animal hair, textile fibers and fabric, rope, feathers, soil, glass, and building materials. The physical contact between a suspect and a victim can result in the transfer of trace materials. The identification and comparison of these materials can often associate a suspect to a crime scene or with another individual."

"The examination of a crime scene for trace materials is a highly respected science aspect of crime scene investigation, is it not?"

"It is. Our unit employs four master's level workers doing trace and transfer for our teams."

"And one of those master's degree people worked with you in the victim's motel room?"

"Yes. And yes, to the second part. We also worked the motel room where Killen Erwin was staying, taking all manner of samples from his motel room to compare to the samples collected from the Blackfeather Motel room at the scene of the murder."

"And nothing matched between the two rooms?"

"That is not correct. There was blood on the pants found at your client's motel room. We later found that blood matched the blood of the victim."

"Let's talk about blood for a minute. When you searched my client's motel room, you were looking for blood evidence, correct?"

"Correct. Plus other items."

"I'm guessing the chemical known as Luminol was used?"

"Correct."

"What is Luminol?"

"A liquid that fluoresces when it comes into contact with blood."

"And you spray this and then look at where you sprayed under UV lights, correct?"

"We did, yes."

"Now I imagine that whoever slit Mary Roberta Erwin's throat encountered a good deal of blood, correct?"

"I would assume so, yes."

"And it would only be natural for some of that blood, even if just droplets, to have gotten on the murderer's clothes, correct?"

"Yes."

"So tell the jury about the blood you found in my client's motel room."

"We examined all clothing there and coveralls in the barn. We found no blood, with the exception of the pants which I've already mentioned. The blood on those pants belonged to the stabbing victim."

"Doesn't that indicate to you that the bloody pants were probably from the earlier fight he'd had with his wife, the one where she hit her head? Otherwise, why would he just leave those pants there for anyone to find? Doesn't that indicate innocence?"

"Objection! Multiple."

"Sustained. Break it apart, Mr. Murfee."

"Sorry, Your Honor. Doesn't the fact he made no attempt to hide the bloody pants suggest to you they were not from the murder scene?"

"It suggests to me that whoever did the murder was probably someone who thought himself beyond the reach of the law. Someone like a district attorney."

Thaddeus had been studying his notes while she answered. When the witness said, "district attorney," Thaddeus' head snapped up. "You say that because my client was the District Attorney and thought he was untouchable?"

"Well, Mr. Murfee, how do you explain the pants with his wife's blood on them?"

"Objection. I'm asking the questions. Move to strike, Your Honor."

Judge Wren agreed. "Jury will disregard the witness' question to counsel. The witness will answer questions, not ask them."

Thaddeus halted. He had had to ask the judge to help control a witness. Even worse, however, was the fact he hadn't been able to snap right back at her with a sensible answer. At that moment, he didn't know *how* he explained the bloody pants in his client's motel room in a way that was believable.

The old Thaddeus would never have been run over like that, he found himself thinking.

A few more meaningless questions and he took his seat.

Christine immediately slammed her knee against his.

"It was nothing," she whispered behind her hand.

"I miss the old Thaddeus," he said. "I really miss him."

45

The trial resumed ten minutes later.

The final "scene witness" was called: a female paramedic who established that the victim was dead at the scene and who testified Exhibits Seventeen and Eighteen were an accurate portrayal of the dead victim. She testified about the nature of the stab wounds as she examined the body for signs of life.

"All hope was gone," she said. "As soon as I saw her, I knew. She was dead, and there was no need for me there."

The paramedic was excused without cross-examination by Thaddeus.

Judge Wren told Rammelskamp to call her next witness, and she leaned to her right and began whispering to Special Agent Waters.

Waters was seated at counsel table with Rammelskamp as the People's representative in the trial. It was standard procedure for the prosecutor to call the People's representative as the state's first guilt witness. Waters would be the pilot at 40,000 feet, describing the overall view.

He would testify about the bloody pants, the partial fingerprint on the knife, the video of the killer's attack, the motel video of what must have been the murderer, the previous aggravated domestic battery on Killen's record, and the story of the cheating wife, which would go to motive even though motive wasn't a requirement in a murder case.

Waters' key role was in giving the jury the times, dates, places, and all the minutiae of the case that needed to be proved in order to avoid the court dismissing the case at the close of the prosecution's case. These matters were called the elements of homicide and each one required proof beyond a reasonable doubt: the killing of an individual without lawful justification if (1) they either intend to kill or do great bodily harm to that individual or another, or know that such acts will cause death to that individual or another; or (2) they know that such acts create a strong probability of death or great bodily harm to that individual or another; or (3) they are committing, or attempting to commit, a forcible felony. Any one of these numbered items, proven beyond a reasonable doubt would send Killen to prison for life without parole when coupled with the previous charge of aggravated domestic battery.

At long last the whispering stopped.

Rammelskamp called Waters to the stand. He was a bull of a man without a neck and carried himself erect and proud. He was wearing his cowboy boots and dark slacks with a white shirt, bolo tie, and cowboy sports coat. The Ray-Bans peeked out of his jacket's breast pocket. He took his seat, pulled the mike close to his mouth, and looked over and smiled at the jury. "Good morning," he mouthed, and several smiled back and returned the greeting. Then he turned his attention to the Special Prosecutor.

Rammelskamp went through his particulars. The jury learned the Special Agent had started out as a State Trooper before joining the Illinois Bureau of Investigation. Worked Robbery-Homicide on high-profile cases. Was this a high-profile case and why? Yes, because it involved a sitting District Attorney.

He then was asked a series of questions about what he had done in the case. With great sincerity, he detailed for the jury what his role had been. He had been called to the crime scene, he said, whereupon Exhibits Seventeen and Eighteen were again trotted out, and the dead body's appearance established yet another time.

Then the pictures were taken down, and the questioning continued. It turned out that his major time expenditure on the case had been working liaison between the Jackson City PD and the Special Prosecutor's Office. That, and he had sought and served the search warrants on the lodgings of Killen Erwin and Barb Daniels.

"Tell us what, if anything, you retrieved from Mr. Erwin's residence."

"It was his motel room. His wife had the house."

"Please go ahead."

"I found pants with the blood of Mary Roberta Erwin on them."

"Was this blood fresh or old?"

"Unknown. But the pants were damp."

"The pants were damp? Was the blood coming out of the pants onto your hands when you picked them up?"

"Gloves, I was wearing latex gloves. No, the blood didn't smear. But the pants were damp."

"Where were the pants located in the motel room?"

"There was a dirty clothes bag that was actually a grocery bag. The pants were in there."

"Anything else in there?"

"Underwear, socks, T-shirts, assorted shirts."

"Any of that stuff bloody?"

"No."

"And where was the dirty clothes bag located?"

"In the closet. Not a closet; just a small opening in the wall with a closet bar, maybe all of three feet wide. The grocery bag was on the bottom. That was all."

"What did you do with the pants?"

"CSI bagged them and sealed them with evidence tape."

"Then what?"

"Initialed them and wrote log information on the tape."

"Then what?"

"Delivered them to the crime lab."

"What department?"

"Biology/DNA."

"Did you ever receive a report back from the crime lab about the pants?"

An objection was made and the usual housekeeping about business record exceptions to the hearsay rule were discussed and the report was admitted into evidence subject to being connected up by the person in the crime lab who had prepared the report.

And then, "What was the finding of the crime lab?"

"The pant's blood belonged to Mary Roberta Erwin."

"Anyone else's body fluids on there?"

"No."

"What about the age of the blood samples on the pants?"

"I don't know if they can do that. There's no reference to age in the lab report."

"Changing topics, Agent Waters. You still with me?"

"Yes, ma'am."

"You also executed a search warrant on the premises inhabited by David and Barbara Daniels, correct?"

"Correct."

"What items were found?"

"The essential item for this case was a T-shirt."

"Tell us about the T-shirt."

"It's a man's T-shirt and contained Mary Roberta Erwin's blood."

"You know this how?"

Waters allowed a small nod in the otherwise regal posture he had maintained on the stand.

"DNA testing. Crime lab, Biology/DNA branch."

"Was there anything else seized?"

"Yes, the T-shirt was found in the garage of the Daniels' home inside a grass collector mounted on a lawnmower. We seized the grass collector."

"So you're saying the T-shirt was hidden?"

"That would be my opinion, yes. Somebody had gone to the trouble of removing the grass catcher and putting the shirt inside and then re-attaching it to the lawnmower."

"Anything else in the grass catcher?"

"Grass particles."

"Were any fingerprints taken from the grass catcher."

"Yes, ma'am."

"Whose fingerprints turned up?"

"Prints belonging to David Daniels, the husband."

"Where were those prints located on the grass catcher?"

"All over, but mainly on the metal frame portions."

"What about Barbara Daniels. Did her fingerprints turn up on the grass-catcher?"

"No."

"Was the T-shirt tested for fingerprints?"

"No."

"Why not?"

"It was wet and wadded up. One CSI looked it over and said it was impossible."

"So it wasn't tested?"

"No, ma'am. It was too wet."

"All right."

Agent Waters then went on to give background on other evidence. Thaddeus listened and made his notes during the long, plodding recitation. Waters talked about the finding of the knife and testing of the knife, and this testimony was just general enough that foundational questions would be seen as interruptive. Waters recounted as well that a video of the murder had been recovered. At this point jurors—every last one of them—stopped writing and their faces came up to look at the witness.

"Say that again?"

"I'm saying we've located video of the murder itself."

"Well, Mr. Waters, where did that video come from?"

Waters again allowed a small nod. "It came from the defense. They located a recording device in the room, and they tracked down the videos that had been shot."

"Do you know how the recording device got in the room?"

Here it comes, Thaddeus thought, she's going to take this

head-on. He knew she had to address that David Daniels had been shooting videos. Coupled with the fact that he was seen leaving the room, his presence would of course raise in the jury's mind the possibility that Dave had done the killing. Thaddeus knew this would be offset by the subsequent video and spotting of the unknown figure, but still, the possibility that Dave was complicit suited Thaddeus just fine. He watched as Rammelskamp did what she could to make Dave's role look innocent when compared to a critical piece of evidence, the DNA.

"Do I know how the recording device got into the room?" Waters repeated. "No, I don't know how it got there."

"Did you ask anyone about the recording?"

"I asked David Daniels. The video evidently came from his YouTube account."

"What did he say to you?"

"He said the recordings were all agreed to by his girlfriends. They shared their 'date-time' as they called it, on YouTube."

"So these videos were consensual?"

"Yes, that's why they always went to room 212, he said."

"Did you ask any of the women about the videos?"

"I did not."

"Why not?"

He shrugged. "No one asked me to."

"Are you ready to play the two videos for the jury at this time?"

"Yes, I have them ready to go on my laptop. Should I step down and begin?"

"Please do."

As Waters went to counsel table and his laptop, Rammelskamp asked the judge to explain the parties' stipulation.

"Ladies and gentlemen, the two sides in this case have reviewed hundreds of hours of video surveillance footage as well as motel room video movies. They have agreed to boil those down, so to speak, into two videos that portray those matters they consider relevant. Each party has retained the right to introduce other portions not stipulated to, but so far that has not been done. Ms. Rammelskamp, you may play the videos. Bailiff, dim the courtroom lights, please."

The lights went down.

Waters clicked his mouse, and the screen came to life as the video rolled.

Rammelskamp narrated, "The first video comes from the CCTV cameras of the motel's security system. The videos speak for themselves."

All eyes watched as Video One played.

9.10/4:44 a.m. A lone figure wearing pants, dark shoes, hat, and shirt was seen, picked up by the video camera approximately twenty-five yards into the parking lot from the stairwell leading up to room 212. The figure was diminutive in stature, maybe five-two or -three and moved gracefully. The figure looked neither right nor left, though that was hard to tell, as he or she was wearing a hat, dark glasses, and had pulled a red bandana up around mouth and nose while approaching. There was a brief instant where the face was somewhat revealed, but it was from too great a distance and in such poor light that the features weren't particularized. On it came, up to the stairs.

9.10/4:45 a.m. From the far end of the walkway on the second level, exterior, the camera there picked up the figure coming head-on. At room 212 the figure turned the doorknob and boldly went inside.

9.10/4:49 a.m. The figure reappeared, walked back the way it had come, passing the stairwell and walking another twenty feet before turning left, then, within a matter of seconds, it reappeared and came back toward the camera until even with the stairwell, where he or she turned left, descended the stairs, and was picked up again by the downstairs camera. This time the view was from the rear and gave no clues about identity: same hat, same dark trousers and shirt. Same slight frame and stature.

9.10/4:50 a.m. In a matter of twenty steps, the figure walked out of view of the camera and wasn't picked up again by any of the parking lot cameras.

The video ended and Rammelskamp again stood.

"At this point, Your Honor, I would ask leave of court to play the second video."

"Please proceed."

Again the screen came to life, and Video Two played.

Dark room. A man sat up on the left-hand side of a bed, stood upright, stretched, and began pulling on his pants and shirt. It was dark in the room, and his features were indiscernible. Five minutes later, the outside door to the room opened, and the man wasn't seen again. Five minutes later, a figure entered the room from left to right. The angle of the camera lens caught the figure just above the waist and just as low as the knees. A knife blade darted up and down in the milky light. The blade itself was black. The figure went around to the right-hand side of the bed, and the knife plunged downward several times and then was seen being drawn from below the event horizon to above. A diamond ring was seen to sparkle on the perpetrator's left hand, ring finger. The entire length of the blade was smeared with blood. Then the visitor departed.

The lights came back up in the courtroom. The room was silent. The jury had just witnessed the murder that brought them there.

Then Rammelskamp's voice pierced the silence.

"Agent Waters, you're aware there was a knife found?"

"Yes, ma'am."

"Tell the jury about that."

"A motel maintenance man found the murder weapon behind a soft drink machine at the motel."

"Objection, foundation."

"Sustained."

"Without saying it was the murder weapon, you're telling the jury a knife was found."

"Well, it tested out to have Mary Roberta Erwin's blood on it."

"Thank you. What else do we know about the knife?"

"We know there was a fingerprint on the knife and that print is a partial match to the defendant's fingerprint. Plus the DNA of the defendant is on the knife."

Thaddeus looked over. The jurors were furiously writing now, nodding and shuffling their feet in excitement. It was the DNA that did it; it always did.

"Let's talk about the print first. Which finger?"

"Index finger, right hand."

"Any other prints?"

"No, you need to understand how the KA-BAR knife is made to understand how other prints possibly weren't left on the handle."

She ignored the KA-BAR knife's engineering and went straight for the DNA.

"You also said there was DNA."

"The defense's own experts found the defendant's DNA on the knife. I haven't seen the report."

"Thank you, Agent Waters, I believe that is all for now."

Thaddeus winked at Rammelskamp as they passed each other: she headed for her seat, he headed for the podium. It was a quick wink, and it was done while her head was blocking the jury. He was telling her that he was about to eat her lunch, to keep her eyes open for what was about to happen to her case.

"Let me just summarize, Agent Waters."

"Fine. Do what you need."

"Well, thank you for that. I will. First, we have David Daniels' fingerprints all over the grass catcher inside which the bloody T-shirt was found by you, correct?"

"Correct."

"Then we have David Daniels seen leaving the scene of the crime in Video Two, getting out of bed first and dressing, correct?"

"Correct."

"And we have David Daniels' lover pregnant with someone's child. Were you aware of that? It's in the autopsy report."

Waters' rigid bearing creaked and gave way an inch or two.

"I have seen the autopsy report, yes."

"Did you ask David Daniels whether he knew his lover was expecting?"

"No, I did not."

"Wouldn't you consider that an important thing to know, given that her being pregnant might motivate him to kill her?"

"Objection. Relevance."

"Sustained. Ladies and gentlemen, motive isn't required in murder cases. That's why I sustained the objection."

Thaddeus plowed ahead, regardless.

"Well, if we add all these together, the hidden T-shirt and her pregnancy, wouldn't you agree that David Daniels would need to be considered as a suspect every bit as much as Killen Erwin? Maybe more?"

"Objection! Calls for a conclusion. Jury question."

"Sustained. Mr. Waters, do not answer that question. Counsel, rephrase. I'm sure there's a better way to make your point."

"Well, Mr. Waters, did you ever consider David Daniels might be the guilty party?"

"I did."

"And yet you agreed with Ms. Rammelskamp that the prosecution should be directed at Killen Erwin, correct?"

"Killen Erwin had the motive. David Daniels had no motive."

"Your Honor," said Thaddeus, "that answer is non-responsive, and I request that it be stricken, and the jury told to disregard."

"The jury will disregard that last response. Mr. Waters, please answer only what is asked. You're a big boy, Sir, and you know better."

Thaddeus tried the same question. "You agreed with Ms. Rammelskamp that the prosecution should be directed at Killen Erwin?"

"I didn't agree, and I didn't disagree. It wasn't my call to make."

"Whose call was it?"

"That lady sitting just to your right. Ms. Rammelskamp."

"Very well."

"Your Honor," said the witness, "can I explain my answer?"

"It's not your turn to explain," Judge Wren said curtly. "You will likely be asked to fill in the blanks by Ms. Rammel-skamp on re-direct."

"Yes, Sir."

Thaddeus decided to go in a different direction.

"Mr. Waters, you are aware that Mr. Erwin was charged with assaulting his wife many months prior to her death?"

"I knew about that."

"Were you also aware that the wife's head was wounded?"

"I knew about that."

"The blood on the pants. Do you know of any reason it wouldn't be from that prior event, the fight between husband and wife?

"I don't know any reason. I just know the pants were damp just hours after she was killed."

"So you need to get that before the jury about the damp again?"

"Well, it's certainly relevant."

"What if the pants are damp because of other items of clothing in the bag that are wet. Did you rule that out?"

"I didn't feel every item in the bag."

"What if Mr. Erwin was wearing those pants the same day you found them and got water on them from a horse trough. Did you rule that out?"

"I haven't been allowed to speak with Mr. Erwin."

"Yes, but my point is, the source of damp could be from any other number of things, isn't that true?"

"I suppose."

"And you didn't rule out those other things, correct?"

"I couldn't."

"Answer my question, please."

"No, I didn't rule out other things."

"So the fact that the pants were damp means absolutely nothing, correct?"

"Objection! Question invades the province of the jury."

"Sustained. Move along, Counsel."

"Did the damp on the pants mean anything to you?"

"Not really. I didn't know if it was from the blood or not."

"Exactly, and you testified earlier that no blood came off on your hands, correct?"

"Yes."

"So wouldn't it be fair to say that you had damp pants with dry blood?"

"I don't know. I'm not a criminalist."

"Well, there was no evidence of damp blood—no smear, as you put it, correct?"

"No, no smear."

"So we know the blood at least wasn't wet enough to transfer to other surfaces, correct?"

"Correct."

"One last matter. The search warrant for Killen Erwin's motel room and barn. Did you or any of the officers with you happen to remove a KA-BAR knife from the barn?"

"No."

"Are you certain of that?"

"Yes."

"Did Dave Daniels ever go into that barn and remove a KA-BAR knife?"

"I wouldn't know that."

"Did you ever ask him?"

"No. I only found out today you're saying it's Mr. Erwin's knife."

"Are you going to ask Mr. Daniels about that?"

"Why would I? The defendant is on trial, not Mr. Daniels."

"That is all for now. Thank you, Mr. Waters."

Thaddeus sat down without further comment.

The judge looked at the jury to get a feeling for their energy. Then he looked at the clock to his right.

"Ladies and gentlemen, it's four forty-five, so we're going to call it a day. Please remember the admonition and please be on time in the morning. We'll start up again at nine a.m."

Thaddeus told Christine he'd catch up with her at the office, that he was going to stop in the men's room. He exited the courtroom and went left toward the men's and women's restrooms at the end of the hall.

Ducking inside with a legal pad clamped between arm and suit jacket, Thaddeus was startled to see David Daniels already there.

Daniels zipped his fly and sauntered to the sink. Thaddeus was already at the urinal, guiding his stream of urine.

"Murfee, we meet again."

"Did we meet before?" Thaddeus said over his shoulder. "I guess I don't remember."

Daniels laughed and lifted water into his face. He was still laughing as he ripped a double-sheet of paper towel from the dispenser.

"No, I guess you don't remember. What about now? Remember this?"

Thaddeus turned his head and saw Daniels had lifted his right leg and turned his cowboy boot sideways to him. The silver capped toe.

"Remember your little friend?" He said in the voice of Scarface from the movie.

Thaddeus zipped up and turned entirely around. "You."

"Me. So what?"

"You sucker-punched me and kicked me while I was unconscious."

"You weren't unconscious. You were moaning. Like a fucking baby."

Thaddeus felt the anger shoot up his spine like a hot rod. He felt his chest tighten, and his breathing stiffen. Rage coursed through him and it was all he could do to restrain himself.

But he knew this wasn't the time or place.

"Well?" Said Daniels, taunting.

"Nothing," said Thaddeus. He went to the basin and washed his hands, never taking his eyes from Daniels in the mirror.

"Shit," said Daniels and he stomped out.

Thaddeus looked up from the sink. He saw in his eyes that a very dark part of him had returned. He had promised himself that he was done with that side of Thaddeus Murfee, but it had been all he could do to keep from killing the guy three minutes ago.

It could wait, said that Thaddeus.

But not for long.

~

"The killer tried to cut her head off," said the Medical Examiner of Hickam County. Dr. Earll Driggs looked back at the prosecutor, anticipating her follow-up, "Why do you say that?" and when it came, he continued with his testimony regarding the wounds.

"So here's what was seen on the table. There was an incised wound on the neck."

"Incised, meaning?"

"Cut. The neck was cut. The left and right carotid arteries were severed. These were ragged wounds, almost a sawing type of wound as if deeper penetration of the blade was desired. Then the killer got the left and right jugular veins. He or she kept cutting, transecting the thyrohyoid membrane, epiglottis or voice box, and hypopharynx. As if that weren't enough, the cut then penetrated the cervical spine. There was very little attaching the head to the body when the killer had finished the job."

"What did these cuts tell you?"

"Not being facetious, but I had my cause of death. More than that, though, and what you're asking about, is the state of mind or emotions of the assailant. Whoever did this was in a rage."

"What does that tell us?"

"That the assailant knew this woman and hated her. Something like that, though I'm certainly not a psychologist, the wounds I observed were furious, very rageful."

"The wounds were anything but careful."

"Correct, anything but."

"What else did you observe?"

"There were also stabbing wounds, seven in number of neck and scalp. The incising or cutting wasn't satisfactory; the assailant felt compelled to stab as well."

"Any defensive wounds?"

"It appeared the victim made a slight attempt at defending. There were multiple injuries to the hands, including an incised wound of the right finger of the right hand. This was a defense wound."

"Anything else?"

"Isn't that enough?"

"Doctor," said the judge, "Please answer as asked.'

"Small bruise to the head. Something hit her head rather sharply."

The doctor took a small sip of the water he had earlier requested. He licked his lips, waiting. Thaddeus considered what he had heard so far. Someone with a great loathing had done this. Those words pointed pretty clearly at Killen Erwin and Barbara Daniels. Thaddeus wondered if the two had conspired to pull off the murder. He would want to discuss that with Christine later.

"You then continued the autopsy?"

"I did. Nothing remarkable except one thing. The victim was pregnant, about nine weeks, judging from the infant and internal changes."

Every eye on the jury suddenly looked up from note-taking. Now he had their full attention.

"So there was a fetus?"

"Indeed. A male child in the womb."

"Was the child viable?"

"Yes."

Rammelskamp leaned up against the podium and wrote furiously. Thaddeus and Christine both knew exactly what she was putting down. She finished and looked up.

The doctor took the pause as his opportunity to add, "I saw

absolutely no reason this child, all else being equal, wouldn't have gone full term. Normal development and nutrient and oxygen supply in all respects. In short, this fetus was thriving."

"Thank you, Doctor. With regard to the remainder of the autopsy, was there any other condition that would have caused this woman's death other than the neck wounds? It sounds like a dumb question, but for the record it must be asked."

"No, Ms. Rammelskamp, there was no other condition that might have caused her death. Death was by incision of the neck."

"Your Honor, I would like to mark the autopsy report and move it into evidence."

"Counsel?"

Thaddeus shook his head. "No objection."

"Very well, the autopsy report is admitted without objection."

"That concludes my questions, Your Honor."

"Mr. Murfee?"

"Doctor, you have testified that whoever did this was enraged, correct?"

"Correct?"

"Which indicates the assailant had some reason to be enraged against the victim, correct?"

"Correct."

"Have you seen cases with wounds such as this where the assailant didn't have any previous relationship with the victim prior to the killing?"

The doctor leaned back and pursed his lips. He wiped away a few errant strands of gray hair that had tumbled from the remaining forelock on his head and were now brushing across his forehead.

"I believe I have seen those cases, yes. I can't specifically recall any one, but I'm sure there have been some."

"So it's entirely possible our assailant didn't know Mary Roberta Erwin before killing her?"

"Possible, but not likely. Someone had had a snootful of her and was intent on seeing her dead as violently as possible."

"All right. Can you tell us anything about the strength of the person who did this? Let me re-phrase. Was the aggressor a powerful person?"

"Yes."

"Would this more likely make him or her a man than a woman?"

"Not necessarily. The assailant was standing, I believe, with both feet firmly planted on the floor. The cuts and stabs were made in a downward motion, much like one would chop wood. A great deal of energy or force can be applied from such a position, given the mechanics of the blow beginning in the powerful legs, traveling up the back, rolling through the shoulders and the upper body all thrusting down at once. A man or a woman could accomplish this much force and wounding, it wouldn't matter which it was."

"How about the fact the victim was all but beheaded?"

"That wouldn't change my answer. A very powerful, very sharp blade was used."

"Have you compared the knife that was recovered from the scene to the wounds you visualized?"

"I have not. That would be outside the kind of inquiry I'm capable of making."

"Then I believe that's all I have. Thank you, Doctor."

"Counsel?" Said the judge. "Any re-direct?"

"No, Your Honor."

"The witness is excused. Call your next witness, Ms. Rammelskamp."

"State calls Esther Kidd of the State of Illinois Crime Lab."

46

"Counsel," said Judge Wren, "how many more witnesses do you expect to call?"

"I believe Esther Kidd will be our final witness, Your Honor."

"Very well."

The witness was located one floor below, in the Clerk's Office, where she was waiting for a cup of coffee. It was a new pot and the bailiff found her and said she had no time. Disappointed, she left the Clerk's office and began climbing stairs.

She entered the courtroom and strode confidently to the witness stand. Thaddeus saw a lovely woman, late forties, wearing a gray suit and a thick gold wedding band. Her hair was styled and understated, and her thin nose and lips gave her the look of a type of culture of bygone days. In a word, she was attractive and, Thaddeus knew, extremely smart. He would have to be very careful with her.

"State your name," Rammelskamp requested when the witness was seated.

"Esther Kidd, Ph.D."

"You hold a doctorate?"

"I do. From the University of Illinois. In microbiology."

"What is your occupation, Doctor?"

"I am a senior analyst for the State of Illinois Crime Lab in Chicago."

"Your area of expertise?"

"Biology/DNA. My team performs all the DNA testing for this northern part of the state."

"Were you asked to do any DNA testing in this case?"

"I was, by you."

"What were you asked to do?"

"I was requested by you to test a pair of pants, a T-shirt, and a knife. A very large, sharp KA-BAR knife."

Here we go, thought Thaddeus. Ever the advocate, these people. It couldn't be a smallish, slightly dull knife. Oh no, it was very large and very sharp. Nice.

"Had you tested this type of knife before?"

"This is the knife used by the United States Marine Corps beginning in World War Two. It is my understanding it is still issued even today."

Thaddeus let it go. Probably the history of the knife was

beyond her expertise, but it was harmless enough, all things considered.

"Tell us about your DNA service."

"We test mostly in conjunction with the DOJ's CODIS apparatus."

"What is CODIS?"

"The CODIS Unit of the FBI/DOJ manages the Combined DNA Index System (CODIS) and the National DNA Index System (NDIS) and is responsible for developing, providing, and supporting the CODIS Program to federal, state, and local crime laboratories in the United States."

"What does this mean, exactly?"

"That certain standards are promulgated for DNA testing and the like. And that a federal database of federal prisoners and some illegal immigrants is kept against which local DNA labs can inquire, make comparisons."

"Tell us about the kind of testing you did in this case."

"We employed what is known as nuclear DNA testing."

"What is that?"

"Nuclear DNA is the most discriminating type of DNA testing. It is typically analyzed in evidence containing body fluids, skin cells, bones, and hairs that have tissue at their root ends. The power of nDNA testing lies in the ability to identify an individual as being the source of the DNA obtained from an evidence item, or by excluding an individual as a contributor to the DNA evidence. That's the high-level view of it."

"How was nDNA testing employed in this case?"

"We used it to determine the DNA of blood and transfer samples."

"Meaning what?"

The witness went on to describe the DNA testing on the pants and shirt. Not surprising to anyone who had been paying even minimal attention to the case, the blood stains on the pants and shirt were from the blood of Mary Roberta Erwin. Thaddeus watched as the jury made its notes, but no one was surprised or evinced any shock at the testimony thus far.

Then she moved into the area of the knife retrieved from behind the soft drink machine. The knife had been tested by the Crime Lab and was also found to have on it the blood of the wife of the ex-District Attorney. Even more importantly, the knife handle was found to store DNA samples that matched the DNA of Killen Erwin.

"In other words, the defendant had handled the knife."

"Well, handled it or somehow the knife was in contact with his skin sufficiently to leave a testable sample on the handle."

"What is the knife handle composed of?"

"You want the official version?"

"Yes."

"Kabar says the oval-shaped leather handle construction on the famous USMC knife is made by first compressing leather washers onto the tang, shaping and coloring them, and then fastening them on with a pinned-on butt cap."

"So the handle is leather."

"Partly, yes."

"And the fact it was leather, did this help store the DNA of Killen Erwin?"

"I don't know that 'store' is the word I would use. But, to your point, yes, the leather is porous and it will tend to be penetrated by the body oils of anyone handling the knife, particularly if they are exerting themselves to where the sweat glands from the hands are depositing sweat into the leather."

"So if Killen Erwin was using the subject knife around his horse business and was sweaty at the time, this might account for his DNA being on the knife?"

"Objection! Speculation."

"It is speculative, but we'll allow it."

"Yes, that's one scenario."

"Are there other scenarios?"

Dr. Kidd smiled. "Probably only limited by our imaginations, Counselor."

"So just to summarize your testimony about the knife: it contained the blood of the victim and the DNA of the defendant, correct?"

"Correct."

"Was there any other DNA on the knife?"

"Not that we were able to identify, no."

"Your witness, Counsel."

Thaddeus moved to the podium and immediately launched right in.

"Doctor Kidd, you don't know how the knife got behind the soft drink machine, do you?"

"No."

"And you don't know how the knife came to be in the possession of the killer, do you?"

"I do not."

"For all you know, the knife could have been stolen from Killen Erwin's barn and used in the attack by someone wearing latex gloves, correct?"

"Yes."

"That scenario would easily explain this case, would it not?"

"Objection, invades the province of the jury."

"Sustained."

"Did you see any evidence that the knife had been handled by anyone wearing latex gloves?"

"Latex gloves wouldn't leave behind trace evidence that would be the subject of DNA testing. Not the exteriors of the gloves, anyway."

"One last question. Can you tell us, from the testing you did, which was first deposited on the knife: the blood or the sweat?"

"No way of telling that."

"And one more. Sorry. If Killen Erwin testified the knife was

his and had been missing from his barn, would that contra-
dict anything you've told us here today?"

"Just that? That the knife was missing from the barn? I see
no contradiction, no."

"That is all, thank you."

"May the witness be excused?" asked Judge Wren.

Both parties responded affirmatively.

Rammelskamp then climbed to her feet again and waited
for silence.

Finally, she said, simply, "The People rest."

It was now Thaddeus' and Christine's turn. They looked at
each other.

She would be first up.

With Killen Erwin.

47

Barbara Daniels visited Killen Erwin on Sunday, visitors' day. The jailers didn't think it odd that the cuckold wife would meet with the cuckold husband during the cuckold husband's trial for killing his wife. They didn't think it odd because, bottom line, jailers rarely pay attention to events outside of their daily world of jails, routines, and prisoners.

The two met with a large plate of Plexiglas separating them. They spoke over a local telephone line, phones on each side of the glass. Killen was wearing orange; Barbara Daniels was wearing denim jeans and a sweatshirt that said "Shedd Water World."

"So, how was New Orleans, Mrs. Daniels?"

"It was perfect. Everyone saw me there."

"Excellent. Did you get any good pictures during your visit?"

"Good pictures were taken. Probably every hour during the day, and several times at night."

"I'm so glad for you. Did your husband manage to make the trip with you?"

"No, he couldn't come. I asked him, but he was busy. By the way, Mr. Erwin, did you get the brownies I mailed?"

"I did. They were delicious. Thank you for those."

"Very well. Okay, it's getting late, and I have to get back to my prayer group. Sunday and all."

"I can't thank you enough for visiting. And I hope I get to see your pictures soon."

"You shall, Mr. Erwin. Maybe sometime during the next week."

"Goodbye, Mrs. Daniels."

"Goodbye, Mr. Erwin."

48

C hristine and Thaddeus met Thursday night before Killen's case was to begin the next day. They were seated in the Silver Dome Inn, lounge side, across the street from the Hickam County Courthouse. It was just after seven and Christine was nursing a draft beer while Thaddeus chewed the ice in his Diet Pepsi.

It was dark in the lounge, they had a booth at the rear, and the noise level was low enough there was no need to shout. In fact, they were able to converse in below-normal conversational tones.

"If he testifies we run a huge risk," Christine said. "We've been over and over it. But to tell the truth, I'm not reading the jury as being wholly in our camp right now. It seemed to me the DNA on the knife was particularly damning. The jury made furious notes while that testimony was coming in."

"I know. I couldn't watch them, but I certainly wasn't liking what I was hearing."

"It puts him in touch with the murder weapon. Maybe even while his wife's blood was on it."

"Or maybe not."

"Okay. So we have the Westlaw records from the night of the murder."

"What do they tell us?"

"They confirmed the IP address as the motel."

"Meaning what?"

"Meaning the computer connection to Westlaw emanated from the motel."

"That's it?"

"Not quite. He also had an online chat with Westlaw support around five in the morning. The morning of the murder."

"So he was actually involved and it wasn't just a bunch scripts he was running?"

"No, the chat was germane to the search he was running. It was contextually accurate."

"What else do we know about Killen?"

"No priors."

Thaddeus shook his head. "Convictions, no. But everyone on the jury knows he was arrested for aggravated domestic battery."

"Which is horrible. If he doesn't testify, we can keep that out."

"Which is a very compelling reason for him not to testify."

"I hate that arrest," she said. "I think it convicts him."

Thaddeus gulped his drink. "Maybe so. I think I'll ask you to make the call on this one."

She shrugged. She ran her fingers around the rim of her beer stein.

"Then I say no," she said. "He doesn't testify."

"As you wish. But we lose the Westlaw search. That pretty well exonerates him."

"Yeah, but does that outweigh the agg battery?"

"Hell, Chris, it's a small town. The jury knows about the agg battery anyway. They all read the papers."

"That's true. Word travels like wildfire down here."

"Don't we know it. We lived here. We know the gossip mill is better oiled than most cars."

"Say it isn't so."

"But it is."

"So, which is it?"

"I like the Westlaw search. Tell you what. I wouldn't ordinarily do this, but Killen's a lawyer. Let's ask him what he wants to do. Testify or not? Let's leave it up to him."

"Hadn't thought of that. I never let my clients make that call."

"Neither do I. But this is exceptional. He's not only a lawyer, but he's also a prosecutor. He knows the risk he runs if he takes the stand."

"True, true. So we agree? We'll let him call it?"

She smiled and stuck out her hand. "Agree."

They shook hands and finished their drinks and left.

49

"**S**tate your name."

"Killen Erwin."

"Mr. Erwin, what is your business, occupation, or profession?" Christine asked, using the exact question she had heard her ex-boss, Thaddeus Murfee, ask so many times of other witnesses.

"I'm presently unemployed."

"Most recent employment?"

"District Attorney of Hickam County."

The jury sat back, arms folded, for the most part, waiting to be convinced. Erwin was wearing gray slacks and a double-breasted navy blazer with a foulard tie, but the jury wasn't fooled. They knew that at night he could be found in jail, sporting the neon orange jumpsuit of his peers. In a word, they knew he was in lockup because the judge had refused to set bail. Everyone read the local news; everyone knew that about the case.

But, Christine could tell it was a good thing they had let Killen decide the testimony question, for he had jumped at the chance to tell his story. And now, judging by the looks of the faces on the jury, and judging by their body language, she was very glad that he was on the stand. For better or worse, she knew it was Killen's call, and she would live with that, as would Thaddeus.

"You were married to the victim in this case?"

"I was."

Christine leaned away from the podium, her arms and hands extended where she gripped it on either side.

"Tell the jury. Did you kill your wife?"

"I did not."

"What proof do you have of that?"

"Well, I have an alibi, for one thing."

"Tell us about the alibi."

"On the night of the murder, I was in my room at the motel, doing legal research."

"How is that an alibi?" Christine asked. Her voice sounded dubious, which she knew would accurately reflect the jury's feeling at that moment. She was joining with them in taking a look at what the man had to say. Dubious, yes, but somewhat willing to allow the truth in.

"It's an alibi because it proves that several times an hour that night and even beginning early the next morning, I was doing my research."

"Do you have proof of that?"

"Yes. You have obtained my search records from Westlaw."

"Who is Westlaw?"

"The legal research company that many lawyers use to do their online research."

"So let me see if I have this right. You can browse to Westlaw and use their database online?"

"Yes."

"And you search how?"

"By sending queries to the Westlaw database. We ask it questions, it gives us answers."

"I'm going to hand you Defendant's Exhibit Six. Would you identify that for the record?"

He flipped through several pages of account statistics.

"These are my legal research account notes from Westlaw."

"For what time period?"

"For the early morning when my wife was killed."

"Were you present when the video was shown of David Daniels getting out of bed and leaving your wife sleeping in room 212 of the Blackfeather Motel on the morning she was murdered?"

"I was present."

"Did you view the entire video?"

"I did."

"What time did Mr. Daniels leave the motel room?"

"About four forty-five a.m."

"Now, referring to your Westlaw records, what time did your research session begin that morning?"

"At four-fifteen a.m."

"Take us through the session."

"All right. According to the records, I sent a search query to the database at four-seventeen, again at four twenty-one, four twenty-five, four thirty-one, four thirty-three, four thirty-six, four-forty, four forty-four, four forty-nine, and four fifty-four. Plus there's a notation about a session I had with customer support during my research. Then there are several queries after that, too. Shall I read them?"

"No, we can give the records to the jury to read. Your Honor, Defense requests that its exhibit six be admitted into evidence."

"Counsel? Any objection."

"Just the objections previously made in our motion. We would renew that same objection now."

"And overruled again. Defendant's Exhibit Six is admitted. Please proceed."

"So, just so I understand, you were at your computer, sending inquiries to the Westlaw database, all during the time we see David Daniels leaving your wife's bed at the motel until after the time we see the figure leaving the motel while wearing the coat and hat. Is that correct?"

"Correct."

"What computer would that be?"

"That would be my desktop machine. In my motel room."

"That wasn't some laptop that you could have easily taken to the motel with you."

"No. The IP address is clearly from the WIFI at the motel."

"So when you tell us you were at the motel during the time your wife was murdered, this Westlaw search is your alibi, as you stated earlier."

"It is."

"Mr. Erwin, did you love your wife?"

"Very much."

"But she had her shortcomings?"

"She was sleeping around for years before she was murdered."

"With who?"

He blanched. "You name it, she probably bedded it."

"Your wife was very promiscuous?"

"That's putting it nicely."

"Even worse, she was flagrant?"

"She was. She made no effort to hide her times with her latest lover. She left the kids and me home alone while she went out and bedded down with man after man."

"Did the kids know?"

"Too young. But it was only a matter of time."

"Tell us about your feelings during this time?"

"Anger, frustration, sorrow. Crying. Drinking too much. Then I began following her at the end. Begging her to come home."

"What else?"

"It was sick. I even tried to cut in and dance with her once when she was dancing with Dave Daniels down at the Copperhead Tavern."

"Did she allow you to cut in?"

"He didn't. They told me to get lost."

"That was the night of the automobile accident?"

"It was."

"Were you driving when the young man was killed?"

"Johnny Albertson? According to one eyewitness, a woman was driving my truck."

"What do you remember?"

"I was in a blackout. I don't remember anything."

"Then there was a night when you and she fought."

"We did. She was taunting me about her lovers, and I lost it. I tackled her. She hit her head on the floor, and I got arrested."

"This is the aggravated battery charge the prosecutor mentioned in her opening statement?"

"Yes."

"Did you ever hit her with your fist?"

"No."

"Or a board or piece of metal?"

"I never struck her, period. Not with anything."

"Ever kick her?"

"No, like I said, I tackled her. But even that was a mistake. I was trying to get her down and make her look at me and listen. I was attempting to tell her what she was doing to me inside. I didn't mean to hurt her."

"But she was hurt. Seriously injured."

"She was."

"Tell us what you did."

"After she hit her head, I went to her and cradled her in my lap. Right there on the floor."

"Was she bleeding?"

"Yes, she bled all over the pants and shirt I was wearing."

"Those have been previously marked and admitted into evidence by the state?"

"Yes, they were."

"Those were the pants seized from your motel room?"

"Yes, they were."

"And the shirt was the one found in Dave Daniels' lawnmower basket?"

"Yes."

"Do you know how it got into his lawnmower basket?"

"No idea. He put it there, I'm guessing."

"Object! Speculation."

"Sustained. Jury will disregard, 'He put it there, I'm guessing.'"

"Where was the last place you saw that shirt?"

"In my dirty clothes bag at the motel."

"You put it there?"

"Sure. That night after we took Mary Roberta to the hospital, I was arrested. Thaddeus later brought me a change of clothes at the jail before I went to court and had bail made. They gave me my clothes back. I was shocked. If I had been the prosecutor and the cops gave some guy his bloody clothes back after an attack on his wife, I'd have fired that cop. But Orbit is a funny little place. Stuff like that happens, and everyone looks the other way. Anyway, they gave me my clothes back after I left the jail. I took them home and put them in the paper bag. Showered and changed. That was pretty much the last I saw of the pants and shirt."

"Were you going to wash them or something?"

"Honest to God, I didn't get that far. I just knew I had to put them somewhere, so I stuffed them in the dirty clothes bag. There was no attempt to hide them. Which I would hope the jury would note."

Christine smiled a small smile. "I'm sure they have noted that. By the way, I notice you have a glass eye."

"Oh, you want to hear about the glass eye? That's what started the fight the night I tackled her. She ran my glass eye down the garbage disposal."

"She did?"

"What kind of person would do that?"

"Did that make you want to kill her?"

"No. I was way beyond wanting to kill Mary. I just wanted her to come home and help me with the kids and stop her bullshit ways. Excuse my language."

"Last item. The knife. The KA-BAR knife. Looking at the knife admitted into evidence, is that your knife?"

"Honestly, I have no way of knowing. Kabar has probably sold millions of those knives. I have no idea if the one in court is mine."

"But you did have such a knife."

"I did."

"What was it used for?"

"Sometimes—rarely—I would use it to clean the crap out of my horse's shoes. There's a tool for that, but sometimes I'd grab the knife and use it."

"Do you still have your KA-BAR knife?"

"I don't. It's gone missing."

"Since when?"

"I don't know. I only know it's not there anymore. You have to remember, the far side of my barn is never locked anyway. Lots of people know that."

"Why not?"

"In case there's a fire, we need to get the horses out and away."

"Is there anything else you want to tell this jury?"

"Just that I didn't kill Mary Roberta. I hated her, but I loved her, too. We were way beyond almost everything. I just wanted her to leave the men alone, quit drinking, and come home to us."

"That is all, Your Honor."

"Counsel, you may cross-examine."

Eleanor Rammelskamp concentrated on the prior fight and the fact the defendant had eventually pled guilty to domestic battery. The prosecutor on that case was Terry Downes, an attorney from Cass County, who had been appointed to serve especially just on that case. The point was made by Killen that the charge was reduced from Aggravated Battery to Battery and that that was when he pled guilty. When asked why he pled guilty, he said because he thought he was guilty of something, and he was willing to pay for it.

"You hated your wife," she then said.

"I did. But I loved her, too."

"Love-hate relationship."

"Yes."

"You were enraged about her sleeping around, isn't that true?"

"Yes."

"And that rage led you to kill her, correct?"

"No, that rage led me to get drunk. I got way in over my head with alcohol. I would rather drink than stab."

"And you were doing legal research the night your wife was killed?"

"The early morning she was killed, yes."

"Researching what?"

"Researching the right of an attorney to run for District Attorney even after he has voluntarily resigned before. Researching election law and so forth."

"You were thinking of running for DA again?"

"Sure, why not?"

"Please, let me ask the questions, okay?"

"Sure. Sorry."

"Now, Mr. Erwin. Did you play football?"

Erwin grinned. "Seriously, do I look like a football player to you?"

Rammelskamp looked at the judge.

"Answer the question, Mr. Erwin."

"No, I didn't play football."

"Yet when you tackled your wife you had enough strength to drive her violently to the floor, correct?"

Erwin couldn't repress a smile. "Mary is four inches taller than me and outweighs me by thirty pounds. I ran for her, but she stumbled."

"Stumbled? Why doesn't that show up in the police report?"

"Probably because I wasn't asked."

"You didn't think it was germane?"

"I wasn't thinking about it at all. I was afraid for my wife's well-being. I wasn't thinking about describing the incident."

"You will admit that today is the first time you've told anyone she stumbled back?"

"Except for my attorneys."

Thaddeus felt his gut tighten. Killen had never actually told him Mary Roberta stumbled. Not even close.

"She hit her head hard enough to suffer a severe head injury, correct?"

"She fell backward when she stumbled. As for my tackling her, that overstates how much I hit her with. She almost laughed at me when I came for her. She brushed me aside."

"That's funny. I don't find anyplace in the police reports where it says she brushed you aside. In fact, in the addendum to the report, made after she was released from the hospital, she says you violently tackled her. Would she just be making that up?"

"We clearly remembered it differently. That's all."

"But you don't deny that she hit her head hard enough to suffer a severe head injury?"

"No, I don't deny that at all."

"You've been violent with her a number of times, isn't that true?"

Killen's face screwed into an angry scowl. "Not at all!" he said, spitting the words out angrily. "I never laid a hand on her until she ran my glass eye down the garbage disposal. But that set me off."

"It made you want to kill her, yes?"

"It made me want to send her to the store for another eye."

"Nice try but most people would be in a rage if someone did that to them. Isn't it true you were enraged?"

"I was pretty pissed. Angry, whatever you want to call it."

"Rage?"

"Rage, maybe. But you don't know me, Ms. Rammelskamp. I don't hold grudges. I'm angry, I say my piece, and then it's forgotten. Or else I drink."

"Driving her to the floor with your shoulder. Is that what you call saying your piece?"

"No."

"Stabbing her multiple times. Is that saying your piece?"

"I didn't stab her. Hard as you might find this to believe, I hated Mary, but I loved her too. It changed frequently and suddenly, depending on her latest stunt."

"So you're saying the rage didn't last?"

"It didn't last. I got over it usually by drinking."

"But not the time you tackled her?"

"No."

"And not the time you stabbed her repeatedly?"

"Objection! Asked and answered."

"Sustained. Move along, counsel."

Much to Christine's relief, Killen had proven quite adept at side-stepping the rage issue. He always managed to interpose that he drank rather than lashed out. Except for the night she ran his glass eye down the garbage disposal. That night he had in fact lashed out.

She left the jury with that, the image of the wife, bleeding and unconscious on the floor, at the husband's hands.

"It's not so far from splitting her head open on the floor to cutting her neck open in a motel room, is it?"

He mumbled an answer about his history of never having hurt her before and how he simply wasn't disposed to violence.

Then they broke for lunch.

"I need to talk to you two," Erwin told Christine and Thaddeus before being led away for lunch back at the jail. The deputies said they had no problem with that; he could meet with them in the courtroom holding cell. They would wait. They had ten minutes.

Inside the holding cell were two benches at right angles to each other. They were metal and shiny from use. Killen took his seat on one bench and Thaddeus and Christine on the other.

"I want you to know. I have another witness."

Christine and Thaddeus traded a look.

"You *what*?" Christine said.

"Yes, I received a call at the jail. Sheriff Altiman let me take it. The caller was Barb Daniels. She wants to testify in my case."

"For the love of God, Killen," said Thaddeus. "Where has this been all this time!"

"I didn't know. Honest. She says she has evidence that can set me free."

"I'm sure that's wrong," said Christine. "Unless she has more of Dave's videos from the murder, and it shows someone's face while they're hacking up your wife."

"She has something better than that."

"What's better than that?"

Killen smiled, and neither attorney smiled back.

"Her," said the defendant. "She is better than that."

50

She came into court wearing the coat and hat. She removed the hat upon entering the courtroom, but she kept it in her hands. The coat was long, below the knees, and was a wine red color, sufficiently dark that the blood stains it held were not immediately apparent.

The bailiff walked her to the witness chair, and she sat down, still wearing the coat, still holding the hat. Thaddeus looked across at the jury. Pens were poised above notebooks, and all eyes were glued on the witness. It was time to begin.

Thaddeus stood and approached the podium.

"Good afternoon, Mrs. Daniels. Would you state your name for the record?"

"Good afternoon. I'm Barbara Seymour Daniels. The middle name is my dad's."

"You are the wife of David Daniels of Orbit?"

"Yes."

"Would you tell us what you know about your husband and Mary Roberta Erwin."

She shook her head.

"They were an item, you know? They were in love, and they were sleeping together every chance they got."

"How did you know that?"

"Oh, well. He told me. Others told me too. They'd see him and her here and there. It was no secret. Not in Gossip City."

Thaddeus paused and turned pages at the podium. He appeared to be searching for something, but the real truth was, he was allowing her testimony to soak in. And he was taking the jury's temperature. As he fiddled around, several jurors shifted their feet uncomfortably. They were anxious for the question/answer program to proceed. He drew a deep breath at long last and then continued.

"How did you feel about that?"

"Enraged."

"What did you do as a result of their affair?"

"I killed Mary Roberta Erwin. I cut her throat. I tried to cut off her goddamn head."

She started crying. He studied the jury. Their faces were frozen in shock and disbelief. Two jurors had tears in their eyes. Staunton Galloway was obviously struggling not to speak up and console the woman, having been through some of it himself with his ex-wife. Thaddeus could hear the gallery behind him and the loud whispered exchanges between media and between spectators. He waited until the sounds died down before continuing.

Rammelskamp looked stunned as if she had just been body-slammed to the canvas. She pulled herself together, finally, and shouted above the noisy courtroom, "Objection!"

"Basis?" said the judge. "Basis of your objection?"

Rammelskamp's fists clenched and unclenched. She opened her Illinois trial practice manual and scanned the table of contents. "One minute," she said, holding up an index finger. Then she looked up again and said meekly, "Surprise. We object on the basis of surprise. The defendant failed to tell us about this prospective testimony."

"Judge, I didn't *know* about this evidence until the last twelve hours," said Thaddeus. "What would the prosecutor have us do, keep this evidence from the jury?"

"Overruled," the judge said, telling Rammelskamp she had no legal right to have the testimony stricken. "Please continue, Mr. Murfee."

Thaddeus placed his arms on the podium and leaned forward.

"Tell us about what evidence you have to corroborate your story."

She stood and removed the wine-red coat. She carefully folded it and placed it on the desktop before her. She then placed the hat down on top of that, presenting a nice, neat offering of evidence that could put her in prison for the rest of her life. Jurors strained to see. They looked incredulously at one another and Thaddeus, waiting for what would come next.

"This is the coat I wore. This is the hat. They have her blood on them."

Pandemonium erupted. One juror stood and pointed at the witness. Another began sobbing. Clearly they had crossed the line between judge and participant. Control had been lost. The judge asked Thaddeus to return to counsel table, that he was imposing a short break. He then sent the jury out.

The coat and hat were seized by Wells Waters.

"Your Honor," said Mrs. Rammelskamp, "obviously the coat and hat portend to be incredibly important items of evidence if they are what the witness says they are. We would ask for a recess during which we might have these articles tested to find out exactly what they are."

"Quite agree," said Judge Wren. "This is a first for me, but clearly we've done all we can do here today. How much time do you need, Counsel?"

Rammelskamp and Waters whispered back and forth. Then she said to the Judge, "Three days. We can get a rush on it and have our findings back in the court's hands in three days. Maybe two, but let's say three just to be safe."

The judge assented, and the items were sent out for DNA testing. Three days later, the DNA results came back. Thaddeus and Christine insisted on admitting the results into evidence, along with the testing. The blood of Mary Roberta Erwin was found spattered across the front of the coat. The DNA of Barbara Daniels was found in the coat. The coat had been laundered, but her DNA was still there. So was Mary Roberta's.

Thaddeus recalled Barbara Daniels to the stand.

"Mrs. Daniels, how did you come to be in possession of the coat and hat?"

"I purchased them. And I wore them when I murdered Mary Roberta Erwin. They've been in my possession ever since."

"Where were you keeping them?"

"In a filing cabinet in my office."

"So that would explain why the police failed to locate the items during their search of your premises."

She brushed a wisp of hair away from her face and for just a moment Thaddeus was pierced with a sincere sorrow for the woman. Apparently she had come to a point in her life where the truth simply had to be told.

"Why are you telling us all this now?"

"I talked to a lawyer and told her what I was going to do. She advised me of my rights and explained what would happen to me. But you know what? Killen Erwin is a good and decent man who just happened to marry a rotten woman. Rotten to her very center! I couldn't just sit by and let him go to prison when it was I who had finally lost control. I had to tell the truth. I'm sorry, Killen, that I waited so long, and you had to go through this."

Killen nodded and looked at the jury. All eyes were on him, and all eyes made contact with him. Their minds were of one accord, and Thaddeus knew the deliberation would be a short one. He finished up with the witness and then Eleanor Rammelskamp took over.

The Special Prosecutor spent the next two hours carefully going through the murder, the acquisition of knife and coat

and hat, and other details that only the real murderer would
know about. Finally she was satisfied and took her seat. The
court was silent at just that moment.

Thaddeus rested his case, and the judge gave jury instructions. The instructions took over one hour. Thaddeus saw
that more than listen to instructions the jury just wanted to
go into the jury room and vote. Then they got their chance.

The jury was out less than thirty minutes.

"Not guilty," said the jury foreperson.

"The defendant is ordered released," said the judge.

Reporters scrambled for the door; the TV lens swung over
to capture the moments after the verdict when Killen Erwin
fell into the embrace of his lawyers. Deputies walked up to
him and shook his hand. Gaffney, the bailiff, circled him
with his massive arms and patted his back.

"Knew you didn't do it, Killen," he said. "Sons of bitches
came after the wrong guy this time!"

Thaddeus and Christine moved off to the side of the celebration. Their faces were anything but joy-filled, unlike the
other celebrants surrounding their client. In fact, when they
gathered their things and silently exited the courtroom, no
one noticed. All the press wanted was a comment from the
defendant-ex-District-Attorney.

The lawyers crossed the street back to the office they shared
in the bank building.

They went into the conference room and closed the door.

"We were had," he said.

"It was well-done," she said. "Give credit where credit is due."

"Now what?" He asked.

"Go back to Chicago and don't look back."

"He got away with murder?"

"But at what expense? Poor Barb Daniels is going to prison."

51

B ut Thaddeus and Christine guessed wrong.

Barbara Daniels did not go to prison.

Instead, she pled guilty to perjury based on her testimony in
the Killen Erwin case. Three years probation and three
hundred hours of community service. It was a first offense
and sympathies strongly favored the wife who had been
cheated out of her husband's fidelity.

How did the authorities come to know she had perjured
herself?

It turned out, as she told Killen Erwin there were pictures.
They were in video format, taken at the New Orleans
Marriott on Canal Street.

Twelve hours of videos, surveillance CCTV, made between
nine p.m. the night before Mary Roberta was murdered and
nine a.m. the next morning of the murder. Starring in the
videos was Barbara Daniels, who was plainly seen in the

date-stamped and time-stamped videos going to her room on the twelfth floor, alone, at nine p.m. the night before the murder, and not emerging from the room until twelve hours later, nine a.m., on the morning Mary Roberta's body was found.

The video was authenticated by Special Agent Wells Waters, who flew down to New Orleans and interviewed the entire video staff and security personnel and confirmed the authenticity and the protocol for video in the hotel. He learned one, that the video was authentic. He learned two, that video was required to stream 24/7 in the hotel and be kept thereafter for thirty-six months until disposal. He learned three, that Barbara Daniels had checked into the hotel the day before the murder and that her signature appeared both on the guest register the day she signed in and on the credit card receipt the morning she checked out. There was no doubt, he reported back to the new District Attorney of Hickam County: she had been in New Orleans when the murder occurred.

Which sent the new District Attorney and Eleanor Rammelskamp scurrying to the law books. They read and re-read everything they could find on Double Jeopardy. They held conferences; they compared notes, they called the Attorney General of Illinois and talked to the senior staff there.

But the result was the same. Killen Erwin couldn't be tried again. Not for the murder of Mary Roberta Erwin.

What about prosecuting him for the murder of the fetus his wife was carrying?

Legally speaking, it was impossible, they decided at long

last. How would they prosecute him for killing the fetus when he didn't kill the mother?

It was troubling, but it soon passed out of the public's consciousness, and new cases appeared on the horizon and the Lady Justice turned away to new beginnings of new cases.

One of those cases was the bludgeoning death of David Daniels.

Someone had caught him coming out of the Copperhead Tavern and had hit him full-on across the face with a two-by-four. They had then used the board to turn his head into a soft pumpkin.

"Talk about rage," said Wells Waters, who investigated and viewed the body.

"Yep," said his assistant.

"Boys," said Waters, "that right there is rage in the first degree."

The red Ford Mustang was halfway back to Chicago by the time the body was bagged and tagged and delivered to the Medical Examiner.

The CSI team sifted the scene and worked the body. Then they reported back to Wells Waters.

"Nothing," they said. "Not a hair, not a fiber, no prints, nothing. Somebody knew what he was doing."

In the trunk of the red Mustang were doctor's scrubs, booties, latex gloves, and a surgical skull cap. All of which had been provided by the driver's physician wife to avoid trace and transfer evidence being left at the scene.

After all, he was her husband.

Someone had all but killed him. She hadn't been able to ignore that.

In fact, she hadn't even tried.

52

In the end, the biopsy was negative.

Katy and Thaddeus celebrated in Chicago with their kids and Christine and her kids.

Navy Pier was the location. The kids rode the rides and the adults drank coffee and chatted.

"You good?" Christine asked Thaddeus.

"I'm good," he said.

"You good?" she asked Katy.

"I'm good," said Katy. "You good?"

"I'm good," said Christine.

"What about the two-by-four?" Thaddeus asked Christine.

"It made a roaring fire. Along with the scrubs."

"What about after?"

"The embers cooled, the coals were gathered and I have them in this bag right here."

They watched as Christine opened the small plastic bag and poured its contents into Lake Michigan.

"Good riddance," said Katy.

"Did we win?" Thaddeus asked Christine.

"Well," she said, "Killen Erwin won. But I don't know that we did."

"He was guilty," said Thaddeus. "And he walked."

"The woman's testimony took me totally by surprise. I thought we had a fighting chance before, but the logical part of me knew that he was probably going down."

Thaddeus lowered his voice; the kids were nearby.

"How did I do, Chris?"

"You were just like the old Thaddeus. There's nothing to worry about."

"My thought processes—"

"Your thought processes are fine."

"He's been having small seizures," Katy said.

Christine's eyes widened. "No!"

Katy nodded. "Petit mal seizures."

"I'm so sorry."

"It's all good," Thaddeus said. "They have me on medication."

Katy said, watching the kids play, "Thad told me about the trial. There's just one thing that's bothering me. How did Killen do the legal research and do the murder at the same time?"

Christine and Thaddeus looked at each other.

"Do you want to field this one?" Christine said.

"No, go ahead. I'm interested in how he did it too."

"Don't you guys talk to your clients?" Katy asked. "Don't you want to know?"

The two lawyers looked at each other.

Then they burst into laughter.

"Never!" they cried.

53

"Let's see," said the paralegal from Saint Louis, "that was eight hours at one hundred per hour."

Killen Erwin proceeded to count out hundred dollar bills until he reached eight. Then he paused. The young paralegal lifted his eyes from the proffered bills and met Erwin's gaze.

"Are we done here?" said the paralegal.

Erwin smiled and added an additional hundred dollar bill.

"Just because I like you."

The paralegal stuffed the nine bills in his jeans.

"So, did you use my research?"

"Not yet. I haven't made up my mind whether to run for election again."

"I heard you testified it was you who did the research."

"What will you do with that information?"

"Exactly nothing."

"Why not?"

"Because, man. I don't want any trouble."

"That's a good reason."

He added one more hundred dollar bill.

The young man stood and shook his head.

"I won't be coming back this way. I won't be talking."

"One last item, friend."

The young paralegal turned utterly white.

"What now?"

"You got a girlfriend? Wife?"

"Girlfriend."

"You going to ask her to marry you?"

"Probably."

"Well, the moment wouldn't be complete without these. Hold out your hand."

Ever so carefully, the young man held out his right hand.

"Turn it over. I have something to give you."

The young man turned his hand palm-up.

Erwin reached into his right bluejeans pocket and came out with a clenched fist. He moved his fist over the young man's hand. Then he opened his fingers and a diamond engagement set spilled onto the young man's hand.

"She will love these," said the young man.

"You'll have to have them cut down. They fit these sausages," Killen said and held out his left hand.

'Why give them to me?"

"I rode a horse once, and she broke my neck. I swore I'd never swing a leg over another nag, and I didn't."

"You were a jockey. I heard that."

"That's why you need the rings, and I don't. I've had my ride. I'll never take another."

"I think I understand."

"I think you do. I'm betting on it."

Erwin picked up the curry brush and drew it along the horse's flank several times. Then he set aside the brush and patted the horse's shoulder. The animal shivered. He turned around. The paralegal was gone.

He smiled and decided to go home. Celena and Parkus would be hungry.

He was learning to cook their favorites, and they were coming out of their shells and talking to him. They seldom spoke of their mom. He never spoke of her. He had ads out to sell the horses. He knew the kids would have to be moved someplace where people didn't know. Maybe California, where people didn't even particularly care.

He turned out the barn lights and shut the door behind him.

The cold evening wind swirled inside his coat. It felt like snow.

Then he stopped and squared off against the wind and lifted his face to the black sky. It sounded like the wind but in it he heard the roar of the crowd as he came around the final turn at Churchill, mud flying, quirts snapping, thundering hooves and all alone out front.

Then the crowd was gathered around him, cameras flashing, roses making their way around Betty's neck.

It would have happened, too, if she hadn't gone down on the turn.

It was the Derby, and he was close.

And Mary Roberta, she never cared about all that.

He felt the tears in his eyes, wet and stinging, and in that briefest of moments he knew regret.

Why, he wondered, would a man choose a woman like that?

He jammed his hands into the pockets of his barn coat and began trudging up the hill toward home.

The sun teetered on the ridge of his roof as he approached.

Then it was gone.

He heard a voice call his name across the pasture. In the dim afterglow, he could just make out a figure at the far end of his drive, where the road ran from the highway back up to his house.

Why stop clear down there? He wondered. Instead of continuing toward home, he went left, back down the drive.

He was almost to the highway when he recognized the Dodge Ram. He froze in his tracks, recognizing the twins' truck and a moment later recognizing the man standing behind the truck's open door, a shotgun pointed at Killen's chest.

"Remember me, Killen?" said Markey.

Killen raised a hand to shield his eyes from the truck's headlights.

"We need to talk," said Killen. "It wasn't me driving when your brother was killed. I have proof now."

"What proof?"

"Police report. Witness says my wife was driving."

"What, the wife you murdered?"

"If you say so."

"Everybody says so. So you know why we're here?"

"I can guess."

"Do you want it here in your driveway? Or do you want to come with us where the kids don't hear?"

"Why don't we talk? Mary Roberta was driving that night."

"You ain't gonna answer me? Fine, we'll do it right here."

Markey flicked off the safety and pulled the trigger.

The spray of pellets caught Killen first in the upraised hand, and the central pattern caught him chest high. He was knocked up and back as if kicked by a horse. A hole the size of a man's fist had come open in his chest.

His last thoughts were of Celena and Parkus. The last will and testament nominated Thaddeus and Katy as guardians.

"Help them forget us, Thaddeus," Killen whispered.

Then he was gone.

54

Whenever they flew out on the Gulfstream, Parkus insisted on riding up front with the pilots. Parkus was five. So the pilot and co-pilot fashioned a third seat in the cockpit atop the console. It was temporary, but it made Parkus happy. All along the flight he would make airplane noises and pretend he was flying the plane. As the pilots threw switches and made comm calls, Killen's offspring mimicked them.

"He wants to be a pilot, Thad," said Celena, who rode in the very back of the plane with Sarai. Completely ignoring the plane and the flight, the two girls would play games on their tablets as the aircraft coursed through the sky. Celena was Parkus' older sister. In the first days, Celena never took her eyes off Parkus, as Mary Roberta's constant absences had abandoned his mothering to Celena. But now Thaddeus and Katy had been added to their lives and Celena, for the first time, was getting to be a little girl. When Thaddeus saw her rolling on the floor with Sarai, a private joke doubling them up with peals of laughter, his heart would swell, and his eyes glisten and he would know the joy of giving in its fullest expression as it came back tenfold to the giver.

Katy and Turquoise sat between the front cabin and the tail, discussing college, dating, veterinary medicine, and clothes. The college sophomore was heavy into clothes. And Katy made no effort to slow her down. Thaddeus observed from the table seat across the aisle that whatever Turquoise wanted, she pretty much got. He would work on his laptop and catch blips of their constant conversation, every so often lifting his head and closing his eyes to remind himself it was all real.

He *did* own the fifty million dollar plane, and they *were* on their way to see Katy's great-grandfather in Arizona, and Thaddeus *was* the father and Katy the mother of all onboard children. They had been given life and it more abundantly, a promise fulfilled.

The twins had left Killen's driveway and emerged at the Copperhead, where they drank too much and confessed to Mitt, the bartender. They told him they had shot Killen, "Like a mad dog," and Mitt had waded into them with his baseball bat. Wells Waters made the arrest, and Hickam County DA Iggie Stoops won his first murder conviction.

Killen was buried, the adoption was final, and it was July. The trout would be flashing through the fast and narrow, slow and shady waters of the Wachuska Mountains, and Henry Landers would be tending his sheep.

Thaddeus reached beneath his seat and retrieved a quilt that Turquoise had made for him. It depicted a chestnut horse standing on its hind legs, pawing the summer air of a green pasture. He reclined his seat and covered himself with the quilt, at last exhausted enough to sleep.

Killen's horses would be joining them in Arizona. Thaddeus had bid at the estate sale and bought every last one of them. Somewhere on the highways below they were trucking two days ahead of the Gulfstream, making their way toward Flagstaff and home.

They were western horses now, and the family was a western family. Thaddeus and Katy had decided they would return to the mountains and give the kids a place of horses and love under sunny skies.

Killen and Mary Roberta would have wanted just that for them.

Thaddeus was sure of it. And he wouldn't let them down.

Each was a small death, maybe.

But the survivors were here and now.

And they were loved.

THE END

UP NEXT: THE NEAR DEATH EXPERIENCE

"This now is the second book by Mr. Ellsworth that has had me blubbering (the other being a book his Michael Gresham's 30 Days of Justis) Read both. You deserve it. "

"I have become an ardent Ellsworth fan since first hearing of the Thaddeus Murfee series on BookBub."

"This book, as well as the other eight books was great, I thoroughly enjoyed reading them. Once I began to read, it was rather difficult to put down."

"This book is wonderful. Anyone interested in human consciousness should not hesitate to read this wonderful story. It will make you cry. But it will give you hope."

Read The Near Death Experience: CLICK HERE

ALSO BY JOHN ELLSWORTH

THADDEUS MURFEE PREQUEL

A Young Lawyer's Story

THADDEUS MURFEE SERIES

The Defendants

Beyond a Reasonable Death

Attorney at Large

Chase, the Bad Baby

Defending Turquoise

The Mental Case

The Girl Who Wrote The New York Times Bestseller

The Trial Lawyer

The Near Death Experience

Flagstaff Station

The Crime

La Jolla Law

The Post office

SISTERS IN LAW SERIES

Frat Party: Sisters In Law

Hellfire: Sisters In Law

MICHAEL GRESHAM PREQUEL

Lies She Never Told Me

MICHAEL GRESHAM SERIES

The Lawyer

Secrets Girls Keep

The Law Partners

Carlos the Ant

Sakharov the Bear

Annie's Verdict

Dead Lawyer on Aisle 11

30 Days of Justis

The Fifth Justice

PSYCHOLOGICAL THRILLERS

The Empty Place at the Table

HISTORICAL THRILLERS

The Point Of Light

Lies She Never Told Me

Unspeakable Prayers

HARLEY STURGIS

No Trivial Pursuit

LETTIE PORTMAN SERIES

The District Attorney

Justice In Time

COPYRIGHT

ABOUT THE AUTHOR

For thirty years John defended criminal clients across the United States. He defended cases ranging from shoplifting to First Degree Murder to RICO to Tax Evasion, and has gone to jury trial on hundreds. His first book, *The Defendants*, was published in January, 2014. John is presently at work on his 31st thriller.

Reception to John's books have been phenomenal; more than 4,000,000 have been downloaded in 6 years! Every one of them are Amazon best-sellers. He is an Amazon All-Star every month and is a *U.S.A Today* bestseller.

John Ellsworth lives in the Arizona region with three dogs that ignore him but worship his wife, and bark day and night until another home must be abandoned in yet another move.

johnellsworthbooks.com

johnellsworthbooks@gmail.com

EMAIL SIGNUP

Can't get enough John
Ellsworth?

Sign up for our weekly newsletter
to stay in touch!

You will have exclusive access to
new releases, special deals, and
insider news!
Join today!

Click here to subscribe to my newsletter: https://www.
subscribepage.com/b5c8a0